THE
ENRICHING

Written by
KATHLEEN STREETER

Based on the original screenplay by
KENNETH STREETER

Archway Publishing books may be ordered through booksellers or by contacting:

Archway Publishing
1663 Liberty Drive
Bloomington, IN 47403
www.archwaypublishing.com
1 (888) 242-5904

Because of the dynamic nature of the Internet, any web addresses or links contained in this book may have changed since publication and may no longer be valid. The views expressed in this work are solely those of the author and do not necessarily reflect the views of the publisher, and the publisher hereby disclaims any responsibility for them.

Any people depicted in stock imagery provided by Thinkstock are models, and such images are being used for illustrative purposes only. Certain stock imagery © Thinkstock.

ISBN: 978-1-4808-3488-0 (sc)
ISBN: 978-1-4808-3489-7 (e)

Library of Congress Control Number: 2016948692

Print information available on the last page.

Archway Publishing rev. date: 10/17/2016

CONTENTS

CHAPTER 1

Them Old Meanies

AN OLD, DUSTY CAR bounced along a narrow road in rural Mississippi, passing lush vegetation and dilapidated shanties. Scrawny, barking dogs leaped into its path. Tom Clausen struggled to roll down his window and called out greetings to some of the poor families who were lounging on sagging porches or watching from doorways. Shouts of "Hey, Mr. Tom!" followed the car as he made his way past the old tin-roofed cabins.

"Howdy! How are y'all? Good to see you," called Tom as he passed. He was a tall, pleasant man, soft-spoken and sincere. He spoke little, but his words carried weight with those who knew him. He possessed an easy way with people, and he touched his hat with courtesy to all who passed his way. When he was a youngster, his life had been saved by a Negro boy. Since that time, he'd carried with him an extra measure of respect and kindness toward the poor people of Anker, most of whom were the coloreds.

It had happened when he was fourteen years old, wild and reckless and not above joining his friends in shouting obscenities at Negro boys. Yet it was in the midst of just such taunting that he had ultimately been rescued from a speeding locomotive just minutes away from crushing him.

On that fateful day, Tom and his friends had been jeering at a group of boys, peppering them with rocks and words. As Tom had scrambled after his friends, laughing hilariously, his foot had become wedged beneath a railroad track and locked tight. He had stared in horror as the beacon of a train could be seen approaching, the shrill whistle sending out a desperate warning. As he struggled, his friends nearby shouted encouragement but did nothing. Suddenly he'd been yanked free by one of the young Negro boys, his eyes huge and frightened. "Ah'll git y'all loose. Never you mind," he'd said. And with a strong tug that sent Tom screaming to the side of the tracks, the boy freed him just as the massive engine roared past. But his rescuer had been caught beneath the wheels, both legs severed. The memory of that awful day remained forever in his mind. The boy later died, and Tom had tried to apologize to the boy's mother, placing the blame on himself. She had been kind, but the hostility in her eyes had haunted him.

In the minds of some, Tom was a fool, a "nigger lover." But to the people in the shanties, he had become a dependable and trusted friend, a man they felt easy with. It gave him a warm sense of pride that the people in the poor, ramshackle houses raised their heads, stood tall, laughed, and called out to him as he passed by.

Tom reached over and stroked his daughter's hair. Elma Mae sat beside him, her flaming-red pigtails flying in the breeze from the open window. He glanced over and marveled at her rosy cheeks sprinkled with freckles, her sparkling blue eyes, slightly crooked nose, and rosebud mouth. Seven-year-old Elma Mae was discussed behind closed doors throughout Anker County, for not only did she lack a mother to "raise her up," but her best friend was the strange Negro boy Tobias, a fact most folks in the county disapproved of. Her mother, Kit, had died in childbirth, and Tom had kept their lives in order, imparting to his daughter his own values, and thinking often of his promise to the only woman he'd ever loved that he'd remarry someday.

But his work with animals and raising his strong-willed daughter consumed his energy and fulfilled his life. He was observant and protective of Elma Mae, who was growing up strong and independent with a mind of her own—"a real handful," people said. Known throughout the county as an exuberant little tomboy, she loved to climb trees and race with wild abandon through the woods, whooping and yelling as she chased her beloved dog, Uncle Pete. She loved to fish, wading into deep water and jabbing her homemade spear into the depths, shouting at the top of her lungs, "I am the timber pool god!" There were days when Tom despaired over his lively daughter, who seemed to make up her own rules, but he took comfort in knowing that her infectious grin and winning ways were like her mother's, who never allowed wrongs to go unheeded.

Tom slowed the car in front of Ricketts General Store. A man stumbled out of a saloon across the street, lurching awkwardly toward them. The saloonkeeper followed him, dusting off his apron, pointing his finger, and shouting at the drunken man. Onlookers paused to stare and chuckle. Elma Mae twisted around in her seat to look over her shoulder.

"That man is drinkin' himself a duck-billed lip, Daddy."

"Yep, sure is." Tom brought the car to a stop.

"Do I have to come in with you?" Elma Mae sighed, twisting one of her pigtails.

Tom glanced over at her and then climbed out of the car. "Suit yourself," he said, shoving both hands into his overall pockets.

Elma Mae watched him leap up onto the boardwalk in one step. She opened the car door and slithered slowly down from the seat, reluctantly following him into the store.

The bronze bell tinkled overhead as Tom opened the door. He turned to wait for his daughter, and he glanced at her with amusement as she poked both thumbs in her ears, wiggling her hands and sticking out her tongue. "Don't go makin' yourself look foolish now, gal," he admonished softly.

"Daddy, George Henry tol' me Chauncey's frog grew six legs by turnin' himself upside down six times," she whispered fiercely.

"Well, we know that ain't true." Tom chuckled, puzzled as usual over his daughter's imaginative stories.

"Them old meanies is in here, Daddy. I don't like 'em."

"Just ignore them." Tom sauntered off into the gloom of the store, stepping around huge sacks of flour, burlap bags of grain and cornmeal, bins of molasses, and baskets full of yams and sweet potatoes.

Elma Mae wandered off among the bolts of fabric stacked against a wall. She turned at the sound of a nasal voice cutting loudly through the stale air.

"Ledyard saw it too … fast as lightnin'!"

Orville Swanny tipped his chair back and reached down to scratch Cottonseed, a wheezing old hound dog that was sprawled at his feet, twitching and whining with bad dreams. Orville and his pals often gathered in Ricketts General Store to gossip, hunched over and polluting the air with cigars, tobacco spitting, and loud guffaws. Orville, the town sheriff's cousin, took pride in that fact and felt entitled to an elevated position among his crony friends. He was a man of cowardly ways, a gossip who gleefully passed on news—true or untrue—to anyone who would listen. The others in the group tolerated him, although secretly they felt a sense of heightened importance at being included in the company of Sheriff Neil Swanny's cousin. The sheriff had recently bestowed on Orville a new position under Shelly Bowles, Anker's top deputy. His duties required him to be on the job each day, but so far, he had displayed only his usual laziness.

Now he stared with distaste at the other men. He stood with a humorless snicker and ambled toward an old cooler in the rear of the store, sweat glistening on his face. He ran his hand over his thinning hair, ruffling it. Grabbing a bottle of Coca-Cola from the cooler, he snapped the cap off beneath the stationary bottle opener and hitched up his trousers. He turned defiantly to the other two men. "Ledyard an' me, we seen it. You can believe us or just sit there starin'. Don't make no difference to me."

Elma Mae watched the men from among the bolts of fabric. She ran her hands along the cloth and hummed softly to herself.

"Gal, we need to look around for that Sunday school dress we been talkin' about." Tom stood in front of her, blocking her view of the men around the stove. He leaned down to her, his voice low and stern. "I don't want you frettin' over those fellers."

Elma Mae rolled her eyes. "Yes, Daddy. But they always talkin' mean."

"And I heard Aaron Lee over at the barbershop sayin' it been 'round Bunny Bayou for eight years now," Orville said, his voice croaky and excited. He looked around at the other men, his beady eyes dancing and hoping for a response. Suddenly he kicked the potbellied stove, causing black smoke to seep from its red-hot seams. "This ol' flip-flop gotta git the boot every day now," he mumbled. The other men sat quietly, ignoring him.

Finally, Percy spoke up. "Y'all likely been drinkin' coffin varnish, seein' Noosemouse mule, that old hayburner. Prob'ly been spooked. Hell, that's all." Percy was a moon-faced man who carried an air of arrogance. His mouth was tight over tobacco-stained teeth, a pencil line of dark mustache on his upper lip. He shrugged and ambled away from the stove. "Eight years," he mused, glancing slyly at Orville.

Ledyard tucked his thumbs under his red suspenders and struggled from his chair, panting from the effort. He lurched over to the window, his twisted clubfoot dragging, and stared out onto the street. His heavy body was always rank with sweat beneath his rumpled shirt and glistening on his unshaven jowls and the hair plastered tight against his skull. He was a bitter, humorless man who only saw things his way.

"Think so, huh?" said Ledyard hotly, turning from the window. "Like he said, don't make any difference to us. We tellin' you what we seen. Believe it or not!"

Orville pulled out a tobacco pouch and snapped off a plug. He glanced across the store. "How are you today, Tom?" he called out. "Been up on Bunny Bayou lately? Strange things happenin' up there."

Tom glanced up, touching the brim of his hat briefly. "Orville," he said, acknowledging him quietly. He turned back to his daughter. "This dress'll do just fine." He held up the garment, pleased with his choice of a dress with pleats and green rickrack trimming. "Like it? Kinda matches your eyes."

"Do I have to wear it, Daddy? You won't make me put that on for all of Sunday, will you?" She poked at the stiff, puffed sleeves. "It's fancy, and—"

"It's a pretty dress, Elma Mae," interrupted Tom. "You can't spend every single day in those overalls. 'Sides, every little girl gotta have a special outfit for Sunday school."

"It's not for tree-climbin'," huffed Elma Mae indignantly.

"Mind your manners, child!"

"You be buyin' that girl of yours a real dress, Tom?" Orville shouted from across the store, shifting his wad of tobacco to the other cheek. "She be a growed woman one of these days and still swingin' from them treetops! And keepin' company with that—"

"I'd be mindin' my own business if I were you, Orville," called out Tom coldly.

Ledyard shrugged and turned back to Percy. "Couldn't be no mule we seen up there," he resumed. "Ain't a man in all Anker can *ride* Noosemouse mule." Ledyard rolled a cigarette in one lick and blew a perfect smoke ring at Percy. The effect of his words hung in the air.

"Did you say *ride* Noosemouse mule?" asked Percy, waving his hand through the swirls of smoke.

"That's exactly what I'm sayin'," said Ledyard, drawing deeply on his cigarette.

"That's right … a tall feller," Orville barked from the other side of the stove.

"Well, if that don't beat all," said Percy slowly. "Now we got a horse streakin' like lightnin' with a tall feller ridin' it through them woods 'n' mud 'n' quicksand … and he ain't been seen for the past eight years! You fellas got addled brains."

"Doesn't matter what you think, Percy," Orville snapped, aiming his empty Coke bottle at a trash can and propping his dusty boots on a stool. "I'm fixin' to find out what's goin' on up there. I got a position in this town, and I'm obliged."

Percy yawned and stretched, dismissing Orville. "'Prob'ly that tall feller is nothin' but the ghost of 'ol Myron comin' back to haunt ya." He chortled loudly at the thought.

The screen door squeaked and swung open. Two men entered the store, grinning and jostling with each other. Jimmy Snaught's arm was slung over the shoulder of his identical twin, Jay. They had shown up in Anker seven years ago, neither one being inclined to say where they had come from. They kept to themselves and were regarded with suspicion. Their name alone had raised eyebrows; there was no kin in this Mississippi county with the name of Snaught. They held themselves aloof and were quick to anger. Their watchful eyes, slack mouths, odd-shaped heads, and heavy eyebrows caused folks to stay clear of them.

Now they paused, surveying the store. Both their heads revealed a pattern of homegrown haircuts, the work of scissors crisscrossing their pallid scalps.

"Howdy, y'all," nodded Jay.

"If it ain't the Snaught brothers," remarked Ledyard. Ugly fools, he thought to himself. Look like they used a couple buckets of barn wash and been scrubbin' with the wrong soap.

Orville and Percy ignored the two.

"You and Jimmy heard anything 'bout that old mule ridin' 'round up near Bunny Bayou carryin' some tall feller on his back, whippin' up folks?" asked Ledyard.

"Nope," said Jay flatly. "Me and Jimmy know for a fact who up there and who ain't. Never seen a mule. Don't know what you're talkin' about."

"Yeah, we got eyes, me and Jay," Jimmy declared, yanking at his top button and stretching his neck. He gazed down at the floor, inspecting his shoes.

"Who wants to know anyway?" demanded Jay, looking around at the men. "You fellas got nothin' better to do than conjure up tales? Me 'n' Jimmy, we passes our time rightly, and stays away from that nonsense. Ain't that right, Jimmy?"

"Yeah, that's right, Jay," said Jimmy. He loosened his shirt collar and crossed his arms, eyeing the men around the stove.

The others propped their dusty boots on chair seats, continuing the gossip that was the limit of their conversation. They held sway in their corner of the store, passing tales among themselves and eyeing the customers who came and went. Today Noosemouse mule was the topic of the day, and they all claimed special knowledge.

CHAPTER 2

Ginger Lee

A GOLDEN HAZE COVERED THE cornfields that stretched to the horizon, the sky of late September like white china. Ginger Lee Swanny drove along the narrow road toward the town of Anker. Insects splattered against the windshield of her new car, a shiny white DeSoto, given to her recently by her husband, Neil Swanny, sheriff of Anker County. She followed the ruts of the dirt road, occasionally tapping her long painted nails on the steering wheel, her eyes frequently darting over the countryside and deeply plowed fields. Her mood was heightened by the smooth ride, the modern rounded headlights and front grille, and the whitewall tires. Her errand this morning had been a quick one, having delivered several jars of her famous apricot preserves to an old friend of her father's, a prominent judge in New Orleans.

Ginger Lee was a tall woman with a full-lipped mouth and a wide smile that was slightly lopsided. Her face caused second glances—not that she was beautiful. Her chin dropped away too quickly, and her mouth was too wide. Her milky-white skin, deep green eyes, and thick, finger-waved blonde hair were what people remembered. She had been in Anker for two years now, having come from New Orleans. Both parents had objected to her marriage to Neil Swanny, but she had persevered, carried away by his good looks and his status as county sheriff. Recently she had begun to regret her marriage, finding Neil to be difficult and often bad-tempered. There was tension between the two, and his purchase of the new car had, in his estimation, solved any problems between them.

Reaching for a cigarette from the pack beside her, she tapped it on the steering wheel and flicked her lighter. She was headed for the general store now to pick up some extra black-eyed peas and a piece of ham hock for supper. Parking carefully in front of the store, she slipped out of the car and headed down the boardwalk, her high heels tapping. Turning into the store, she brushed past Orville, who was slouched on an old chair in the doorway, his hat tipped low over his eyes. Ginger Lee stopped briefly, her eyes flashing as she looked sharply at him.

"Aren't you supposed to be working today, Orville?" she asked, her voice testy. "Damn sakes, Neil went to a lot of trouble to get you that new position."

Orville didn't answer. He stared at her with disinterest, languidly sucking on a toothpick.

Ginger Lee angrily tossed her cigarette onto the dust of the street. "Huh!" she uttered, passing him by and disappearing into the store.

Squeezing past shelves of household goods and sacks of flour, she leaned over a long counter next to a huge red coffee grinder and called out to Herbert Ricketts, proprietor of the general store. He emerged from the dark interior, wiping his hands on a worn apron.

"Pleased to see you, Miz Swanny," he chirped, pushing his glasses up higher on his nose. "Here's the peas 'n' ham, just like you likes 'em."

She stopped and turned back toward the counter, taking brief notice of the men lounging around the potbellied stove.

"Thank you, Herbert. How is Sharleen doing these days?"

"Well, she's a-busyin' herself just like always. Send my greetings to that man of yours, hear?" said Mr. Ricketts.

"Certainly will, Herbert. And a good day to you." Her soft drawl floated on the air, and she gave him her best crooked smile.

Orville looked up as Ginger Lee swished past him briskly, headed for her car. "Like I told you a couple days ago," he called out, "one of these days soon now I'm plannin' to head up to Bunny Bayou, have a look at that lightnin'-fast—"

"Damnation, Orville," she interrupted, turning back to face him. "Are you still leaving folks in a nest of commotion over that damned story?" Her voice hiked to a shrill note.

"I'm tellin' you, Ginger Lee, Percy thinks it's some ol' spooked horse. Hell, I know better. I'm gonna find out the truth!"

Ginger Lee turned in disgust, pulling car keys from her purse. Tossing them into her hand, she glared at Orville, her mouth tight.

"Orville," she drawled slowly, "you are a full-grown man. 'Stead of chasing spooked horses and hanging around with those cronies of yours, y'all should be over at the station helping Shelly and Soddy with their paperwork. That's what you been hired for."

Orville's face reddened. "That damn Soddy is always shoutin' at me," he whined, "tossin' out orders. I ain't just any old hired hand, Ginger Lee. I am Neil's cousin—family—and we Swannys deserve to be respected, hear?"

Ginger Lee opened the car door, slid behind the wheel, leaned out the window, and fumbled with her pack of cigarettes. "Now you listen to me," she shouted at him, "I plan to let Neil know you're lying around Ricketts's all day, and if I have my say, there is not a green thumb of pay comin' in your pocket!" She slammed the car door, her attention suddenly riveted on a young Negro woman standing on the boardwalk, about to cross the street. With her was a curiously beautiful boy who was the dark, rich color of an eggplant.

He held the woman's hand and clutched a large piece of white paper in the other.

"My, my," murmured Ginger Lee to herself, "there's that odd Negra child. I never—"

"Don't you go tellin' Neil nothin'!" Orville bellowed from the doorway. "If you do, you're gonna regret it. I'll surely see to that!"

Ginger Lee scoffed. "Lazy good-for-nothing," she retorted, rolling up her window. Familiar faces stared at the two of them from the boardwalk with smug half-smiles and whispers. She ignored them, starting the engine and slamming her foot down on the gas pedal. The car leaped forward as she briefly glanced back at Orville. There was a short, high-pitched scream. The young Negro woman pushed the little boy out of the way, throwing him off balance as the big DeSoto bore down on them and came to a sudden halt, the engine dead. The Negro woman stooped down to help the child to his feet, a protective arm around him. She crouched beside him, dusting off his overalls and small leather shoes.

For a moment Ginger Lee sat frozen, only her tapping fingernails on the steering wheel betraying the tension she felt. She rolled the window down, her eyes locked on the astonished gaze of the little boy.

"Damn you, boy," she uttered slowly, her words soft and drawling. "Why you crossing right in front of me? I could have run you over!"

The Negro woman straightened up, staring at her. "We never meant to cause y'all any distress, ma'am," she said quietly, pulling the child close to her. "I think we be all right." She was breathing hard.

"What's your name, child?" Ginger Lee asked.

The boy continued to gaze at her. She felt suddenly hot and uncomfortable, drawn somehow to his eyes, which were the color of rich amber. She shook her head impatiently. "Well?" she asked uneasily.

"My name be Tobias," the boy stated softly.

"You be more careful from now on, hear?" Her voice was brittle, the words scolding. "And you too," she added, glancing at the woman and shaking her finger. 'Course, from the unusual looks of that boy, she thought to herself, any car would come to a screeching halt. She inserted the key into the ignition. The engine whined over and over, the car vibrating. Ginger Lee frantically stamped on the gas pedal.

"Come on, come on," she whispered, flipping her hair. "This is my new car! No reason …" Angrily she slapped the steering wheel, suddenly aware of the stares from the boardwalk. She snatched the keys from the ignition and whirled out of the car.

"What y'all looking at?" she said loudly to several people standing nearby.

"Better get Neil to buy ya somethin' that don't die when y'all is 'bout to run over some coloreds!" a voice called out.

"Oh, shut your mouth!" Ginger Lee snapped, looking back at her car and shaking the car keys.

Tobias scrambled after the paper that had fallen to the ground and then reached up for his mother's hand again. He looked up, watching Ginger Lee as she strode angrily past the townsfolk. For a moment he placed his hand on the hood of the stalled car. Instantly the low purring of the engine could be heard. Ginger Lee turned, staring back at her car in disbelief. Her car keys lay in her open palm. Everyone was staring now as the white DeSoto sat idling smoothly. No one spoke. Tobias and the young Negro woman walked quietly past and disappeared from view.

Behind her came Orville's sneering voice. "I told you, Ginger Lee. That feller on the horse got some voodoo spirits jumpin' around. Must be lurkin' 'round that fancy car of yours too!"

CHAPTER 3

Tobias and Jewell

TOM LEANED DOWN, INSPECTING the racks of dresses that hung against the wall. Elma Mae generally rebelled at the idea of wearing anything but her well-worn overalls. Weeks ago he had sent away for a pretty pink dress from the Sears catalog—ruffled, with puffed sleeves and a sash. For Sunday school, he'd thought. Most little girls loved to dress up in their finest. But Elma Mae had let it hang in her small closet, observing it with disdain. Now he turned to catch her attention, but she had twisted away from him and was calling out from the dusky gloom in the back of the store.

"I seen 'em," she piped up, turning toward the men sitting around the stove.

"Now we gettin' somewhere," sneered Ledyard, his eyes narrowing as the little girl stepped forward. "Tell me, gal, what y'all see?"

Elma Mae's face reddened under Tom's stern gaze, knowing that she shouldn't have been listening to the talk around the stove.

"Well, they ... they big, they is," she stammered, "and move faster'n squirmin' fish, and they is ..." Her voice began to fade.

Tom bent low, whispering hoarsely in her ear. "Don't go fallin' off at the mouth now, Elma Mae!"

Ledyard whirled around, pointing his finger. "See? What'd I tell you? Lightnin' fast, like the little gal said."

"It was a Noosemouse mule, wasn't it, girl?" Percy called out lazily.

Elma Mae shook her head vigorously.

Percy moved closer to her, his voice cloying. "Noosemouse mule jes got spooked, that all," he crooned.

Elma Mae took another step backward, her blue eyes blazing. "I seen 'em! Seen 'em lots of times!"

Orville entered through the screen door and sauntered over to the cooler. "We gonna take some buckshot and ride on up to Bunny Bayou, see for ourselves," he said over his shoulder. "I'm tellin' you, it wasn't no horse, and it sure ain't Noosemouse mule!"

Leaning close to Elma Mae, Percy whispered as if sharing a secret. "Was just an old spooked mule, wasn't it?" He chuckled and looked back over at the men, grinning mischievously.

Tom stepped in front of him, his face flushed and angry. "Leave her be!"

Percy stared back at him. "You oughta give that girl of yours some teachin' and a good whippin'. She's tellin' tales, crawlin' for attention."

The men around the stove turned as the screen door squeaked and Tobias entered with his mother, Jewell Valentine. They all fell silent, their eyes following the two. Tobias walked quietly behind Jewell, his eyes lingering in their direction. His head was bald and shiny, his skin a deep, rich purple. He had been the center of conversation around Anker for several years, ever since Jewell had begun appearing in town, carrying him as a baby—and later as he toddled after her on her weekly errands.

"Where y'all git that child, Jewell?" the colored folks would ask. "He's purple! Never seen no purple Negra chile! You sure he one of us?"

Jewell would smile softly, returning their gaze. "He's one of us," she would say, "only he's different from you and me. He's important ... of greatness." Her words confused them, and they would move away from her, shaking their heads.

"It don't do to have a child like that in this town, ma'am. He ain't 'ceptable," a tall colored man had said one morning as she'd approached the hardware store with Tobias toddling beside her. He spoke gently and earnestly.

"I intend to keep him, thank you, sir," Jewell had answered.

She turned now and spoke quietly to the small boy. "Stay here beside me, Tobias. Soon as I pick up some syrup for Grampa Perry's cough, we'll be headin' home."

Jewell was a slender young woman of twenty-six years, with an inner grace and strength. Her black, kinky hair was tied up in a kerchief, her eyes alert and watchful. She carried herself with a quiet dignity and seldom mingled with others. Born in Anker County, she had grown to adulthood on a small farm several miles from the town, where she tended to her father, Perry Dorling, who had purchased the small tract of land many years ago on the shoreline marsh of Bunny Bayou. Jewell and her husband, Myron Valentine, and her oldest son, Josh, had taken over the field work from her ailing father several years ago and had worked hard to put food on the table and see to it that the little farm brought in a small profit.

Myron and Josh had been found dead near the Bayou a year ago. Now it was Jewell who was responsible for Grampa Perry and seven-year-old Tobias. As the only provider for her small family, Jewell called upon her inner strength to withstand the suspicion and hostility she encountered in the town of Anker. Her attempts to ask for help in solving the deaths of her husband and son had been met with a casual air of disinterest. Except for Tom Clausen, most of the townspeople thought very little about it. "Just a coupla Negras out by the bayou," they said with a shrug. "Probably ran into some trouble of their own makin'!"

Tobias looked up at his mother imploringly. "Mama, I sees Elma Mae over there with her daddy. Can I show her what I drawed?"

"All right," said Jewell, " but only for a minute." She kept a close eye on Tobias, her one remaining son. She knew the deaths of her husband and elder son had not been committed only out of contempt and hate; there were other, deeper reasons as well. Grampa Perry knew it too. One afternoon shortly before the two had disappeared, a portly man in a gray suit had come calling at their farm. He was from Texas, he'd said, and he wanted to "test the soil" in their neatly plowed fields. She remembered listening as Myron and their visitor sat at her kitchen table until late that night, lighting the kerosene lamps as they pored over a large, important-looking paper that appeared to be a map of their farm.

"Oil under these fields, Mr. Valentine." The visitor had stabbed his forefinger at the map. "Worth lots of money! You are living on a valuable piece of property."

"What's he mean, Myron?" Jewell had pressed him to explain the next morning.

"Jewell, a lot of black, sticky goo under our fields—it's oil! Folks can start livin' real good if they dig down deep enough!" His eyes had sparkled with excitement as he'd thrown his arm around her. "Might be just the way to improve all of us, and find your daddy a cure for his eyes!" Jewell's heart had leaped at the thought.

It was Grampa Perry who had first suspected the connection. "Happened right away, Jewell," he'd said. "Couple days after that feller sat here a-talkin' to Myron, why, him and Josh—they was found down by the bayou, life squeezed out of 'em. Done on purpose. 'Oil' story got spread 'round these parts. And that Sheriff Swanny and his cronies, they all ears. Don't want no Negra folks livin' good. 'Sides, couple them boys, they Klan. 'Member that, Jewell. Tobias, he still a youngun and needs ta go fishin' and play in the woods, but you keep track a him, hear? This town full a folks who suspicious anyways. They don't understand 'bout Tobias."

Jewell watched Tobias dash to the back of the store, clutching his drawing.

"Elma Mae!" he called out.

"Hi, Tobias!" shouted Elma Mae, turning away from the racks of dresses.

"Gotta show you what I drawed, jes today!"

Elma Mae ducked under Tom's arm and ran toward Tobias.

"Y'all come back here, Elma Mae," scolded Tom. "We aren't done choosin' your dress."

"I gotta see what Tobias drawed! He makes them butterflies 'n' stuff. Did a new one today, I'll bet."

The two children huddled together near Jewell while she made a few selections of dry goods.

"Howdy, Jewell. Pleasure seein' you today." Tom's eyes were warm and friendly as he moved to the counter.

"Thank you, Mr. Tom. I was hopin' to see y'all. Brought with me this parcel for you an' Elma Mae. Corn not much good this year, but we're managin' to find a few that is fresh."

"Well, thank you, Jewell."

She nodded, looking down at the children and laughing softly. "These two. There's never a dull moment when they gets together! Come on, Tobias. We gotta go now, hear?"

"That boy of yours, Jewell," said Tom, "I swear he gonna accomplish somethin' high rankin' someday. Like he was born to make them pretty pictures."

Elma Mae looked up at her father. "And it's always butterflies, ain't it, Tobias?" Her high voice floated out over the store.

The men around the stove looked up, alert and listening, nudging each other.

"Hush, child," said Tom, aware that Ledyard had risen and was moving toward them. His crippled foot gave him a sloping, menacing gait.

Jewell turned to Tobias and crouched down in front of him. "Give Mama your drawing, Tobias." Her voice was unsettled and slightly anxious.

Jimmy and Jay stood in the shadowed corner of the store, talking with each other in hushed tones as they watched Ledyard approach Jewell and lean against one of the big wooden barrels. "Howdy, ma'am," he said pleasantly enough. "What you got there, boy?" he asked softly, looking down at Tobias. "How 'bout lettin' me see?"

Jewell straightened up, her hand resting protectively on Tobias's purple head.

"If you wants to," said Tobias politely.

"Just for a minute!" hissed Elma Mae in Tobias's ear, her eyes locked on Ledyard.

Ledyard leaned down and studied the drawing, his eyes narrowing. "Uh-huh." He chuckled and then turned his gaze on Tobias. "Never seen nothin' so peculiar as this boy of yours," he rasped, looking over at Jewell. He pinched some tobacco from a small pouch, taking his time and staring at her. His thick fingers rubbed out some tobacco shavings onto a cigarette paper, and his eyes shifted to Tobias. Slowly he rolled the cigarette and licked it, spitting a flake of tobacco from his lip and running a wooden match along the barrel. "You sure he one of your kind?" he asked, puffing a cloud of smoke over them.

Tom put his hand on Jewell's arm. "It's time to go now," he said, his voice low and calm.

"I wouldn't bring this boy in here no more if I was you," Ledyard said, looming above Tobias. "Just ain't a good idea. He scarin' us!"

The other men exploded in laughter. Tobias reached for Jewell's hand, meeting Ledyard's stare.

Elma Mae's face flushed, and her fists doubled tightly. "Daddy, ain't you gonna do somethin'? He talkin' mean 'bout Tobias!" She faced Ledyard. "Y'all is cabbage guts! I oughta flatten yer nose!"

Ledyard threw his head back and called over his shoulder. "Hear that? Gal says she gonna beat me up, says I cabbage guts!" He swiped the back of his hand under his nose, sniffing loudly. "Your gal here, she's dallyin' with the Devil, Tom."

"I'd like my drawin' back, if you please," said Tobias, holding out his hand. His face was solemn.

"You would, huh?" Ledyard studied it closely again as he wiped the back of his neck. He was beginning to feel clammy and uncomfortable under the boy's intense gaze. His right hand itched and burned, and he shifted the drawing to the other hand before stuffing his right hand into his pocket. His forehead was dripping with beads of sweat. He looked down at Tobias and stammered, "B-b-boy ... can't have no nigger chile lookin' at me like that!" Ledyard paused. "What this mean, anyway, these winged varmints? Betcha traced 'em from some catalog."

"You wrong, mister. I drawed 'em myself."

"He sure did!" screeched Elma Mae furiously. "Who you callin' a nigger?"

Tom steered Jewell and the children toward the door. He turned back to Ledyard, his face flushed. "You've said enough now. Go on back there with your pals. You have no cause to turn on this child with your hateful words."

"But my drawin', Mama—that man still has it!" Tobias clutched Jewell's arm. She knelt down and slipped her arm around him.

"We got to go now, Tobias." She looked at him sternly for a moment and laid her hand gently on his cheek.

"Ledyard, give the drawin' back to that little purple turnip," bellowed Orville from the back of the store.

"Believe I'll just do that." Ledyard dropped the drawing on the floor as Tobias, tearing himself away from Jewell, lunged toward him. The big, hulking man ground his boot into the paper. Suddenly the general store was filled with the sound of strange musical notes, a faint tinkling of cymbals. They seemed to come from everywhere. Ledyard turned, searching for the source of the soft music, his big, muddy heel tearing the boy's drawing.

The Snaught brothers glared around the store from beneath their heavy eyebrows, muttering to each other. Tom paused, his face mystified.

"Daddy, you hear that?" asked Elma Mae, still seething with anger. Tom didn't answer.

Then all was still. "Somebody playin' a harp?" Ledyard paused, looking around at the others, his eyes bulging. Then he laughed loudly. "There ya are, boy, good as new!" He stamped again on the small drawing.

"No-o-o!" wailed Elma Mae, hurling herself at Ledyard, her small face twisted in rage, her pigtails swinging. She kicked him fiercely in the shin as Tom tried to restrain her.

"Why, you hot-headed little savage," shrieked Ledyard, clutching at his knee. He turned on her as Tom pushed his daughter out the screen door.

"You ruined my drawing, mister," Tobias cried out, tears running down his cheeks. "That Elo. You ruined Elo," he wailed, turning into his mother's arms. Tom whirled around in confusion and anger, and he was suddenly confronted by Ledyard lumbering toward him.

"See what y'all has caused, Tom, actin' all lovey-dovey to this purple boy, this ab-er-a-shun?" Ledyard hurled the word out slowly.

Tom stepped in front of him. "I won't have you talkin' that way. He's just a boy. Leave him be!" The two men stared at each other, Tom's jaw visibly throbbing in anger.

"Your daddy was nothin' but a fool, boy," Ledyard shouted out to Tobias, "a blistered mole. Folks here in Anker say 'good riddance'!"

Tom grabbed his shirt, jerking him upward, his eyes blazing. "Leave him alone, I said!"

"He ain't even a Negra boy!" Ledyard scoffed, twisting away from Tom's grasp. He glared at Jewell and Tobias. "Who are you, anyway?"

Tobias looked up at him, his eyes brimming with tears. Jewell drew him close and headed out the screen door. Sniffling and wiping away tears, Elma Mae took Tom's hand. "If I was growed up, I'd whip them old grunts like a bulldog knowin' his chores," she said, her voice trembling.

"No more of that now, Elma Mae. We're through here." Tom put his arm around her small shoulders and headed for the car.

A purple butterfly floated above them, its wings glowing with brilliant green and gold markings. It hovered, its velvety wings slowly opening and closing. Tom paused, staring at its unusual beauty.

Tobias reached out his hand and held it still as the butterfly settled on his thumb. He nodded slowly, his small purple finger barely touching the wings. Twisting away from Jewell, he turned and faced Ledyard for a moment. "I have me a teacher. Name Elo. He be kind and very wise, and he say to you this: 'Know, mister, yer heart will leap at yer downfall. It will be among the wood splinters.'"

Ledyard stumbled back toward the stove, scowling and muttering. "Ricketts! Don't let them two come in here no more, hear? They stirs things up." He made his way over to the stove and kicked his wooden rocking chair into position, slowly lowering himself.

Herbert Ricketts spoke firmly from behind the counter. "I'll decide that, Ledyard. Seems to me you fellas are the ones stirrin' up trouble."

Without warning, Ledyard's rocking chair collapsed under his weight, sending him sprawling onto the floor, clawing for support . The room lapsed into silence as the men looked on.

Mr. Ricketts stood dumbfounded, covering his mouth to hide a laugh. Then he slid his hands into his pockets and headed into the back of the store. The group around the old stove sat stunned, their jaws dropping open. Suddenly they exploded with laughter, doubling over and pointing at Ledyard. Pitifully he reached up, his hand dangling in midair.

"Help me up, fellas," he pleaded. All but Orville ignored him, replaying the pitiful comedy, pointing and mimicking. Grudgingly his friend hauled him up from the floor. "Always knowed you'd end up in a woodpile, Ledyard," he said with a snicker.

CHAPTER 4

From Out of the Drawing

TOBIAS AND ELMA MAE climbed into the backseat of Tom's old Ford and tucked in tightly together. Elma Mae swiped at her tear-soaked face and angrily crossed her arms, scowling out the window. Tobias settled himself beside her, smoothing his crumpled drawing across his lap. They started out of town with Jewell in the front seat beside Tom.

"Them men is—" began Elma Mae.

"Elma Mae, there'll be no further talk 'bout that, hear?"

Tom straightened his rearview mirror and looked over at Jewell. "Are you all right?"

"I'm all right, thank you, Mr. Tom," she said wearily.

Tom leaned closer to the windshield and then poked his head out the side window. "Elma Mae, ain't that Hoedig up there?"

Elma Mae unlocked her arms, her eyes growing large. "Hoedig! Did you say Hoedig, Daddy?" The little girl was excited now, and she reached for Tobias's hand.

"Yep, it's him," said Tom, chuckling.

Elma Mae twisted over Tom's shoulder and peered up into the sky. "Up there—that's Hoedig, Tobias. He flyin' that funny plane. Wow! Missus Swanny 'tol me 'bout him. You know Missus Swanny, Tobias? Her name's Ginger Lee, an' she the sheriff's wife, Daddy says. She's real pretty."

"I don't trust that sheriff," Jewell whispered quietly.

"She say Hoedig washes his face up there in that airplane! Can you see a feller flyin' in the sky, washin' his face?" Elma Mae crowed in delight. "Scrub-a-dub, scrub-a-dub-dub," she sang to herself, rocking back and forth on the car seat, rubbing her cheeks. Tobias laughed, joining in her merriment, the drawing put aside for the moment.

Tom drove slowly past newly plowed cotton fields and occasional rows of corn, the stalks drooping and dead-looking. It had been a poor growing season due to a blazing hot summer. Farther on, low-lying fog covered the landscape.

"Pretty, ain't it, Jewell? It's good to look on somethin' natural from the good Lord and forget about those hateful fellas at Ricketts's."

"It don't s'prise me, Tom," replied Jewell. "Folks never take much care to be kind to my son. It cause me to worry, but he always calm and never has no back-talk to give out." She sighed, waving her hand in the direction of the fields. "Just wish our corn crop had prospered this past year. We doin' poorly now. Used up our profits from last season. Grampa Perry, he failin' too."

"Sorry to hear that, Jewell. If there's anything I can do to help, hope you'll tell me." He turned his attention to the two children in the backseat and listened to his daughter's banter.

"What did you mean, sayin' those words to ol' Ledyard, Tobias? That part about the wood splinters—it sure came true! That ol' meanie got clobbered!" Elma Mae shouted indignantly.

Tom turned his head for a moment to speak quietly to the little boy. "Seems almost like you … I mean, what you said, Tobias."

Tobias looked calmly out the window. "Just as it were said by my teacher, Mr. Tom. That man, that ol' Ledyard, he say things to hurt my mama. I know he got hate in his heart. What I said, it come to Mister Ledyard. I knowed it would."

"Tobias …," Jewell began, turning to look at him.

"Ain't no need to worry, Mama."

Elma Mae squeezed Tobias's hand. "Next time Daddy makes me go to Mr. Ricketts's store, I'm gonna punch every one of 'em till their dogs is houndin' at the south wind."

Tobias laughed. "You say funny things, Elma Mae." They playfully began to wrestle with each other, nudging and poking.

Jewell sat quietly, listening to the two of them giggling together, her heart glad and at peace for a few moments. If only it could go on, she thought to herself.

Tom turned to her, slowing the car over the bumpy back road.

"Y'all been changin' Tawny's wrap on a regular basis, like I showed you?"

Jewell nodded. "Yes, sir, I have. Tawny, he's farin' better now, I'm sure of that. Thanks to you, Mr. Tom. That old horse never had better carin'.'"

They drove on in silence, content to listen to the two children in the backseat, their peals of laughter causing amused glances between the two of them.

"How old your boy now, Jewell?"

"He goin' on his eighth birthday tomorrow."

"I bet I older'n you, Tobias!" chirped Elma Mae from behind them.

"Mebbe," said Tobias, studying his crumpled drawing that lay open across his bare knees.

"He's a fine boy, Jewell," continued Tom. "Polite and mannerly as any boy I ever knew of."

"Thank you." Jewell laughed softly. "It ain't a callin' for lots of folks, raisin' up a child."

"No, ma'am! I know that! Life throws some snags we're not expectin'."

"Surely you is right." Jewell sighed. She listened with special interest to Tobias now, who was carefully pointing out his beloved trees to Elma Mae as the car moved along.

"That one there … that a magnolia, Elma Mae." His purple finger pressed against the glass. "And that one—it a chinaberry. That one over there a sweet gum tree."

Elma Mae whooped with delight. "How you know them trees?" The two of them continued their lively observations, their heads bobbing back and forth at the passing landscape.

"Jewell, I don't believe I ever had a chance to tell you plain and simple, but I always had a likin' for your two men, Myron and that boy of yours." Tom rested his arm on the car window ledge. "I'm real sorry 'bout that accident. Just seems like—"

"Wasn't no accident," interrupted Jewell quickly. She glanced at Tom, wiping at her eyes.

"I know," said Tom quietly.

"My heart been in mighty grief—Josh growin' to be so handsome, and my Myron a good husband, honest and proud. I ain't never been akin to death before. It hard."

From the backseat, Elma Mae let out a squeal as she bent low over the drawing that Tobias had spread across his knees. He moved his finger slowly across the paper, smoothing out the wrinkled, torn corners, badly damaged by the angry grinding of Ledyard's boot. A beautiful butterfly rose slowly from the paper, its purple wings unfolding in velvet elegance and fluttering around their heads. Tom came to a stop as they watched the brilliant creature float among them and then disappear.

Jewell gasped and looked sternly back at him. "You aren't s'posed to do that, Tobias! Folks won't never understand."

"By gum, did y'all see that?" Tom exclaimed. "Biggest butterfly I seen in my life! Never seen a butterfly so fine—purple wings, gold spots 'n' all. Where'd it come from?"

"I told you, Daddy! I told ya!" Elma Mae bounced up and down beside Tobias.

"What're you blisterin' about, gal? Just calm down, Elma Mae."

"But I been tellin' you, Tobias got this power, and he can—"

"Now hush," he admonished impatiently. "I'm your daddy, Elma Mae, not a dumb cluck!"

The car turned in to a single dusty lane with drooping corn crops alongside the road. The roof of Jewell's small farmhouse was visible in the distance. Jewell sat quiet and subdued.

Tom came to a stop beside a weathered mailbox and turned around to face the children. "Tobias, that butterfly, where'd it go? I didn't see it fly out the window."

"Nope! It flewed back into the drawin'," said Elma Mae importantly.

"Uh-huh. I was askin' Tobias." He eyed Elma Mae sternly. "Tell me about your picture," he said gently to the boy.

Elma Mae cupped her hands to her mouth, rocking on the seat and squeezing her eyes shut.

"Okay," said Tobias, placing his finger on the drawing and tracing its outline. "This butterfly, he be Elo, Mr. Tom," he said, speaking softly. "He very wise and kind. He can be anywhere. Sometimes he very big, sometimes small. He in the woods or in the trees, even in my drawin'. He a teacher, Mr. Tom, grand and—and dang funny too," Tobias giggled. "He talks to me."

"Tobias!" uttered Jewell, shutting her eyes.

"Now 'n' then he stutters," continued Tobias. "I think it's 'cause he gets so excited 'bout all the learnin' he helpin' me with. Sometimes he even gits kinda scared. This little one, she is Queen Trumpeter of Zinfoneth. She has a special horn." He pointed carefully to a tiny butterfly drawn at the bottom of the page. "And these here are the

Cupbearers. Folks don't know 'bout 'em except me." Tobias looked up, his eyes round and earnest.

"Wow!" breathed Elma Mae, craning her neck to have a better look at the drawing.

"Elo didn't scare ya, did he?" asked Tobias.

Tom looked back at the boy, almost lost in the intensity of his gaze. "No, Tobias," he said slowly, "Elo didn't scare me." He laid his hand on Tobias's smooth purple head for a moment and then turned to Jewell and took a deep breath. She remained still beside him, her eyes still closed.

"I'll be comin' by to check on Tawny real soon," he said quietly.

"That'll be fine, Mr. Tom, real fine. And thank you," she whispered, her eyes still downcast.

Tom watched silently as Tobias took his mother's hand and set out down the dirt road.

Elma Mae scampered into the front seat beside Tom. "We goin' fishin' tomorrow, Tobias?" she yelled out the window. "You 'an me and Chalmers?"

"Sure hopin' to, after my chores." Tobias waved back to her.

Tom leaned on the steering wheel, one arm slung over the top. The old car idled as the two sat in silence watching mother and son walk down the road hand in hand.

"C'mon, Daddy, why we just sittin' here?" inquired Elma Mae impatiently. He reached over and briefly stroked her hair.

"Dunno, just thinkin', I guess." Lost in thought, his eyes widened as a cloud of butterflies rose from the field, shimmering in the afternoon sun. For a fleeting moment there was a faraway sound of ethereal music. Tom leaned toward the open window.

"C'mon, Daddy!"

Tom held his finger to his lips. "Shh, listen! You hear that?"

"What?" exclaimed Elma Mae, her face puzzled.

"That. Listen. I'm tellin' you, child, now listen."

They sat for a moment, unmoving. Faint, sublime music surrounded them and echoed softly over the fields.

"It's cuz of Tobias, Daddy, like I told you," Elma Mae said softly. Tom swung the car around and headed off toward his farm. *The boy*, he thought to himself, staring out over the fields. *Perhaps I should listen to Elma Mae, and yet—it can't be, these stories she tells. They're just children! Yet the child often tries to explain—*

Tom had ceased to hear his lively daughter's chatter as they drove toward home.

Jewell stopped on the road and crouched in front of Tobias, whisking the dust from his small, wrinkled shirt. She looked at him seriously, her eyes pleading, close to tears. "You been tellin' Mama it not wise to show folks your gift."

"I knows that," he said, looking down at his dusty shoes, "but the season here. I be eight years old tomorrow, and ... and they comin', like I always knowed."

Jewell fidgeted with his top button, her hands agitated as she breathed quickly in tiny gasps.

"We needs to leave Anker—us and Grampa Perry—to where they can't find you!"

Tobias reached up and put his small purple arms around Jewell's neck. She leaned down to his embrace, crying quietly.

"Mama," he spoke tenderly, "anywhere I be, they find me. But it all right. It a joyous thing, not fer tears comin' down your cheeks. " He nestled his head against her.

Jewell rose to her feet, wiping her cheeks and staring out at the tall stalks of dead corn standing brittle and rotten, the husks sucked dry and wizened, lying in heaps on the hard clay dirt. She looked sadly down at the broken rows choked with weeds and dry dirt.

Cornfields look like I feel, she thought. *My chile not mine anymore, but he my only reason to keep goin'.*

Tobias slipped his hand into hers and looked up at her. "Don't be sad, Mama," he said as a radiant purple butterfly, tiny and delicate, lit on his shoulder. Tobias twisted, gazing down at it. "Oh!" he exclaimed. He stood perfectly still as if listening. The butterfly rose in the air, and Tobias stepped into the field.

"Watch this, Mama," he called back. He stooped down to one of the furrows, his small shoes sinking in the dust. His purple hand reached down into the sunbaked dirt and cupped a small clod in his palm. His childish voice sang into the splintered corn stalks.

May the frail flourish, the earth nourish, the crop be green and golden. To you we are be-be-beholden."

Tobias looked up at Jewell and then out at the rows of corn. "This from Elo," he told her, resting on one knee and staring out at the skeletal stalks as he let the dry dirt sift through his fingers. Jewell bent down beside him.

"Tobias! What are you doin'? Why'd you sing that song? I never heard you—"

"Feel the dirt, Mama. Dig your hand down deep, like me."

Jewell plunged her hand into the dusty furrow and clutched a piece of parched clod. "Ugh!" she exclaimed. "Tobias, this silly. Just gettin' grimy. We got to be goin'!"

"Spit on it, Mama."

"I won't!"

"Then look." Tobias spat on his dirt-covered hands and closed them into small purple fists. Slowly he opened his hands to reveal rich, dark earth lying in his palm. "This be what Elo told me. This be for nourishin'."

Jewell looked down at his hands and gasped in astonishment. "But Tobias, a minute ago it was just—"

"Dust. I know, Mama," he interrupted, giggling in delight and lunging toward a dead cornstalk.

"I doin' it, Elo! I doin' it," he chanted. Busily he pushed the new fertile soil around the base of the dead cornstalk, his hand closing tightly around the roots, his shiny purple head bent low.

"Now you may grow, and grow strong you will," he uttered as he rose to his feet and took Jewell's hand. "We be watchin' now, you 'n' me, Mama."

"What we s'posed to be watchin', Tobias? I don't see no change."

"You will. It will come."

They headed down the road again. Suddenly at the base of the dead cornstalk there was a slight shifting of the soil, and a brilliant green leaf began to coil outward, inching slowly up the tall, withered stalk. More leaves appeared and wrapped themselves around and around the dead stalk. Up and down the deep sun-scorched rows, the earth surged, heaping chocolate-colored, rich dirt along the deep troughs of dust. The vast field seemed to be alive as hundreds of new shoots and leaves sprang from the parched earth. Jewell stood in bewilderment, gripping Tobias's hand.

"My 'chile, my 'chile," she repeated over and over to herself. They stood looking out over the field, which was now ripe with tall golden cornstalks. A gentle breeze sighed among them, shimmering in the distance. Far out on the horizon, the once ruined field had sprung into new life.

A few miles away, across the fields, Birdie Foy stood in front of his sagging shanty with his hands on his hips, watching with narrow, darting eyes as the dusty soil surged and the cornstalks whipped back and forth.

"Jumper! Come here, boy." Birdie tipped back a canteen and removed his old straw hat. He wiped his sweaty face and looked out at the cornfields.

"Jumper!" he yelled again. "Whatcha got in this cooler? Ol' devil rum got me seein' things!" He inspected his dented canteen and sniffed at the contents. "Somethin' goin' on out in them fields!

Minute ago I was near to weepin' at the sight of that old dead crop. Now look at 'em! Miracle of the Lord!" The old Negro farmer stumbled backward and turned to face his son. "The Lord bringin' down some mighty bounty for us, Jumper. Do you see what I sees?"

Jumper ran toward the cornfield. "Gawd Almighty," he yelled. "It ain't the rum, Papa. It real, it real!" He dashed into the field, laughing and waving his arms over his head.

Jewell's hand flew to her mouth, and a faint cry escaped her lips as a curious popping sound filled the air. With a soft thud, two ears of corn landed at her feet, dark green in their husks, silky tassels sprouting from their tips. She stooped and picked one up and then carefully folded back the layers to expose rows of bright golden kernels. The flowering crowns along the stalks in the field began to whip wildly back and forth. More ears of corn exploded, shooting skyward from their leafy cocoons. Jewell shaded her eyes and looked up. All along the road, the sky was filled with soaring green husks. Soon the road was littered with them.

"Dear God!" breathed Jewell.

Tobias broke away from her and scrambled to load up an armful. He was exuberant, laughing with excitement.

"Mama," he called out, "we gonna have corn for supper, ain't we?"

Jewell stroked the silken tassels lying in her palm. "Yes, son, we gonna," she answered quietly.

Overhead a great swarm of purple butterflies dipped and swooped, their wings whirring in the hazy sunlight. For a few seconds they enveloped Jewell, a velvet touch on her face. "Oh!" she exclaimed, touching her cheek. "What was that?"

"The *Enriching*, Mama." Tobias watched the butterflies disappear.

CHAPTER 5

Dampened by Tears

OUT ON THE ROAD again, Jewell and Tobias followed the ruts of the road that led toward their farm. The miracle of the cornfield had left Jewell stunned and unable to speak as her son chattered happily and trotted along beside her.

He been tellin' me the season comin', that it be a joyous time, she thought. *He been leadin' me for a long time now, and today I sees it with my own eyes. But it dangerous for the chile with bein' so purple and beautiful, and with what Elma Mae said—the powers. What is I to do?*

She quickly wiped at her eyes dampened by tears. They passed through the few acres of fields that belonged to her and Grampa Perry, bound in by a horizon of wild hedges and dense woods beyond. The land that rolled gently toward the tree line was planted in corn, cotton, sorghum cane, sweet potatoes, and field peas—the precious gifts of nature that kept them fed. With Myron and Josh gone, Jewell worked hard in the fields—with the help of Jumper, Birdie Foy's son—to supply enough food for their table. But it was hard, and their meager living was a constant worry. Now people said there was that "mighty black goo" beneath their land, but she often wished it had never been discovered.

The two of them passed the barn and approached the small farmhouse. Wagon wheels with splintered wooden spokes, a rusty plow, and scattered buckets lay in jumbled confusion. An old truck, once the prized possession of Grampa Perry, stood near the barn door, its wheels missing, but supported by four blocks of wood. Tobias loved the rusting flatbed. Grampa Perry and Myron had never gotten rid of it, both in agreement that it was a perfect playground for Tobias when he wasn't off in the woods climbing trees or at the fishing hole with Elma Mae and Chalmers.

Now Tobias jumped into the driver's seat, his short legs dangling as he gripped the old steering wheel. Turning and twisting the wheel, he soared off into his make-believe world, making buzzing noises. Jewell smiled to herself and walked on toward the farmhouse. She said nothing to her son as she left him to play, but she walked with her head down, in deep thought.

Tobias watched her, knowing she was sad. His usual exuberance disappeared, and he sat forlornly on the seat of the old truck, resting his chin on his fist. Soon he climbed down and entered the barn, tiptoeing over to one of the stalls. Peeking over the top, he was face to face with a handsome, chestnut-colored mare. He reached up and gently stroked her nose. "Hi, Tawny," he whispered. Barn swallows flew in and out of the door. Slanted sunlight laid paths across the hay-strewn floor. Tawny whiffled. "Mama comin' real soon to check your wrap," said Tobias.

"Excuse me, Royal Master," came a low, polite voice from above in the dusty rafters. Tobias looked up, startled, and broke into a wide smile. Perched on a single beam, its graceful wings folded, was an enormous butterfly standing over six feet tall, glowing in hues of rich purples, dusted with green and gold, and speckled with dots.

His wing tips were lined in deep azure blue, and his wrinkled face was like a walnut with waving antennae. On his wire-like hands were miniature white gloves, and he wore a matching vest, complete with pockets the size of tiny purses. The creature had a startling air of importance.

"Yes, Elo," said Tobias.

"For a few frightful moments I was highly alarmed," said the creature in a scratchy voice. "*Dis-disquieted* would be a better word, for I found myself stuck in your drawing. "Then a man's ugly boot stomped on me, and I was utterly frozen. The look on his f-f-face was simply un-unnerving! Did you hear the Enriching, sire?" His strange eyes rolled in deep sockets. They resembled crystal prisms, and they glowed as he spoke. "Thankfully, Elma Mae helped me to get unstuck when she let out that frightful squeal in the backseat of Tom's car. Goodness! It gave my ears such a start!" He sniffed. "You must prepare a proper time and formally introduce her to m-m-me. She is quite chattery but certainly helpful." Elo floated lazily to the floor of the barn as Tobias stood smiling at him.

"You sure did wink a raised eyeball in Mr. Tom's car," Tobias said with a chuckle.

Elo stood taller. "Yes, well, Royal One, I am very pleased to see your attention to your learning. It was a stunning display of your power before your eighth birthday, bringing the corn to life—and taking appropriate measures to punish the one who spoke with an evil tongue. I am very proud of you." Elo began to pace back and forth. "Although, I was afraid that without my teaching gloves, you might miss some important instructions, therefore causing me enormous agitation and worry that you could not hear me, even though I had placed myself very comfortably on your shoulder."

"I heard every word you said, Elo," said Tobias. "Dang! Mama was standin' right there too!"

"Yes, yes, sire, you are most correct." Elo scraped his throat and nodded. He stopped and looked up, his tiny brow furrowed in concentration.

Tobias squinched his face, squeezed his eyes shut, and clapped his hands over his ears as Elo's high voice called out: "Speech, mountain and splendor! Our trumpeter come forth!"

Dropping his hands, Tobias looked around with anticipation as Elo grumbled to himself, his eyes darting back and forth.

"Hmm, where is she?" Elo wondered. He repeated his command: "Speech, mountain and splendor! I call forth the Queen Trumpeter of Zinfoneth!" He turned to address Tobias. "It is possible that she too is stuck in your drawing, sire." With his gloved hands locked across his tiny vest, Elo began to pace back and forth across the barn floor. He stopped, leaned close to Tobias, and held up one gloved finger. "It is entirely possible that she is still attempting to use her wings. This planet has the most unusual air currents." He stared at Tobias and then back at his tiny finger. "Eek!" he shrieked, his prism eyes rolling in terror. He flung himself across the length of the barn and disappeared behind a feeding trough.

"Elo! What wrong with you?" cried Tobias, dashing in the same direction.

Elo's trembling voice from behind the trough. "I saw a strange finger standing in front of me."

"But that be *yer* finger, Elo!" Tobias laughed and looked down at him.

Elo straightened his wings, his face glowing red with embarrassment. "Oh, forgive me, Royal One. I did not intend to frighten you." He drifted slowly to the top of the corral.

"You din't frighten me, Elo," Tobias said calmly. "You jest forgot yer finger was attached to yerself." He giggled.

"The proper word choice is *did not*. It is not correct to say *din't*." Elo looked sternly at Tobias.

"Did not," repeated Tobias.

"Yes, well, I did think for a moment that the finger looked somehow very familiar," Elo said, his polite voice slightly gruff.

"I comin' up to where you is." Tobias clambered up the wobbly slats to the top of the corral. The boards creaked and swayed as he clung, testing each foothold. "Stay where you is," he said, panting. "Don't go flyin' off."

Elo watched from his perch, his face pinched with concern, and his strange, cavernous eyes raising and lowering. "Royal One, must you give me such a fright? Is it not possible that you may forego such a risky ascent?"

Tobias reached the top of the corral door, settled himself into a comfortable position, and swung his legs back and forth. "I likes to sit up high," he announced. "Tomorrow I will be eight years old—of royal height."

Elo regarded him with devotion. "You are already cited as Ninth Ambassador to Nuctemeron." He spoke softly and placed his tiny gloved hand on Tobias's cheek.

"What be an ambass ... ambassador?" The small boy's face crinkled as he tried hard to pronounce the word.

"An ambassador, sire, is the voice of the Cripons. There will come a time when you will be king."

"Then, you be teaching me how to be king!" He regarded Elo seriously, resting his chin in his hand.

Elo smiled. "Yes, how to be king. But kings have other duties besides ruling: kindness, love, helping others, lifting sadness ..." His fingers suddenly explored the pockets in his vest, and he frowned. "I really should have my teaching spectacles on in order to finish the list."

"That's okay, Elo," said Tobias.

"You still have much learning to accomplish," continued Elo, still searching his vest pocket.

"Is he kind, Nuc-tem-er ...?" asked Tobias.

"Nuctemeron is treacherous," Elo replied, "and not one to be trusted in the matters of our origin, we of the Cripons."

Tobias considered Elo's words and nodded slowly, his shiny purple brow puckered.

"Nuc-tem-er-on," he repeated to himself.

"Remember," Elo said, "you will grow and learn to use words that are keepers of fire and sword. You will raise the banner for the Cripons." He turned his gaze intently on Tobias, his huge eyes rolling beneath the heavy lids.

"I likes to look at you, Elo. I likes to look at your eyes especially," Tobias said. He reached out and cautiously touched the edge of Elo's wing.

"Well." Elo chuckled, sounding slightly ill at ease. "May I fly above you, Royal One?"

"Of course. Is it fer teachin'?" asked Tobias.

Elo floated gracefully to a high beam in the center of the barn. He placed a pair of tiny spectacles on his wizened face, adjusting them carefully. "I had intended that we work on speaking proper words today, but being stuck in your drawing caused me to forget the scroll and my pointer. So we shall simply discuss the art of love. As ninth ambassador, you will need to be well schooled in—" Elo paused. "Royal One, is there something on your mind? Is something bothering you?"

Tobias sat on top of the corral, lost in thought. He had not been listening to Elo. "Sometimes," he said.

"Shall I sound the horn? They ride at all times, and they will come immediately," Elo said, appearing distressed.

"No," said Tobias. "It my mama." He looked up, his eyes filling with tears. "She very sad."

"I am listening, Royal One."

Tobias continued. "See, my mama, she's knowed from the time I been born to her that I be noble and most folks ain't, but she ain't accepted it. Now I gonna be eight years old tomorrow, and I sees her weepin' about me, even though I been tryin' to tell her. I loves her, Elo."

Elo made a strange sniffling sound. Tobias's eyes widened. "Is you weepin' too, Elo?"

"No, no." He removed his tiny spectacles, cleared his scratchy throat, and adjusted his wings. "Your mama is strong, just like your daddy was. She is staunch—like a tree, sire. She is passing through a time now that has been coming closer and closer each year. And now it is here. As I teach you more about yourself, you will be able to help her know that you will always be at her side. The power of love is already deep within you, Royal One, and she will feel that always. With time, she will let you go, but know, Tobias, that she will forever feel your presence. The rest of her life will be joyous and beautiful because of you." He tucked away his spectacles in his vest pocket and paced back and forth on the wooden beam. "I think I hear her calling you now, Royal One."

"It be Mama all right, callin' me fer supper." Tobias remained on top of the corral, his small shoulders drooping.

"We will speak more of this yesterday." Elo floated down past him.

Tobias brightened and wiped his eyes. "You means tomorrow, Elo." He laughed.

"Of course, of course," said Elo, rising tall, his wings unfolding. "Tomorrow!" Suddenly he was very small and perched on Tobias's shoulder, his voice reedy and far away. "Remember, the cupbearers shall ride with raised swords of honor. I shall find Queen Zinfoneth, and the trumpet call will be blown in your honor, sire. Soon now." With a faint whiffle, Elo was gone.

CHAPTER 6

The Wisdom of Grampa Perry

J EWELL STOOD LOOKING DOWN at Tobias. In the darkened bedroom she watched him sleep, his small head resting peacefully on his pillow. Tenderly she tucked the light blanket under his chin, marveling at his rich purple skin and small, graceful hands. She bent over and kissed him lightly, passing the tips of her fingers over his closed eyes. Softly she closed the bedroom door and returned to her kitchen table, her scuffed shoes treading lightly across the pinewood floor.

She wore a simple dress of cotton print fabric, held together high at the throat with a brooch. Her hair was done up tight since she had been in town today. Jewell was always keenly conscious of carrying herself proudly and dressing carefully on the days she appeared in the town of Anker with Tobias. Many of the townsfolk noticed how beautiful she was, but the mystery of her purple child had surrounded her since his birth, causing cold stares and unspoken hostility.

Now she sat silently in a straight-backed chair, sliding the kerosene lamp closer and sipping from a chipped white mug. The table was covered with oilcloth, frayed at the edges and almost bare in one or two places where elbows had rested over the years. A stove of rusting iron sat against one wall, a blackened kettle on top. On nails behind it hung a few pots and flat baking pans. An odd assortment of drinking glasses lined the small, unpainted cupboard, none of them the same size or pattern. Jewell's prized collection of dinner plates was stacked beside the glassware, imitations of Blue Willow ware. She picked absently at a bouquet of wildflowers that stood in a Mason jar in the middle of the table, half smiling at Tobias's delight as he had come in from play several days ago and presented them to her, their petals wilting in his clutched fist.

Grampa Perry rocked in his old chair by the hearth, the rhythmic creaking the only sound in the room.

"Where'd you git that corn we had fer supper, Jewell?" he asked suddenly. "Mighty good, gal. Don't believe I ever sunk these old teeth into such kernels! Like heaven it was!"

"Tobias, he—" She stopped herself. "Mr. Ricketts had him some overflowin' baskets, Daddy."

"Prob'ly from ol' Birdie Foy over yonder. Must've had hisself a dandy crop this year—yes, sir!" He continued to rock, his sightless eyes turned toward the window.

Grampa Perry was a frail old man. He wore a pair of crudely mended dark glasses. His kinky hair stood up in tufts, and his grizzled cheeks were unshaven since he could only fumble with a razor. His place of choice was almost always in this rocking chair, angling his head back and forth as he listened to the activity around him. Frequently he ventured onto the small porch, carefully feeling his way with his cane over the pine boards, his unseeing eyes turned toward the fields.

Jewell was Grampa Perry's only child. Her name had been specially chosen by her parents as a tribute to her beauty. As Jewell grew to be a young woman, Grampa Perry knew he had been blessed, and he thanked the Lord every day for her kindness and sweet disposition. When she'd given birth to a beautiful, deep-purple baby, Grampa Perry's astonishment had immediately given way to overpowering love for the tiny child who unlike anything he had ever known. Only once had he expressed his amazement to Jewell shortly after Tobias had been born.

"He purple, Jewell! What on earth?"

"He is, Daddy," she had interrupted, smiling secretly. "He s'posed to be. He not like us." Then she'd handed her father the tiny, gurgling infant wrapped snugly in a worn blanket. "Here. He bring you peace and contentment like you've never knowed."

Grampa Perry had rocked the baby in his old chair, the baby slipping into a deep sleep. A feeling of unearthly tranquility had enveloped him, his tired body freed from the never-ending aches and pains from years of toiling in the fields. Shortly after that day he had lost his sight, and now he could only sense Tobias growing into a boy. But every day he looked forward to the sound of his merry voice and the feel of the small arms that hugged him. At the boy's touch, he felt a sudden peeling away of old-age ailments and worries. As the years passed, he gradually came to sense things about Tobias that were known only to Jewell.

Now he removed his glasses and wiped them on his sleeve and resumed his rocking.

Jewell looked up, watching him from across the room. "Why you wipin' your glasses when you can't see nothin', Daddy?"

"I don't take kindly to that question, Jewell," answered Grampa Perry, sounding testy.

"I only sayin' you couldn't see a owl if it were perched on your knee."

"I know what you sayin', gal. Why you so sour? Gets me wonderin' about your day."

The kitchen was silent again, with only the sound of the squeaking rocker. Jewell sniffed, wiping tears from her cheeks, and bent low over her account book.

"What y'all over there swimmin' in tears for?" Grampa Perry asked.

"Lotsa things, Daddy." Jewell stifled a sob.

"We gonna manage, gal. I knows y'all is worried, but—"

Twisting in her chair, Jewell turned to interrupt the old man. "We should sell Tawny, and this land—take Tobias and go to the city. I sure to find work there." She sank back in her chair and buried her face in her hands.

Grampa Perry grunted, a scraping sound in his throat. Poking his cane around the floor, he searched for his coffee mug and leaned over to pick it up.

"Cleanin' houses for them," he declared with contempt.

"That's right, Daddy, but we gotta eat." Jewell looked up, her voice rising. "Y'all know Myron was plannin' to do that anyway."

"Nope!" Grampa Perry shouted suddenly. "No chile of mine gonna disgrace herself cleanin' up after white folks!"

Jewell looked at him sadly. "Why we gotta pass bad words, Daddy?"

Grampa Perry gripped his cane and pounded it on the floor. "Don't like bad words neither, chile, but these acres been in my line since shackles bound yer great grampa. I never leavin' what's mine. Be here tomorrow, next year, twenty year ..." His voice trailed off.

Jewell stood abruptly and moved to the sink. She tied an apron around her waist and began to stack the supper dishes, glancing back briefly at Grampa Perry. "Fine, Daddy. That's all fine. I knows those things, but you—"

"Besides, the season is here," interrupted Grampa Perry.

Jewell whirled around, her eyes riveted on him. "How you know that?" she demanded.

Grampa Perry stood and hesitantly made his way to the window, his feet shuffling. He stood silently for a moment. "I knows about Tobias, Jewell. I knowed it from the first when he a small bundle in my arms. He give me a ... a kinda peace ... can't rightly describe it. Has ever since. I hears him talkin', things the boy been sayin'."

"That don't mean nothin'!" Jewell argued.

"Jewell, chile, they is comin'! They comin' soon. Ah can sense it. Nothin' y'all kin do about it. He not of this world."

Jewell shoved past him, half sobbing. She clutched Tobias's drawings, crumpling them, and moved quickly to the fireplace.

"What you doin'?" Grampa Perry's voice was tense.

"I burnin' these drawings, Daddy—these butterflies Tobias always makin'. They part of why you sensin' all this. They alive!"

"Don't you dare, gal!" Grampa Perry groped for her arm. "If you puts that to the flame, a mighty wind gonna sweep over you, the likes you never knowed before. You gonna be ankle deep in tellin' that young pepperstorm why his drawin' in ashes."

Jewell stopped, breathing hard, her eyes closed. She walked back to the table, flinging the wrinkled drawings onto the chair. With a strangled cry she collapsed, sinking to the floor. She bitterly regretted speaking with Grampa Perry. Better to have left it alone, she thought. Don't wanna hear what he knows. He just an ol' man who can't see. How could he—

Grampa Perry's voice cut into her thoughts. "I can sense yer wrath, darlin', but this here ain't some shovel-n-oats. This is about Tobias. He yer blood—mine too—so settle them tortures. They ain't yours to change."

"Damn you, Daddy!" Jewell headed for the door, grabbing the drawings from the chair.

"Damn me? What got into you, woman?"

Jewell smoothed out the drawings as she paused at the door. "I knows you can't see this, Daddy," she said, her voice trembling, "but on this paper be our Tobias. He drawed it real good. He here, purple

like we knows him to be. Front of him there be a ... a ... somethin'
like a boat, or a funny-lookin' steamship with all these bright colors
an' shinin' a-golden. Tobias, he kneelin' front of that big boat, with
them butterflies he always makin' all around him. Strange-lookin'
folks is around him too, all wearin' somethin' like ... like suits made
outa tin, all shiny and bowin' down. They all there around Tobias,
some of 'em purple too. This drawin', Daddy, it don't look like it
done by a child, but I seen Tobias doin' it, right over there on the
fire hearth!"

Jewell stood silent, staring at Grampa Perry. Neither of them
spoke. She reached out and closed his hand around the drawing. "It
safe with you, I know. I has no right to try and destroy it, Daddy."

She stepped out the door and picked up a shotgun that leaned
against the wall. With a heavy heart she headed for the barn, feeling
weary and defeated. Her head was aching, her feet plodding. Holding
an old lantern high above her head, she made her way through
the dark and entered the barn, her eyes searching immediately for
Tawny as she called out his name. The horse raised his sleek head
above the stall, whinnying lightly. The sight of him softened her
mood as she scooped a bucket of oats from the grain bin.

"Ah, Tawny," she said, stroking the mare's nose and laying her
face against the sleek animal. "I come to check on you, give you some
of these good oats." She slid into the stall and set the bucket down,
smoothing Tawny's side. Leaning low, she looked closely at the
mare's bandaged ankle. "Whoa, girl, whoa." She laid a restraining
hand on Tawny's neck as the horse shifted restlessly. "What's wrong,
girl? What is it?" She stood back, half-chuckling to herself. *There
you go, Jewell*, she thought, *talkin' to a horse like she of a mind to
answer.* Picking up the lantern, she stepped a few feet out into the
darkness, the shotgun cradled in her arm.

"Who's there?" Jewell called out, peering into the dark. She
heard a distant shuffling sound and called out again. "I got me a
double barrel, and it's loaded! We ain't havin' no barn raisin', hear?"

With a sigh of relief she lowered the shotgun as Grampa Perry appeared out of the dark shadows, his cane stabbing cautiously as he picked his way toward Jewell.

"Daddy, what you doin' out?"

"That you, Jewell?"

"Course it me, Daddy. You heard me callin'."

"Had to tell you." His breath came in short gasps. "After you walked out the door, I knowed they was there. I heard 'em."

Jewell eyed him suspiciously, lowering the lantern. "Who'd ya hear?" she demanded.

"I heard them horses ridin' by—like the wind they was. Wasn't no ordinary ones like Tawny. Besides, this the middle of the night. Nobody out scamperin' around like that at this hour. Ain't no newcomers, neither. Been around since Tobias come to us."

Jewell caught her breath. "Daddy, get that thinkin' outa your old head!"

Grampa Perry stared into the dark. "Heard 'em before, Jewell—couple years back. Never told you. Believe it were right after Tobias started drawin' all them butterflies. You remember? He only a wee twig then, mebbe two year old."

"This gotta stop now, Daddy." Jewell shook his arm, but her eyes scanned the pitch-black woods off in the distance. She suddenly shivered in the cool night air.

"C'mon, I goin' to bed now. Prob'ly ol' Birdie Foy out huntin'. Now 'n' then he known for doin' some strange things. Fond of that ol' rot-gut rum and all."

But Jewell was afraid now, and exhausted. Through most of that day she had carried the knowledge of her gifted son as a burden on her heart. Her own eyes had looked upon his unusual powers. There was the butterfly in Tom's car that seemed to rise from Tobias's drawing, with Elma Mae screeching in delight. Then the cornfield. And of course that frightening man at Herbert Ricketts's store, who had ended up on the floor. His eyes had been so full of hatred. Had she dreamed that? It seemed now so long ago. Now her daddy had come to her with this story after the two of them had quarreled over her refusal to acknowledge what she had always known in her heart.

"Who is they, do you s'pose, Daddy?" she whispered.

"I been ponderin' that, Jewell, for many a year. Could be them fellers in the tin suits, the ones you tol' me about that Tobias drawed."

"Better git goin' now, Daddy." Picking up the lantern, Jewell was silent as Grampa Perry clutched her arm. She steered him back to the house through the dark night.

"He eight years ol' today," Grampa Perry said as they climbed to the porch.

Jewell put out the lantern, and presently the house was dark and sleeping.

Tobias stirred in his bed, the light cotton curtains billowing in soft folds across his face. A breeze whispered through the room. He sat bolt upright, wide awake. Past the open window, close by, tall and erect, rode twelve knights, moonlight shining on their suits of armor. The front row of six carried long lances and banners of silk, held close and rigid. The banners were emblazoned in rich purples, greens, and gold. They snapped briskly in the night breeze. Purple plumes waved gracefully from their helmets, and each wore a purple mantle draped across the shoulders.

Tobias watched the two rows of majestic horses trot slowly past, the first row cantering into the dark as the second row stopped for a moment to raise shining battle swords in salute as they rode by the small face at the window.

There was a whiffle of wings. Elo was at the foot of his bed, his face stern.

"I sees 'em, Elo!" said Tobias excitedly.

"Yes, sire, for your birthday," said Elo, placing his twig finger to his lips. "This is not the time to converse. I am here to present you with the Five Stones of Royal Passage that will bestow upon you power and wisdom. You will soon learn how to place these stones in their proper position." Elo's heavy eyelids slowly opened and closed. "This was the prophecy of King Suryes of the Cripons, an ancient one who ruled on our planet of Elios in a time so distant we cannot fathom. When you have mastered the positioning of the Five Stones it will be the time of departure for you, me, Queen Zinfoneth, and the cupbearers. The ship will be waiting."

Elo bowed low and placed a pouch of gold mesh in Tobias's hand. It was bound with a purple ribbon. Then he straightened, standing tall. "You may look into the bag, sire. It is your eighth birthday. The Five Stones of Royal Passage are to be used to bring love and joy. With the passing of days, you will learn to achieve other ways for their effectiveness."

Tobias untied the ribbon and stared into the small bag. "Oh, Elo" he breathed softly, spilling the glowing stones onto his blanket. "Can me an' Elma Mae play with 'em? Chalmers too?"

Elo's curious little face creased in a smile. "Certainly," he said, "but be aware that they have great powers."

Tobias carefully placed each stone back into the bag. He looked up at Elo. "It be a fine present." He paused for a moment, the small bag held tight in his fist. "Elo, does you think you could get Mama a present—even though it be my birthday and not hers? I knows she cryin' some. I told you she be sad. When she be sad, I be sad. Mebbe somethin' to hep her feel better?"

Elo nodded and placed his tiny twig finger on the boy's cheek. "Royal One, will you please repeat after me?"

Tobias nodded. "Uh-huh."

"*Do* you think, not *does* you think."

"*Do* you think," repeated Tobias.

Hunched over, his eyes rolling, Elo gestured with his fingers. "It *is* my birthday," he said, pronouncing each syllable. "Not—it *be* my birthday."

"It *is* my birthday."

"When she *feels* sad, I *feel* sad.

"When she *feels* sad, I *feel* sad," said Tobias.

"Very good, sire." Elo straightened up.

"To *help* her feel better. The word is *help*, not *hep*."

"To *help* her feel better," said Tobias obediently.

"Now it is time you begin to place your words carefully upon your tongue—and I believe I have something in mind for your mama." He bowed low and was gone.

CHAPTER 7

The Sheriff

T
HE SUN GLARED DOWN on the faded blue police car
as it rumbled along a weather-beaten bridge and came
to a stop. It stood silent for a few moments in the humid
noonday heat, the engine idling. Then the car door swung open, and
Neil Swanny, sheriff of Anker County, stepped out and stretched
to his full height, his barrel chest bulging and heaving with deep
breaths. His unshaven face glistened with small beads of sweat. He
hitched up his trousers and spit a long stream of brown tobacco
juice over his shoulder.

Sheriff Swanny was a vain man, often stopping in the midst
of his daily runs over the dusty back roads of Anker County to
check his appearance, and now he leaned toward the window of his
car, admiring his reflection in the glass. He smoothed his sweat-
stained shirt and carefully parted his greasy black hair with a comb,
dabbing at stray wisps as he angled his head from side to side. He
straightened and sucked in his belly with a look of smug satisfaction
on his face.

"Gotta get the missus to do a better job on these uniforms," he mused.

Although the sheriff's wife, Ginger Lee, had always devoted a good portion of time to pressing her husband's uniform, creasing the pants, and shining his shoes, Neil Swanny was beginning to feel that she no longer cared how he looked, nor did she seem to appreciate the high position he held. The creases in his trousers were not quite as sharp, his jacket was rarely brushed, and his normally spotless shoes were being neglected. Ginger Lee even seemed to be slightly bored with his presence nowadays. As with most everything in his life, he believed that he deserved attention, from her and from the people of Anker County who had voted him into the office of sheriff.

With the coming of August and the annual Mint Julep Festival, Ginger Lee always created a stir among the onlookers as the wife of the county sheriff. For the past two years since she had arrived in Anker, she had regularly appeared as queen of the Magnolia Festival, waving to the residents of Anker, seated beside him in the parade that made its way down Main Street. Neil was proud of his New Orleans wife, but to him she was a reflection of his own image.

Each year, as he regularly predicted, the white folks in Anker lined up alongside his police car as they inched their way along the parade route. Some actually saluted. As for the colored people who occasionally showed up for the festivities, he ignored their silent stares and sober faces.

He reached up to polish the single red light on top of his car and smiled to himself. He was glad he'd purchased the new white DeSoto for his wife. That gift would surely cause her to be more appreciative of him again, he was certain. Carefully dusting off his trousers, he opened the car door and slid into the seat. He grabbed the handheld radio, wiping the accumulated dust from the dashboard as he pressed the radio button. His raspy voice carried into the muggy air of the surrounding woods.

"Soddy, Neil here ... over."

The radio crackled back at him, full of static. Neil sighed, rolling his eyes. A slow, drawling voice came back indistinctly. "Yeah, Neil. Where in tarnation are you? We had some problems here in town this mornin'. Over."

Neil heaved a sigh and ran his fingers through his oily hair. "All right, tell your sheriff about it, Soddy," he said patiently. "Have anything to do with old Ringling callin' again about strikin' oil? Over."

"Nope, wasn't him. Over."

Neil laughed and slapped his knee. "Old fool can't figure out it's just plain ol' Mississippi mud he's seein' squeezin' up through his garage floor."

"Wasn't no shallow dish like Ringling, Neil, not this time—no, sir! Had to do with that durn hooley-ann. Over."

"Hooley-ann? What y'all talkin' about? Over."

"Well, if you'd let me finish, Sheriff, damn sakes. My pappy always said a hooley-ann is a man who got no guts, always stirrin' up matters he ain't got nothin' to do with. My pappy always said—"

Neil interrupted. "All right, all right, Soddy, you really tryin' my nerves, mister."

The radio crackled, spitting static. "It's that cousin of yours, Neil, that damned Orville. He's rilin' folks up to an afternoon sweat, talkin' about that horse again. Got some of these folks in an uproar listenin' to his tales. Over."

Neil's voice rose to a higher pitch. "Orville oughta be run outa town. Never did like him bein' my kin anyway!" He tossed the radio down on the seat, his jaw tense and jutting. He lurched clumsily out of the car and kicked at the splintered wood boards of the bridge. A gritty cloud of dust settled over his well-shined boots. "Orville— that damned fool," he muttered. "Him and his fairy tales. Nothin' but make-believe. I got a mind to grab my night stick and ..." His voice trailed off, and he yanked at his necktie, opening his shirt collar.

Composing himself, he sauntered over to the railing of the bridge and stared down at the stagnant water, ignoring the incoming pleas from Soddy.

"Neil ... come in. Git on back to me. Where are you, anyway? Over!"

Suddenly the sound of an engine above him filled the sultry air. Neil glanced upward, shading his eyes. He backed up toward the car, staring at a small plane that was pitching and buzzing over his head.

"Don't you go doin' your arrow-plane antics again, Hoedig," he hissed to himself. "I'll run you in for disturbin' the peace." Neil's eyes narrowed as the sound of the plane grew louder. "You never gonna learn your lesson, are ya, Hoedig?" Neil spun around, watching the plane. Reaching into the car, he grabbed the radio as the plane buzzed directly above him, seeming to hang in midair.

Instinctively Neil ducked as the plane dropped low just above the treetops, kicking up debris from the ground and ruffling his hair. He spun around again, jabbing his finger in the air. "That's it!" he shouted. "I'm gonna be at your heels by midday, Hoedig! Ain't no place to hide. Thirty days in the county jail, and that means no Sunday dinner! Swallow that, ya turnip!"

"Neil, who y'all talkin' to out there? You got a finger on the button. You need to calm down about Orville. Over."

The sound of the plane could be heard nearing the bridge again. Neil watched with squinted eyes. "I'm talkin' about Hoedig, Soddy." He spoke quietly into the radio, his tone low and sinister. "You know that foolhardy old pinhead. He's flyin' that crop duster like he's daffy or somethin'. Puttin' a nail in his own coffin, that's what he's doin'. Boilin' down on his county sheriff, nearly takin' the hair right off my head. Over."

Neil jerked his head up as the plane roared above him, appearing empty as it whipped up and down. Hoedig was barely visible in the cockpit, but he could be seen lifting a bottle to his mouth, tipping his head and taking long swigs as the plane dipped and bounced close to the trees. Passing his grimy gloves across his goggles and patting his black leather helmet, he raised the bottle as in a toast, seeming unconcerned as the little plane zigzagged above Neil.

"It's a Mississippi mornin', and I'm up here a-soarin', lookin' down on my county sheriff," Hoedig sang loudly in a drunken slur above the roar of the engine. He leaned his head out from the cockpit and shouted down at Neil. "Whoopee, Sheriff, you look like just another old varmint down there! You raisin' my hackles, Sheriff—me and my kin!" He took another swig from his pint, the plane pitching and rolling. The engine began to sputter. "It's a Mississippi mornin', and I'm up here a-soarin', lookin' down on my county sheriff," he sang out again. The plane began to dive, the engine spitting. "Lord almighty!" he screamed suddenly. "Someone playin' a joke on me? Look at the size of *that critter! Look like somethin' outa pre-his-tor-ic*—someone call the gov'nor!" Hoedig's voice was louder now. "My gawd! Never seen nothin' like …"

"He's comin' back, Soddy!" Neil shouted. "Can't you hear that ragtag engine on your radio? Over."

The plane grazed the nearby treetops, skimming low over Neil's car. "Gonna run him in, Soddy. Thirty days. Break out the extra mattress in the jail. Over." Neil dropped the radio and squatted low, his hands gripping the open window of the car. The sound of the plane faded away. He twisted away from the car and ran down the length of the bridge, shouting as the engine sputtered and coughed, trailing off over the tree line. "Hope you crash in the hickory trees!" he shouted gleefully. Swiping his sleeve across his forehead, he stood and watched the plane rise again, the engine coughing, and then disappear. Suddenly, all was quiet.

"Uncle and underbrush, Hoedig! You gonna be lucky if y'all don't break your head buzzin' yer sheriff. Think I'll just let you simmer out here for a spell if you go down. Oughta teach ya." Neil shaded his eyes, scanning the tree line. As he turned and headed back toward the car, a deep shadow passed over him. A flapping sound echoed overhead. He cocked his head and looked up, spitting tobacco juice. "Agh," he choked, wiping his hand across his mouth. Hovering directly over his head was a giant Pandarus butterfly, its velvet wings moving gracefully. He stood frozen, uttering tiny gasps, and then reached cautiously for the car door. The huge creature shifted slightly, blotting out the sun.

"Wha—what we got here? Somebody set loose a big ol' moth. Must've been hibernatin'." He grabbed the radio. "Soddy! Soddy! Get the boys out here! Over," he called frantically, his voice high and trembling. The radio was dead. "Mebbe it's the army!" he panted as he scrambled into the car. "Damned military boys always tryin' somethin'." He threw the radio on the floor and gunned the motor. "Gotta get the hell outa here!"

The car sped onto a narrow road between tree stumps, tall reeds, and clumps of wild raspberry bushes.

The radio crackled again. "Whatsa matter, Neil? You ain't answerin' me. Somethin' wrong out there? Over."

Neil drove on, ignoring Soddy. The car lurched sideways, the engine whining as he forced it past heavy underbrush and low-hanging tree branches. "C'mon, c'mon ... don't go fallin' apart on me now," he snarled.

Suddenly the entire windshield split with a cracking sound. Neil pitched forward as the car died, the engine winding down to a sputter. The sound of grinding gears broke the stillness of the quiet marshland. He leaned his head against the steering wheel, moaning and whimpering, his neatly combed hair falling over his forehead. Yanking on the door handle, he shoved his weight against it. The door was stuck shut. Soddy's pleas from the radio went unanswered.

Inside the sweltering car, Neil reached for the other door, mangling his cherished hat as he bounced across the seat, attempting to get out. The hat was a symbol of his authority, and the sight of it crushed and shapeless nearly moved him to tears. He tossed it in the back seat, wiping hot beads of sweat from his face.

When he finally managed to squeeze out the door, he found himself surrounded by prickly undergrowth and hordes of insects rising up out of the dead tree stumps. They buzzed around him, attracted to his sweat-slick face. Desperately he retrieved the crumpled hat from the backseat, jammed it onto his head, and began to stumble along the soggy ground, dodging yellow jackets and mosquitoes. A feeling of nausea rose in his throat. There seemed to be no shade, and looking back he discovered that he had lost sight of his car. "Help!" he croaked, dropping to the ground.

Suddenly the sound of a voice floated eerily through the summer haze. Looking around, Neil found that he was beside an old limestone wall thickly entwined with ivy and old vines. Picking his way to the end of the wall, he slowly made his way to a huge, moss-covered tree, its branches sweeping low to the forest floor. He tried to ignore the constant whining of insects around his head, following the strange voice ahead of him. His eyes grew large, and his mouth dropped open, his tongue flicking on his parched lips. Odd cackling sounds emerged from his throat. Instinctively he reached for his gun, his hand shaking.

Standing on the other side of the tree was the huge butterfly he had encountered at the bridge. It dazzled in hues of lavender, its wings gossamer, and it towered above Neil. A curious head, shaped like a peanut, was adjoined to the narrow body. The head was dark-skinned, with patterns and overlays. The enormous eyes had no perceivable pupils, but they rolled back and forth, emitting rainbows of color. It seemed to be speaking, the voice thin and reedy.

Neil moved closer, as in a trance, and cowered beneath the tree branches. The strange voice spoke as the wondrous wings moved slowly back and forth.

"Now, sire, I have given you the Five Stones of Royal Passage, and we are taking the course by which your birthright has led us, and soon, little faithful one, we shall—" The creature paused, and the odd face seemed to rumple into a frown. "No, no, no. I must be more clear. I must teach him to understand. It is the mastering of the stones that will allow our ship to know its course … to take the long journey back to our planet of Elios."

The huge butterfly seemed to be speaking to no one. It moved forward a few feet, shifting its weight from side to side, rubbing tiny, wire-like fingers together, and raising them to its brow. The puckered mouth pursed, and the rolling eyes raised upward. They glowed, turning slowly in the deep sockets. "Oh, where are my gloves?" it said.

Neil clutched at the tree trunk, trembling as he stared in disbelief. "Gawd almighty," he whispered, his body flattened against the old brick wall.

The wings fluttered again briefly. Elo raised his head. "You must continue the advantage of … oh, what is the word?" The creature seemed to ponder, tapping its wire finger on its lip. "Let me see. Let me see. Be wise. Think! As ambassador—no … your royal title! Yes, yes, that's it!"

Again Elo shifted his weight and clasped his tiny hands together. "Soon you shall become a Lord of Fire. From the long-ago time of this prophecy, time has advanced more quickly. King Suryes claimed that a Cripon would rise again from a planet called Earth, which would cause—" Elo lifted his head and pursed his lips together. He seemed to be inhaling a raspy, deep breath.

"Speech, mountain, and splendor. Speech, mountain, and splendor. I call forth Queen Trumpeter of Zinfoneth," the high reedy voice shrieked. The sound echoed through the trees, ear-splitting and jangling. Neil sagged against the crumbling wall. Twigs scratched against his face as he desperately tried to call out anything to anyone, but no words came. He heard a ruffling noise, and then all was still. He slumped over in a dead faint.

The afternoon sun was low when Neil emerged from the deep undergrowth, his hair wild and stuck with leaves and debris. He squinted into the trees, randomly firing his pistol in all directions. "I'll git ya!" he hollered into the woods. "I'll kill that bumble-back moth, comin' down here with no cause and aimin' to take good white folks to cork an' bottle with the demons of hell." He rushed in among the trees and emptied his .38 pug-nose pistol of bullets until the chamber clicked over and over, the nozzle smoking. Sudden fear drained his face of anger, and he stood quietly, trying to calm himself. Dusk was creeping over the forest.

"What was I seein'?" he wailed into the trees. Whisking his hair back with trembling hands, he stealthily began to make his way forward, stumbling over the rough ground and glancing back nervously every few feet. At the sight of his police car standing askew between fallen trees, he cried out in relief and broke into a furious run.

CHAPTER 8

Hazer's Field

A N OLD DENTED CAR, its headlights blazing into the darkness, jostled off the side of the narrow mountain road and came to a stop just inside Hazer's Field. Close behind, a beaten truck followed, whining and gnashing its gears.

Jimmy and Jay Snaught climbed out of the car, their boots oozing in the muddy grass. Percy shouldered his way out of the backseat and hitched up his trousers, clutching a pint of bourbon. He tipped his head back and took a long swig. As he wiped his mustache, his eyes swept the field and the forest in the distance.

"It's up here!" Orville shouted. "Y'all just wait 'n' see."

"You think so, huh?" answered Percy. He ran his fingers through his hair and squinted into the darkness. Scratching a match, he guarded the flame in his palm for a moment before lighting a fat cigar and sending out wreaths of smoke.

"Yeah, Orville, ya think so?" echoed Jay, eyeing his brother from under heavy eyebrows. He snorted to himself and scratched his chin, mottled with a week's growth of beard.

Ledyard swung down from the cab of the truck, favoring his good leg. Orville emerged from the other side. His dog, Cottonseed, squeezed past him, limping slowly toward the nearest tree, where he sprawled. Orville stood on the running board, gleefully swinging the door back and forth. "Take 'er easy there, Cottonseed. You know you don't have much breath left," he called out to the old hound. He turned his attention to the group near the blue Dodge. "Did y'all hear that horn blowin' as we was comin' up Highway 2?" he shouted over their heads. "Me and Ledyard did. Cottonseed—even he was a-barkin'.'"

"Calm down, Orville," Ledyard said with a snort. "I didn't hear nothin'. Them ears of yours been livin' inside a trombone since you was born. That's why you talk nonsense all the time." Ledyard laughed loudly.

Orville leaped to the ground, slamming the truck door. His eyes blazed at Ledyard. "Don't go givin' me your snorts, you gimpy oaf! Better remember who I am in this town! Seems to me you was pleadin' for help weeks back, sittin' there in that heap of splinters. I aim to tell folks near 'n' far how tears was runnin' down yer chinny-chin-chin. I heard me a horn blowin'. No ordinary horn neither."

"Yeah," called out Jimmy, "what that odd-lookin' purple boy say to you anyway, Ledyard? Seems like you was real spooked … and then your chair broke!" The others cackled and hooted.

"You damn fools," muttered Ledyard, turning away, "have your fun! If anyone's odd around here, it's you two.

Several hours passed while the night air chilled, and the five men jigged and pranced in the clearing of Hazer's Field, tossing talk back and forth and hugging themselves to keep warm. The moon was high, and shadows fell across the rutted road. Now and then they stared across the field into the woods, their eyes darting, unsure, a sense of foreboding among them. No one was willing to talk about what they expected to find. Ledyard leaned against an old tree stump, his head down, still brooding over Jimmy's remark.

Jimmy and Jay perched on the hood of the car, swinging their muddy boots and mumbling between themselves. Their occasional high snickers caused suspicious looks from the others.

"This is a waste a time," said Percy, sauntering over to the old car. "I got a mind to head back to town, throw down a few at Boggie Taylor's, and go git some shut-eye." Slapping absently at the back of his neck, he tossed his head as a crimson butterfly rose from his shirt collar and floated past his ear. "Somethin' bit me," he muttered. Soon he was snoring, his legs sprawled out of the car door, his head thrown back, and his mouth sagging.

Jimmy laid back on the hood, his arms behind his head, and closed his eyes. "Think I'll do me some snoozin' too."

"Do you think they're nearby?" asked Jay, his voice low.

"They'll expose themselves," said Jimmy. "The time is nearing."

Ledyard had nodded off beside the tree stump, and Orville was in the front seat of the truck with his boots propped up through the open window.

A low fog settled over Hazer's Field, swirling eerily through the tall grass and underbrush.

An odd clicking noise swirled past Jay's head. "Jimmy, you hear those crickets? Damn, they're pesky!"

"Everything here is pesky," mumbled Jay, his voice drowsy. "Pay them no attention." He scratched his stubbly chin. Suddenly a small coil of butterflies encircled his head—clicking, buzzing, fluttering, and tightening around him in a whirl.

Jimmy sat up and began to howl, his voice oddly high-pitched. The butterflies around the old Dodge scattered, and some fell to the ground.

"Now if that ain't the strangest wail a feller ever heard," said Ledyard, suddenly awake. "Where y'all git tonsils like that?" Jerking his head from side to side, he began to swat frantically as he was engulfed by swarms of butterflies.

Jimmy and Jay watched him silently through narrowed eyes, their mouths twitching. They stayed where they were. "Thought them red moths was gonna have your head for dinner," remarked Jay moments later as Ledyard slumped heavily against a tree, his arms still flailing in the air. "Looks to be a roundup here in these mountains with critters flyin' around at night," observed Jimmy dryly, ignoring Ledyard's plight.

"Red moths?" shouted Orville from the truck. "There ain't no red moths around these parts! Hell, there ain't no red moths anywhere!"

"Why'd they pick on me?" Ledyard whined. "Stung right through my pants."

"Might have been butterflies, but butterflies don't click 'n' sting," Orville said loudly. "They goes round to flowers, gentle and such."

An unearthly sound of a horn bellowed in the distance, resounding over the field. Cottonseed dragged himself from the tree, his nose high in the air, baying and yowling. The surrounding trees of Hazer's Field began to toss as a sudden gust of wind blew through the woods. The truck was suddenly swallowed in a menacing horde of red-banded butterflies.

Jimmy and Jay scrambled into the Dodge, pushing Percy's inert body across the car seat. "I find the sound similar to what is heard in the Halls of Surtaq," said Jay as they settled in the backseat.

Jimmy nodded. "The earthlings would not recognize it." They slammed the door shut and sat looking out, their identical faces bland and watchful.

With the insects swarming around him, Ledyard managed to slide back inside the truck with Orville, slamming the door and rolling up the window. He picked up a pint of whiskey from the seat and took a swig, staring coldly at Orville. "Got no courage, boy," he stated. "Shoulda helped me plan our escape."

"Escape?" asked Orville, his voice shaking.

"Yeah, from that lightnin'-fast horse we seen. Oh, you thinkin' these strange moths are just out here for their exercise? You and me, we know a few things, Orville. You yourself been warnin' the folks in town. Somethin' not right up here in this field. This gale came outa nowhere after that damned horn blowed, and them red bloodsuckers, they been sent ahead of that horse. He a bad one, sent from hell's own serpent. Known to kindle folks' minds to repent—yes, sir! And why those moths red? Just think about it." Ledyard paused, staring at the windshield that was crawling with red butterflies. "I see you ain't moved, Orville. I ain't surprised. I know you got no spine, boy!"

Orville stared at Ledyard, his lips trembling. "What we gonna do, Ledyard? Can't let them red bugs just eat us alive. And where you s'pose Cottonseed gone to?"

Ledyard took a long swig and flung the bottle to the floor of the truck, staring morosely out the window. He glared at Orville with contempt and said nothing.

"What I mean is, whatcha thinkin' we should—"

"Shut up, Orville!" Ledyard leaned close to the windshield, studying the huge butterflies that lay like a blanket across the glass. "Damned river of grief," he muttered. He turned and pulled his shotgun from the rack behind him. "I got somethin' for 'em, ya crybaby!" Rolling the window down in quick jerks, Ledyard sprayed buckshot into the swirling mass, the crackle of double barrels echoing into the night. "Finished 'em off, see, while you're sittin' there suckin' your thumb and cryin' for your mama. You ain't no good to this town at all, Orville. Never did understand why Neil gave you that job as deputy. So what if you're kin? When somethin' needs doin', I take charge!" He got out and slammed the truck door, furiously grinding the few remaining insects beneath his boot. Orville followed cautiously, leaning against the door.

"Take them famously feared Snaught brothers over there," continued Ledyard. "What do you really know about 'em? I heard 'em talk like they was from the North Pole. Hush-hush this, and hush-hush that. Coupla yellow-bellied cowards like the rest of you, so don't go feelin' alone, Orville. Your dog prob'ly smartest of the whole lot. He prob'ly lit out for home. Or take Percy over there—passed out 'n' missed the party." He clawed at his shirt pocket and pulled out a flattened pack of cigarettes, seeking one that wasn't broken. "I'm headin' back to Anker. I ain't waitin' around for that spooked horse to show up." Looking down, he inspected the ground, pushing his boot among the dead butterflies. "What the hell—biggest flyin' critters I ever seen."

Orville stepped down from the truck as Cottonseed came slowly out of the woods, dragging his hind leg. "I sure am glad to see you, ol' boy." He bent down and stroked the dog's head. "Thought for a Tennessee moment them bugs had eaten my best friend. Come on, boy, in the truck." Suddenly he twisted around, his eyes wide. He grabbed Ledyard's sleeve. "You hear that? Same horn blowin'—louder, though, and damned creepy!"

Ledyard shook his arm from Orville's clutch and held up his hand. "Gotta say, it's real unnatural and—"

"Sh-h-h." Orville cut him off as the high wavering note sounded again.

Jimmy looked over at Jay as they sat together in the backseat of the Dodge. "You know what that sounds like to me? We need to be watchful."

Orville and Ledyard stood still and tense. They looked at each other as the far-off sound of horns continued, bouncing off the trees across Hazer's Field and the valley. Ledyard slowly reached into the truck and snapped on the headlights.

Jimmy and Jay emerged from the car, their faces slack-jawed and waxen. They stood silently, side by side.

Without warning there was a heavy sound of galloping hooves. Two tall figures on horseback swept across the yellow glare, their images a blur. Ledyard froze, trying to comprehend, when suddenly a longsword cut through the darkness, flashing in a lightning-fast motion. Ledyard felt his shirt ripped from his body. He fell heavily, clutching the car door.

The ground shuddered now with the pounding of horses. Four riders whirled past the men, their speed cutting through the darkness with the sounds of hoofbeats and the strange, whipping wind.

Jimmy was knocked to the ground by one of the huge steeds. Jay stumbled as a sword slashed at his face. He let out a high whine, inching his way beneath the truck as the thundering hooves hemmed him in. More figures tore past, silent except for the snorting and huffing of the horses.

From inside the truck, Orville ducked low with only his eyes peering over the window ledge. He was having trouble breathing. He felt Cottonseed's cold nose against his face, whining piteously. "Nobody believed what we knowed to begin with, Ledyard 'n' me." His whisper rasped into the old dog's ear. "Somethin' evil happenin' round this county, Cottonseed."

Then the clearing was quiet. Except for the low cries and moans of the men, all was still.

Orville inched the truck door open warily and crept out, gasping for breath. Illuminated in the glare of the headlights were twelve knights, each in a shining suit of medieval armor. They sat unmoving and gigantic, all of them astride mighty horses, facing the group of cowering men. The horses were draped in rich purple tunics, their bridles garnished with tassels of gold.

"Ho-ho-holy be-bejeebers!" Orville gaped at the horsemen as he slowly rose to his feet. He jumped back as a long lance hit the ground in front of him, stabbing powerfully into the soil and missing his boot by inches.

The knights parted, six on each side, and turned their steeds. Sweeping into the darkness, they left a floating mist of pale violet behind them.

CHAPTER 9

Porch Settin' and
Peach Juice

I T WAS HOT AND humid as Ginger Lee drove out of the driveway in front of the Southern Baptist church, an imposing brick building with manicured lawns and fragrant magnolia trees. An ornate sign in large Gothic lettering adorned the entry. "Come and be saved. Your souls are thirsty for Jesus," the banner proclaimed to the members of the church, who were all white folks from the "better" part of town. On Sundays the pews were packed, and frequently the church held a midweek bake sale featuring homemade cakes, cookies, sweet corn puddings, jars of pickles, and seasonal jams.

Ginger Lee pulled the big white DeSoto out onto Main Street and drove slowly through town. It was unusual for her to pass up her weekly visit to Marabelle's Beauty Parlor, but this morning she'd had a special reason to drop by the bake sale and buy one of the angel food cakes made famous by Miss Genevieve Stark, head of the church choir. Reaching out, she placed her hand momentarily on the plain white cake box on the seat next to her and headed down Main Street. Her destination was Jewell Valentine's farm.

Anker was in the Black Belt of Mississippi, not far from Tuscaloosa. It was an ordinary, small southern town surrounded by a patchwork sea of cotton fields, cornfields, and timberland rolling off in the distance. Its buildings were solid, and the streets were wide but dusty from constant use as people from the outlying farms came to town on a weekly basis, many of them simply to pass the time and gossip. The white citizens of Anker lived in neat, well-kept houses away from the colored part of town that clustered near the dirt road that ran from the highway past the railroad tracks and the town dump.

Ginger Lee passed the beauty parlor, Ricketts General Store, the small gasoline station, and the hardware store. Up the main street stood the old courthouse surrounded by lovely bushes of angel's trumpet, the dark glossy leaves awaiting the winter bloom. These things caught her attention in the morning sun, but she had no particular fondness for the town. She had managed to tolerate her husband's insistence that she engage in the summer parade down Main Street, well aware that he coveted the attention he always got from the bystanders. But mostly she kept to herself, spending time clipping, pruning, and caring for her Royal Crown magnolias, well-known all over town for their pale-violet beauty. She rarely ventured much beyond the town limits.

Funny, she thought, that last night she'd kept seeing those two in her mind—the woman and her purple boy—and couldn't sleep. She'd tossed and turned all night. Neil had been in a sour temper this morning and had been for days. He blamed Ginger Lee, of course, for being so restless. His eyes of late appeared red-rimmed and puffy, and his usual clean-shaven face bristled with patchy stubble. He had become irritable and more easily angered than usual. She had decided to keep her distance.

Remembering the pair again, she grimaced. She could have hurt them really bad, she thought. The image of the purple boy especially obsessed her—the strange child with skin so purple he appeared to have a golden sheen, his amber eyes penetrating and serious. She had heard talk of him many times—the whispers and questions, the ridicule. Neil himself had mentioned him just a few weeks ago. He had come home for supper and casually informed her that a colored man had been found dead in a marsh somewhere out near Bunny Bayou.

"Name was Valentine. That odd-lookin' purple boy belong to him. Prob'ly ran into trouble of some kind. You can never tell about those folks."

Several days later she had dropped by Neil's office. All the talk among his pals was about "another Negra been found, another Valentine." This time it was the son. She had been stunned to notice an air of complacency and slight amusement among the men as they passed the story around. It didn't seem to matter. "Y'all talkin' about murder!" she'd said, confronting a scrappy little man who seemed to be especially talkative. "Appears to me mighty strange that two men from the same family were—"

"Don't go frettin' yer pretty head about trivialities, Missus Swanny," said the man, taking her firmly by the arm and ushering her out the door. "Ain't for you to worry about."

She thought again of the boy and the young woman holding his hand. Must be his mother. But she wasn't like him … not like him at all. The boy had gazed at her as she'd sat fuming in her car, and it had seemed that her eyes were locked on his, that she couldn't look away if she tried.

She shook her head to chase away the thought, flicking her long, painted fingernails. Out on the country road, squinting against the sun, she stopped the car in front of an old mailbox. The name was chipped and faded, barely discernible. Leaning closer, she was able to make out the name: Valentine. A narrow dirt lane led off into the fields, and in the distance she could see the small roof of a house and a barn. She turned in to the lane, glancing out at the cornfields as she passed. Suddenly she jammed on the brakes and sat staring in amazement at the tall, majestic cornstalks, their colors golden and green, a luster about them that seemed unusual—miraculous, even. Her knowledge of rural Mississippi was limited, and cornfields were cornfields, nothing more. But she knew this had been a drought year. Mr. Ricketts's store was full of such talk: bankruptcy, dead fields, and "no corn for profit" throughout the county and the whole state. But who owned this field, she wondered to herself, this stunningly beautiful cornfield that stretched out to the horizon? It obviously bordered the Valentine farm, but the two men had been found dead. Were they the owners? And if so, how …

Checking her lipstick in the rearview mirror and fluffing her short, cropped, blonde hair, she slowly approached the small farmhouse with the peeling paint.

Jewell wiped her sleeve along her forehead and climbed down from the ladder. She had been nailing loosened boards and applying whitewash to the barn.

"Kin I go up again and pound?" asked Tobias, swinging his small hammer as she descended. "I loves to climb that ladder!"

Jewell smiled. "No, son, it pretty much done now. Far as I know, I believe you've done all your chores." She gathered up the bucket of nails and whitewash, and pulled Tobias close, kissing the top of his head. "This be a special day, Tobias. You growin' up—eight years old—and I gonna give you somethin' real special, somethin' your daddy made for you to keep forever."

She reached into the pocket of her dress. "Close your eyes now, and hold out your hand."

Jewell laid a small, beautifully carved wooden medallion in his palm. It was made of hickory, smoothed to a satin finish, with an inscription carefully carved on its face.

"To my son Tobias, Born to Myron and Jewell

This be to remember Your Folks who Loves You. 1934"

Tobias stared down at it, his eyes shining. "Oh, lookee! From my daddy!" He held it up, studying the carefully carved letters. "I gonna carry this in my pocket all the time!" he said, slipping it into the pocket of his worn blue overalls, "an' I gonna show it to Elma Mae and Chalmers. They knows I misses him."

"Your daddy carved that for you last year before he died. Intended to give it to you himself, Tobias."

"Thank you, Mama." Tobias put his arms around Jewell's waist and pressed his face against her.

"I promised Grampa Perry I'd come and set awhile with him this mornin'," she said, heading for the house. After their discussion of the child last night, she had felt tired and confused. She hoped to find peace and quiet in a simple rocking chair beside Grampa Perry.

Tobias skipped around the barnyard, having swept it clean this morning with his favorite tall broom. He had fed Tawny and pitched some new hay into the trough. "I goin' fishin' today," he called out to Jewell. "Elma Mae and Uncle Pete, they prob'ly already down at Pencil Creek."

"Who Uncle Pete?" Jewell called back, adjusting the kerchief that covered her hair and whisking her faded blue dress.

Tobias laughed. "Oh, I forgot! Uncle Pete be Elma Mae's dog. He always with us at Pencil Creek. Chalmers, he comin' too."

He squatted down, pulling the mesh bag from his pocket. Reaching inside, he picked out one of the shiny balls and placed it in the dust in front of him … then another … and another. Five glowing lustrous globes winked up at him, emitting tiny shafts of light.

"Tobias! Where did you get those?" Jewell was suddenly back, standing above him, her voice stern. "I never seen marbles like those."

"They from Elo ... fer my birthday." Tobias picked up one of the globes and examined it closely.

"Tobias," said Jewell again sternly, "is this about the butterfly you always drawin'? What you talkin' about, 'for my birthday'? You don't get no gifts from butterflies!"

"Yes, I does!" he said, continuing to turn his new treasures over and over in his hand. "They from Elo. He my teacher."

They both looked up suddenly at a car approaching the house, the tires grinding into the gravel. The glossy white car came bumping into the barnyard and stopped, its motor purring. A blonde woman sat looking at them from behind the steering wheel. Tobias jumped up and stuffed the bag of stones into his pocket. His eyes grew wide.

"Mama, ain't that the car that just about runned us over?" he whispered fiercely. Jewell passed her sleeve across her forehead and stared hard at the woman, a glint of recognition in her eyes. "I think so, chile. I think so. You better git along now, down to Pencil Creek." She regarded the woman soberly, not trusting this visitor.

"I think I wait awhile," said Tobias, scuffing at the dirt, sensing his mother's unease.

"'Lo there!" Ginger Lee climbed out of the car and advanced toward them in her spike-heeled shoes. She picked her way cautiously over the uneven ground. "I'm Ginger Lee ... Ginger Lee Swanny." She extended her hand.

Jewell and Tobias watched her silently.

"I ... I ... well, I saw y'all weeks ago. You were crossing the street and ... and y'all must remember," she stammered. "I wasn't exactly having myself a grand day. Almost ran you both over." She laughed self-consciously, aware of Jewell's slightly hostile eyes upon her.

Jewell remained silent, her eyes taking in the expensive dress, the exquisite lace of the collar, and the high-heeled, patent leather pumps with pointed toes. A pale pink purse hung from her arm, its gold clasp engraved with initials, GLS. She noted the woman's too-white complexion glowing with rouge spots, and the astonishing green eyes that almost begged her for a response. She'd come out here to apologize, thought Jewell, to apologize for scaring her and her child out of their wits. Well, she could at least say thank you. It was more than most white folks would do.

On the other hand, she could tell already that the woman was curious about Tobias. She reckoned that since she was married to that sheriff, maybe he'd sent her out here to snoop around. Jewell didn't hold any respect for that man. She wished the woman hadn't bothered to come.

Ginger Lee smiled, still holding out her hand. Tobias shifted his gaze to the white car as Jewell stepped forward and clasped her hand briefly.

"My name's Jewell, ma'am ... Jewell Valentine. Tobias be my son."

"What beautiful names—Jewell Valentine ... and Tobias," gushed Ginger Lee, looking down at him as his mother pulled him to her side, his purple skin glowing in the hot sun. "I don't believe I've ever heard that name—Tobias. Not anyone I've ever known. What does your name mean? Do y'all know?" she asked.

Tobias met her gaze, his small face serious. "Elo, he say it mean king—king of the Ancients."

"King of the Ancients," mused Ginger Lee. "That sounds like a mighty powerful name for such a little boy!"

"Had me a dream before he born, and I knew his name was to be Tobias," said Jewell quietly.

"Can I touch yer car, missus?" asked Tobias.

"'Course you can. You can sit behind the steering wheel if y'all care to." She smiled at Jewell as Tobias dashed to the big car, whooping with delight.

"And Tobias," Ginger Lee called after him, "sitting there on the front seat is a box holding an angel food cake! It's for you and your mama."

"Wow! And Grampa Perry!" shouted Tobias, climbing into the front seat. Purring noises immediately erupted from him, his small head barely visible inside the car as he rocked the steering wheel back and forth.

"My son—nothin' he loves better than pretendin' to be drivin' somethin'," said Jewell, beginning to warm up to the other woman. "He can spend hours in that ol' backwheeler you sees over there, growlin' and purrin'. Used to belong to his grandpappy when he was a youngun, and then to his daddy. 'Fore his daddy died, him an' Tobias, they be putterin' around that ol' flatbed together for hours. Seems like most younguns loves engines."

"Something about the sound," said Ginger Lee, laughing.

Suddenly Grampa Perry's high, thin voice rang out from the porch. "Jewell, are ya done nailin' them boards?"

"Comin', Daddy," she called. "Have a visitor just now."

"That who ya talkin' to?" shouted Grampa Perry.

Jewell glanced shyly at Ginger Lee for a moment. "My daddy, he blind, and he likes to have me do some porch-settin' with him now 'n' then. Promised him this mornin' after my chores. Would you care to join us, Missus Ginger? Mebbe a cool glass of peach juice?"

"It'd be a privilege, Jewell. Pretty muggy this morning," said Ginger Lee. "Could use some shade, and my! Sippin' peach juice sounds mighty welcome."

"Tobias, time to come outa Miz Swanny's car now, hear? We all gonna set on the porch awhile an' have us some fresh juice." Jewell shaded her eyes and watched him wiggle down from the car seat.

"Oh, let me get the cake!" exclaimed Ginger Lee, making her way back to the car, her high heels tottering on the gravel. "Y'all can call me Ginger Lee," she called back as she handed the cake box to Tobias. "Would you like to carry this to your mama and your grampa, Tobias?" she asked.

"Yessum, I'd be pleased to, missus," said Tobias politely. He walked slowly and carefully toward the porch, balancing the box on his outspread hands.

"My, but he's a polite child, Miz Valentine," Ginger Lee murmured to Jewell. "So many younguns these days tend to be rude and snappy. Take my baby brother's youngest. He's probably the age of Tobias, yet he's spoiled and disagreeable. Can't stand to be around the boy." The two women walked slowly together toward the porch.

Grampa Perry looked vacantly out over their heads, sucking on a well-chewed pipe. "Who that?" he demanded. "Who ya got there, Jewell?"

"It's a lady from town, Daddy. Name is Ginger Lee Swanny."

"Ya don't say!" quipped Grampa Perry.

"This be my daddy, Perry Dorling."

"Pleased to meet you," said Ginger Lee. She settled into the porch swing that hung on long, quiet chains, adjusting her skirt and noting the dust that now covered her shiny black pumps.

"Hmph!" responded Grampa Perry, his head angled in her direction. He fumbled in his shirt pocket for a match. Tobias passed silently into the house behind his mother, bearing the cake box.

"I'll just be a minute," called Jewell from the kitchen, "fixin' us somethin' cool."

"That be Tobias that just passed by?" called Grampa Perry. "Why ya walkin' like that?"

"I be carryin' a cake, Grampa, in a big box. Made by angels." Tobias appeared back at the screen door.

"What? Whatcha mean, made by angels?" Grampa Perry's voice rose, high and querulous.

"I only means what the missus tol' me."

"He means angel food cake," said Ginger Lee with a low laugh. She leaned toward the old man. "I was over at the church bake sale this morning and thought y'all might like something special."

"'Cause it my birthday!" shouted Tobias gleefully from the kitchen. Ginger Lee heard the tinkle of glassware as Jewell and Tobias spoke quietly together.

"I see," said Grampa Perry. "How'd ya know it be the chile's birthday?" There was suspicion in his tone.

"Well, I … I didn't, really. I just thought y'all might … well, I was driving out this way anyway, and …"

Grampa Perry leaned close. "Y'all nevah been out to this farm before. I nevah heard my gal say your name till now. Some special reason you drop by to visit Jewell 'n' the boy?"

"I … I …" She stopped, unable to think of what to say. "My! I must say I've never seen such a grand corn crop in my life as y'all has," she exclaimed loudly, hoping Jewell would hear her and come to her rescue. She was beginning to feel uncomfortable as the old man lapsed into silence, unmoving, staring at her with his sightless eyes. She had experienced a deep sense of satisfaction at first, meeting the curious little boy and his mother, and had even had a fleeting vision of spending long afternoons on this porch with a real friend, sipping coffee and watching this wondrous child at play. But the grandfather was making her squirm. She was sure he was scrutinizing her, even though he was blind.

She heard excited voices coming from the kitchen and hoped that Jewell would appear soon. She had no idea what to say to the old man, but she sensed that he was deeply suspicious of her reasons for coming out here. Well, she thought, I certainly cannot announce to him that I nearly ran over his daughter and his grandson. I'll just have to leave it be. He can think whatever he pleases. She suddenly looked over at Grampa Perry and gave him one of her best lopsided smiles. Then she remembered that he was blind.

Tobias placed the white box carefully on the kitchen table and lifted the top to peek inside. Swirls of pink frosting lay in peaks, nestled among sprinkles of glitter. He gasped. "Look at this, Mama! Can I have me a piece right now? 'Fore I goes fishin?" He hopped up on a chair, swinging his short legs.

"Sure you can, son. But better hurry. They prob'ly already hooked all them fish!" Jewell put a tall pitcher of peach juice on the table, opened the cupboard doors, and reached toward the assortment of cheap drinking glasses she used for her family. They were no longer there. Instead an array of tall crystal glasses and graceful long-stemmed goblets stood before her eyes. Slender ribbons of gold rimmed each one, and a tiny deep-purple butterfly was etched on each of the fluted sides. Beside her carefully stacked, old, chipped plates of dinnerware were sets of fine bone china, with the same gold band around each piece, and the same delicate butterfly etched in translucent beauty.

Jewell stood frozen in front of her cupboard, her eyes moving back and forth across the shelves. She gasped and grabbed for a chair and then sank to her seat, her hand to her chest. "My dishes ... everything ... they all changed!" she cried out. "They all new and ... and glistenin'!" She clapped her hand over her mouth, "Tobias, look, chile! Look what in Mama's cupboard!" She pointed, her hand shaking.

Tobias jumped down from his chair, licking his fingers. He came to Jewell's side, his mouth smeared with pink frosting. "What, Mama?" he asked, following Jewell's hand. "Oh, they all different! All shiny and pearly-lookin'," he exclaimed. "Elo, he told me ... that this for you."

She turned and wrapped her arms around him, stroking his smooth head. His skin was like velvet beneath her hand, his voice muffled against her.

"I loves you, Mama."

Cupping his face in her hands, Jewell kissed him. She searched his eyes, her breathing rapid. "Tobias, you must tell me ... you must tell me about Elo, who he be. How this fine crystal get into my cupboard?" She spoke slowly and gently to him. "Who is Elo, Tobias? The cornfield—you talkin' about Elo out there on the road— and those shiny marbles you said came from him."

Tobias looked back at her, his eyes unwavering. "Elo teaches me. Every day. He a wise ancient, and he showin' me how ta be royal. He might be here in this room right now, only you cain't see him." His small brow puckered. "Do you like your dishes, Mama? They real fittin' ta serve cake for the town lady, ain't they?"

Jewell sighed, holding him close for a moment. "Yes, chile, they real fittin'. And thank you, Tobias. You tell Elo."

"I will. I will!" Tobias scampered to the screen door. "Goin' down to Pencil Creek now. Elma Mae and Chalmers prob'ly already there."

"Be home by supper," Jewell called after him, watching him skip merrily out on the porch. "And y'all be careful and stay together, hear?"

The two women and Grampa Perry sat in the shade of the porch. Jewell had served them cake and peach juice. Tobias had skipped down the front steps an hour ago in high spirits, run across the barnyard, and disappeared. He had stopped briefly beside Ginger Lee.

"That cake sure tastes good, missus. Mama gave me a big piece cuz I goin' fishin' now."

Ginger Lee smiled. "Next year when y'all turns nine, why, I'll bring you another one."

Grampa Perry chuckled. "Where y'all off to, boy?"

"Fishin'! At Pencil Creek!" Tobias was halfway across the barnyard.

Ginger Lee stood and watched him go. "That youngun—y'all must know how special he is, Jewell."

"Oh, yes, I knows."

"And Miz Valentine … Jewell," said Ginger Lee, "I must comment on your outstanding china and goblets. Why, I've never seen such elegant plates and fine crystal glasses—all gold-rimmed with the beautiful, tiny purple butterflies. They are just enchanting! Where on earth did you get them … if you don't mind my asking?"

"They was a gift," Jewell said simply.

"My, my," continued Ginger Lee. "Why, y'all could shut your eyes and imagine dinnerware like that on tables for royal folks!" Ginger Lee settled in the rocker again, inspecting her nails and whisking the dust off her shoes.

"What she talkin' about, Jewell?" asked Grampa Perry.

"Never mind, Daddy. Just us womens prattlin'."

A rusty tractor rumbled into the barnyard and stopped. A tubby old Negro man swung down from the seat and headed for the porch. He wore a broken straw hat that shaded his stubbly chin. Dark suspenders were clamped onto his patched pants. Piercing black eyes peered out from under the brim of his hat, and he laughed as he approached the house.

"Hey, ya twitter-pecks!"

"It's Birdie Foy!" said Jewell as she rose from her chair.

"Whatcha all doin' loungin' around here today?" he called out, climbing the steps. He swept off his tattered hat, his merry eyes twinkling.

Jewell nodded. "Howdy-do, Birdie. We just coolin' off. Come on up and set awhile. This lady here a friend from town." She motioned toward Ginger Lee.

Birdie's eyes grew round, his hand rubbing his unshaven chin. "Thought that shiny white car somethin' we don't see in these parts, ma'am." He swept low in front of her in a mock bow. "I lives over yonder," he said, jerking his thumb toward the field. "Just stoppin' by to—"

"That old Birdie?" interrupted Grampa Perry.

Birdie stepped over to him and put a hand on his old friend's shoulder. "Where that young saplin'? He around here?"

"Gone fishin'," said Grampa Perry.

Birdie sighed and turned to Ginger Lee, running his hand over his grizzled head. "Ma'am, that chile ... do you know, these ol' bones has never experienced no pain, no hurtin' since the first day Jewell put that wee babe in my arms. No more'n a couple days old, he was. He sleepin' 'n' dreamin' like he b'long somewheres else." Birdie leaned closer to Ginger Lee. "Missus, I eighty-one years old now, and that old-age stiffenins I was troubled with—why, they never bothered me again after Tobias born, goin' on eight years now."

Ginger Lee looked up at him, her eyes wide in astonishment. "Y'all mean, Mr. Foy, that holding Tobias took away your arthritis?"

"Zactly!" Birdie slapped his hat on his head and headed back down the steps. He turned and looked up at Jewell. "Got somethin' on my mind, gal, I'm needin' to tell you. That's why I came by." He pointed out to the fields. "Them corns ... they was dry and dusty day 'fore yesterday, not fit fer a ragtag crow. Wind rattlin' through 'em sounded like ol' skeletons. Now look at 'em. Right in front of me 'n' Jumper yesterday, they growed 'n' bloomed, and corns started shootin' off 'em. We had some fer supper. Never tasted anything like 'em. They like from some magic place, Jewell. Nothin' to explain it, neither."

Jewell stood at the screen door, her eyes closed. The group on the porch was quiet.

"Better tell him, Jewell. He suspectin', I kin tell," piped Grampa Perry after a long moment. His voice was high and shrill.

"Hush, Daddy," said Jewell. "Just never mind." She leaned close to Birdie over the rail, her voice dropping to a whisper. "I know you thought you were seein' things—like a pipe dream, and scary-like. It be Tobias, Birdie."

Birdie nodded and stepped back. He looked at Jewell thoughtfully. Touching his hat, he said quietly, "I think I be a-knowin' that, Jewell." He shuffled back to the tractor, whistling, his hands deep in his pockets. "Y'all take good care of that boy, hear?" he called back. "I be comin' by again real soon, Jumper and me."

Ginger Lee turned to Jewell, her eyes wide. "Land sakes! What on earth is he talking about? I myself just came to a halt driving out here today. Just had to slam on my brakes. Those cornfields Mr. Foy is talking about, why ... they are just plain dazzling! I heard him say they were dead a few days back!"

Jewell remained silent.

"Ain't nothin', ma'am," said Grampa Perry, blowing his nose loudly into a large handkerchief. "The cornfields, they just havin' a particular good year. Birdie, he likin' his whiskey. Now 'n' then he experiences visions. Fields just takin' their time this year."

The three sat awhile longer, Jewell lapsing into a melancholy quiet, and the old man saying nothing, just rocking and mumbling to himself. At last Ginger Lee picked up her purse and slowly rose from the rocker. She felt an urgency to get back in her car, drive to town, and think about this visit. "Thank you, Jewell," she said. "Good afternoon to you, Mr. Dorling. Time I was getting on."

"I'd rather ya call me Grampa Perry if y'all gonna be here on a regular basis. You plannin' to come back?"

Ginger Lee cleared her throat. "I'll remember that, Grampa Perry. I'd be honored." She reached for Jewell's hand, and the two of them started across the barnyard. "It's been a pleasure spending the afternoon with y'all."

"Cake was mighty tasty, missus," called out Grampa Perry pleasantly. As Ginger Lee slid into her car, the old man's voice came to her, high and querulous. "Did I hear your name be Swanny? Ya kin to the sheriff?"

"He's my husband." Ginger Lee turned back toward him. "I'm not real proud of that sometimes. There's folks here in Anker that don't always look upon him kindly. But I ... I'm planning to come back if y'all will allow me."

"Pay no mind to Grampa Perry," said Jewell. "He known for speakin' out. Just comes right out 'n' asks questions. Doesn't think to be delicate-like."

"That's all right, Jewell. My own daddy is a lot like yours. He's a judge in New Orleans where I was raised up. Has a question—why, he doesn't hesitate for one minute." She started the engine and paused for a moment. "Just need to tell you before I go ... how real sorry I felt about nearly running you over ... you and Tobias. I had no right to be rude."

Jewell touched her arm lightly. "Stop frettin' about it. Have to admit you gave us a real fright, but we was all right, Tobias 'n' me. Just needed a little dustin' off."

She watched as the car eased down the narrow road.

"Bye, Jewell," Ginger Lee called, waving over her shoulder. She drove toward Anker, lost in thought, several times glancing out over the golden cornfields, idly noting a graceful horde of purple butterflies hovering above the tall stalks. A bit unusual, she thought. They looked like the etchings on Jewell's beautiful goblets.

She lit a cigarette and inhaled deeply, her eyes squinting on the road ahead as she reflected on her visit. She looked again out over the golden fields of corn. Mr. Foy had said they were dead a couple of days ago and had then bloomed to life right in front of his eyes. The old man didn't seem to be talking "whiskey visions" either. He'd seemed anxious to share his news with Jewell, plain as day. Claimed that the baby Tobias had cured his aches and pains. Still, these colored folks, they were known to weave spells. She smiled to herself. The enchanting purple boy kept reappearing in her thoughts. They had all spoken of him kind of secret-like, almost as if the boy had supernatural leanings.

As her mind lingered on Tobias, she suddenly gripped the steering wheel and sat taller. Hadn't he been standing right in front of her car that day when her motor simply came back to life? The car had been dead! The scene was suddenly vivid in her memory: the astonished faces of folks nearby, herself whipping around as she headed for the general store, the sound of her car starting with nobody in it, and the keys in her own hand.

Snuffing out her cigarette, she smiled to herself, envisioning the reaction of her few women friends if she were to tell them this story—or Marabelle at the beauty parlor, who hungered for bits of gossip, passing tales all over town and loving every minute of it. She could see their raised eyebrows, their sly glances and whispers. She rolled down the car window, letting the cool breeze blow through her hair.

Parking the car in front of her house for a moment, she sat and admired her beautiful magnolias behind the white picket fence. She was not looking forward to seeing her husband this evening. Her visit to the Valentine farm had given her some added insights about him. Nothing had been said directly, but those kind people were harboring unspoken resentment toward Neil. Grampa Perry ... there'd been something in his tone.

CHAPTER 10

The Glass Tree

ELMA MAE AND CHALMERS lingered among the daisies and buttercups in the field near the narrow river and wooded ridge. The sky was cloudless, a quiver of birdsong filled the air, and bees flitted among the flowers. Little Chalmers had grown tired of waiting by the side of the road for Tobias and had spied Elma Mae in the distant field, her pigtails swinging as she ran toward the fishing hole. Running and shouting he had caught up with her, and now they settled themselves on a big tree root under the shade of a huge cypress to wait for Tobias together.

Elma Mae lay back in the dry grass, her arms behind her head, whistling through the gap in her front teeth. Chalmers sat alert, watching for Tobias.

"See this?" She pointed to her mouth. "My tooth felled out yesterday, after I wiggled it so much Daddy made me stop. It was botherin' him." She giggled. "Put my tooth in a glass o' water when I went to bed, and this mornin' it gone! But a nickel was there, a real shiny one."

Chalmers leaned down, inspecting the gap in her teeth. "Will my tooth fall out like yours?" he asked.

He was a skinny child, six years old, barefoot, and wearing only a pair of too-large overalls. He admired Elma Mae and Tobias, both of whom he considered to be quite grown-up and brave. The two older children loved the little boy and looked after him, aware that he was easily frightened and timid. But they always let him go along with them on their adventures around the woods, climbing trees and playing hide-and-seek in the cornfields. Today they were on their way to their favorite pastime: fishing and playing in the big oak tree at Pencil Creek.

"Yep," said Elma Mae.

"I won't get no nickel, though," he said, dispirited.

"Why not?" demanded Elma Mae.

"My daddy ain't got one."

"Silly, the fairy brings it, not your daddy."

Chalmers leaped to his feet. "I sees Tobias."

Tobias ran toward them, his purple head shining under the summer sun, his short legs pumping. "A town lady bringed me a birthday cake!" he shouted, panting. "She say it were angel food. That's why I late."

"Wow!" said Elma Mae.

"With pink frosting 'n' sparkles," continued Tobias. "She real pretty too. Her hair gold, and she wearin' them shoes with sticks. She came in a big white car with red seats inside." He shifted his willow fishing pole to his other shoulder and dashed ahead of them. "C'mon," he shouted, "I gotta be back by supper."

Elma Mae raced after him. "Tobias gonna beat us to the fishin' hole!" she shrieked as Chalmers struggled to keep up. Overhead a swarm of purple butterflies dipped and soared.

High on a bank above the river, Tobias lay on his stomach beside a pool. The bank was formed by the sudden drop of the earth as it collected water from the torrent of the river. He stared into its depths, hoping to see a fish. Elma Mae and Chalmers sat close by, dangling their lines into the murky water, their bare feet clinging to the bank. Behind them was a great oak, their favorite climbing tree, its giant branches gnarled and steady, offering delightful places to sit and call out to each other, a breathless challenge as they swung limb upon limb to the top. Chalmers always stayed on the lowest branches, but today he was excited. Tobias had promised to help him plant his small feet firmly on the higher branches and follow him and Elma Mae to their hidden places concealed by leafy foliage.

Tobias swung his pole out of the water, a tiny fish dangling from the hook. "Yippee!" he squealed. "Got me one!" He let the fish slip into his hand, and the three of them bent over it, murmuring together. "It just a baby. Gonna throw it back."

"No," complained Chalmers. "Why you wanna do that?"

Tobias regarded him for a moment. "Don't you need your mama?" Chalmers nodded, squinting up at him.

"So do fishes. This just a little one." They watched as Tobias let the fish go to squirm through the still water.

It was late afternoon by the time Elma Mae placed her small catch into a knapsack, tiring now of the fishing hole and ready to explore the great tree. Tobias and Chalmers were creeping on hands and knees beside the blackberry bushes, peering at the myriads of bugs and ant colonies. The ground was clean and swept, and the pines sighed around them, the air fragrant.

"I have somethin' to show ya," called out Tobias, picking himself up off the ground. He dug deep into his pocket and pulled out the small mesh bag given to him by Elo. The polished wood carving his father had made, his mother's birthday gift to him, fell to the ground unnoticed, his foot accidentally kicking it aside.

Leaning close, Elma Mae studied the small bag and poked her finger at it. "Jeez, Tobias," she said in awe, "did the town lady give you this too?" She looked up at him, her blue eyes wide.

"Can I pick it up?" asked Chalmers. "Mebbe the tooth fairy been to Tobias's house too."

"Yeah, maybe he right, Tobias. See … I lost my front tooth just yesterday." Elma Mae poked at her bare gum, giving Tobias a wide grin. "The fairy came with a nickel last night. You lost any tooths, Tobias?" She continued to examine the small bag, her freckled face squinched.

Tobias laughed. "This ain't from no fairy. It from Elo."

Elma Mae gasped. "You mean that purple butterfly you drawed? The one that flew out—"

"What's in that little bag?" Chalmers bent low over the mysterious pouch.

"Look!" Tobias emptied five round stones onto the forest floor. They rolled together, shooting off rays of bright colors.

"What they s'posed to do, Tobias? Did Elo tell ya?" inquired Elma Mae. "They like a bunch of rainbows."

"Yep, he told me … an I s'posed to practice," said Tobias importantly. "Y'all can watch."

Tobias passed his hand through the air above the stones. One of them rose in front of their eyes, shivering, with small points of light shooting from it suddenly above the treetops. They heard a faint musical note in the distance, and in an instant the soft thudding of horses' hooves whispered past the clearing.

Chalmers gasped and ran into the bushes. Elma Mae sat rigid, holding her breath. She leaned toward Tobias. "Did ya hear them horses?" she whispered loudly.

"Yup," answered Tobias, concentrating on the stone that lay before him.

"Will the marbles jump off the ground for me too?" she asked.

Tobias lowered his hand, and the stones lay still, small lights winking from them. Elma Mae held her hand over them. "They does that only for me, Elma Mae. See, today my birthday, 'member? An' Elo, he teachin' me. He … he bringed 'em."

"Wow!" exclaimed Elma Mae, gingerly reaching for one. She held the small stone up to her face while tiny shoots of light continued to wink around it. "I been tellin' Daddy about your magic, but he don't believe me." She carefully placed the stone on the ground. "But when that butterfly flew outa the drawin'," she said, looking slyly at Tobias, "now he wonderin'. I can tell; I watched his face." She giggled.

The two sat together with heads bowed over the small treasures. "Was Elo ridin' one of them horses that we heard?" whispered Elma Mae.

Tobias laughed as they scrambled to their feet. "Mebbe. They was the Cupbearers on the horses. But usually you can't see 'em. They rides like lightnin'."

"I … I seen 'em," said Elma Mae excitedly, staring into the woods.

"I wanna go home!" Chalmers emerged from behind the blackberry bush. Brambles clung to his overalls, and his tiny arms were scratched and berry-stained.

"Chalmers, you just a fraidy-cat!" scolded Elma Mae, her hands on her hips.

Tobias put his arm around him, picking the thorns from his hair. "Don't be scared, Chalmers. We won't let nothin' hurt you." He gathered up the stones, placed them carefully into the bag, and put them in his pocket. "Let's go climb the tree!" he said.

Suddenly a small dog hurled himself into the clearing, barking, his tail wagging furiously as he greeted Elma Mae.

"Uncle Pete!" she cried joyfully. "You found us! I forgot all about ya today." She wrapped her arms around the dog as he nuzzled her face.

The children dashed in and out among the trees, chasing Uncle Pete, balancing on old logs, and tossing pebbles into the water. They crept up the bank that stood high above the water and looked down.

"Keep hold of my hand, Chalmers," Tobias said. "That deep water down there. Mama said never—"

"I am the timber pool god!" howled Elma Mae, balancing at the edge of the bank, her arms flung out.

"Who that be, Tobias—the timber pool god?" Chalmers asked wonderingly, clinging tightly to his hand.

"It nobody. She always does that." He patted Chalmers on the head. "C'mon! Beat you to the tree!" He clambered up into the branches and reached down for Chalmers's hand. Elma Mae passed them, whooping with joy. They finally settled themselves in their favorite places, with Chalmers tucked close beside Tobias.

There was a rustling of wings. In the dusky light among the branches, Elo appeared soundlessly on a branch just above their heads. The transparent rays of the morning sun created patches of gold on his huge, delicate wings. He folded them carefully and stared down at the three of them, his tiny face creased. He wore a plaid vest today, its buttons the size of silver dollars. In one wiry hand he held a strange silver scroll, and in the other was a long, slender pointer.

"Good afternoon, Royal One," his raspy voice sang out. "I have been observing you at play." He bowed his head.

"I skeered a' him. He gonna hurt us!" Chalmers held onto Tobias, his eyes huge.

Tobias bent down to the frightened little boy. "He not here to harm ya, Chalmers."

"It's Elo!" gasped Elma Mae loudly from her place at the end of the branch.

Elo turned his tiny, walnut-sized head, his eyes directly on Elma Mae. His wrinkled face widened in a smile. "Well, how do you do? You must be Elma Mae. And you are Chalmers, are you not?" His brow gathered in tiny furrows as he continued to stare at the little boy.

"How ... how you know my name?" Chalmers asked.

Elo's voice turned husky as he spoke firmly. "Tobias has told me of you and Elma Mae." He nodded at her. "I will know you better as time goes forward." He directed his gaze at Tobias. "Royal One, today I have brought my scroll and my pointer. We are going to have a lesson on proper words."

Tobias settled himself more comfortably against the tree trunk, his arm around Chalmers. "Okay, Elo, but before we start, well, Chalmers, he scared of you, even though I tells him not to be. He kind of a fraidy-boy. Can you 'splain to him how you my teacher, my friend, and how wise you is?"

"He will learn these things as time passes. And about himself as well." Elo rolled his eyes upward and tapped his tiny finger to his lip. He paused and chuckled and turned his wizened smile toward Chalmers.

"Now, Royal One, today we must make serious progress." Elo carefully placed his spectacles on his nose and grasped the pointer in his wiry fingers. Chalmers and Elma Mae stared at him in astonishment.

"Well, my children," began Elo, his voice higher now and sounding like a breeze blowing through the trees. "I already know you, even though we have never formally met until now. You see, I frequently travel along with you if you are with Tobias. Often I am very tiny—sometimes on Tobias's shoulder or perhaps on his head. I sometimes travel on your pigtails, Elma Mae. I find your red hair becomes me well."

Elma Mae crowed in delight and grabbed one of her pigtails.

"Has you traveled on me too, Elo?" asked Chalmers.

"Yes," said Elo thoughtfully. He adjusted his spectacles. "Often on the top of your left ear."

"Oh!" exclaimed Chalmers, putting his hand to his ear. He smiled broadly at Elo.

"Children, I am teaching Tobias the ways of the royal passage," Elo continued. "Tobias is a royal ambassador and is—"

"What be an ambass ... ador?" interrupted Chalmers, stammering out the word and staring up at Tobias.

Elo nodded to Tobias.

"An ambassador, Chalmers," said Tobias carefully, "is a voice to the peoples. He there to help his peoples and tell 'em of their kingdom."

"Tobias is learning to master all the secrets of the Cripons, so when the time comes, he will be ready to embark," stated Elo, bowing low on his limb above them.

"Em-bark?" shouted Elma Mae.

Elo jumped back on his branch. "You must not screech, my child. Just as your dog must desist from making all those bothersome noises." He looked sternly down at Elma Mae, raising his tiny hands to the sides of his face.

Elma Mae stared down through the branches, noting that Uncle Pete was leaping at the tree trunk, whining and barking. "I apologize, Elo," she said, looking downhearted. "He only want to be up here with us. But what do you mean, em-bark? What does that mean?"

"He will be leaving," pronounced Elo firmly. "Soon now—when he masters the positions of the Royal Passage."

"He can't leave," Elma Mae wailed. "Me 'n' Chalmers 'n' Uncle Pete—"

"Do not be sad, Elma Mae," said Elo, noting the tears in her eyes. "He has great powers already, and you will always know his presence. He will forever be a part of your lives, you and Chalmers—and Uncle Pete."

Tobias sat swinging his legs, staring intently down through the branches. "I showed 'em the rocks, Elo. We played with the one that shoots off golden arrows. Is it okay if Elma Mae and Chalmers watch me practice?" He paused for a moment. "You sure have yourself a lot of fancy coats, Elo," he observed.

"They are my royal vests, sire. Do you like them?"

"Oh, yes, very much Elo, very much."

"Me too," Chalmers said.

Elo laughed, like the sound of a tin cup being scratched. "Thank you, Royal One. And Chalmers. I decided to wear this one today in honor of your birthday ... and meeting your two special friends." He bent his head to inspect his vest and then looked up again to meet Tobias's eyes. "You must learn to call the 'rocks' what they are: Stones of the Royal Passage. And you must apply yourself to practice—no longer play from this time forward. Elma Mae and Chalmers may be at your side as you train yourself to the excellence and the powers of the Stones, but as I have already explained, you must find the correct positioning for each one. Time grows short."

The children watched as Elo seemed to be grumbling strangely to himself, his fingers picking at his vest. "Where, oh, where are my reading spectacles?" he said.

Tobias laughed. "You wearin' 'em, Elo. They be on yer nose, not in yer pocket."

"Oh. My apologies, Majesty." His voice crackled in embarrassment. "I seem to forget at times, sire. Within the small bag I gave you, there is a special gift. You must always know that birthdays are milestones, and your eighth one is what we have been waiting for. Each Stone has a character of its own. But there is one in particular that was created by the Ancients from our planet Elios for occasions such as this."

"What do 'okay-shuns' mean?" Elma Mae leaned closer to Elo.

"Give me a moment, my dear. Sire, it has special, significant powers. Spill the Stones into your hand."

Tobias emptied the Stones onto his palm, and Elo picked one up with his tweezer-like fingers and held it up to the sunlight. "Ah, it is this one." He smiled and peered through it, turning it over and over. "I recognize its texture. If you please, sire, hold out your hand."

Tobias obeyed, and Elo placed it in his palm.

"That looks like one of them jawbreakers at Mr. Ricketts's store in the big glass candy jars," Elma Mae observed.

Elo let out a high, wheezy laugh. "Royal One, curl your hand around this ball for a moment. Then blow on your fist. Upon finishing, open your palm."

Tobias did as he was told. They watched as the ball took on a glow that was almost blinding. Shafts of green and purple encompassed the tree, sweeping through the branches. It rose from Tobias's hand and made small sounds—faraway giggles and blowing noises. The ball floated above their heads, spreading its journey among all the branches—a quick touch on this leaf, another on that leaf. Soon it was out of sight, but they could hear it rustling and jiggling in the branches behind them, above and below. It was suddenly quiet. Tobias looked down at his palm as the ball reappeared, looking like a big, round jawbreaker, just as Elma Mae had said.

Elo sat smiling at them as he slipped on his tiny white gloves, folded his hands, and twiddled his thumbs. "You may look around you now. You will perceive that your favorite oak tree is quite different from a few moments ago."

The branches on which they sat had turned to brilliant colored glass, the leaves tinkling gently back and forth, shimmering in the sunlight, all of them in various hues, smooth and polished. Tiny glowing crystal orbs shaped like cherries dangled among the leaves.

Elo pointed his finger at the strange, brilliant clusters. "These are known as smoots, children. Each of you may take a few."

"They be like gumdrops!" whooped Chalmers.

"Soft and sweet, Chalmers, like gumdrops, but smoots only grow on the glass tree. When you chew on them, they will taste of orange, strawberry, or blueberry. But you must never swallow them, for they are only for blowing magnificent floating bubbles."

"Wow!" breathed Elma Mae. They all began to grab at the glistening hanging orbs.

Elo held up one gloved finger. "The glass tree will always be yours, even after Tobias embarks. You will forever be safe among its branches. Smoots are for your pleasure—yours alone—and are to be tasted wisely. And, my Royal One," continued Elo, appearing to clear his throat with tiny gargles, "the Stones of the Royal Passage hold the key to many events to come. This you will learn with the passage of time." He adjusted his great wings and held out the scroll, unfurling it slowly down among the branches. He tapped his tiny pointer on its shiny surface. "Lessons! They begin now!" Elo's wispy voice sounded stern, vibrating through the trees in a staccato beat.

"Why he carryin' that shiny stick?" Chalmers asked. He looked up at Tobias and whispered, "Do he be mad at ya? Sounds kinda cross."

Tobias straightened his small shoulders. "Nope. Just gettin' my attention. Sit there quiet now and listen."

The scroll suddenly appeared among the tinkling leaves, hanging in midair, its surface glossy and translucent. For a moment it shivered and then hung still.

Elma Mae inched her way closer to Tobias. "Wow!" she erupted at full volume, immediately covering her mouth.

"Tobias, today we are learning proper words," Elo intoned. "As an ambassador, you cannot speak in your usual diddle-daddle fashion." He tapped the scroll.

"*Ain't* is properly *are not* or *is not*. *Cain't* is *cannot*; *de* is *the*; *y'all* is *you*; *I gonna* is *I am going to* … and so forth. Repeat, please. Oh, and *thet* is *that*!"

The scroll glowed as Elo moved his pointer, each word appearing in bold letters. Tobias repeated carefully, halting and stumbling, paying close attention. All three children sat tall and solemn, their clear, childish voices ringing out together, repeating after Elo. He busily whisked the pointer back and forth, calling out words, pushing his spectacles up, bowing and buzzing, leading them on.

"This is fun, Tobias," Elma Mae said softly. "Me 'n' Chalmers, we learnin' too."

As the day grew later, Elo finally came to a halt and tucked his pointer beneath his wing. He stepped toward the scroll, moving along the branch.

"I feel much encouraged, Royal One, and tomorrow we shall—" He stopped in front of the scroll, his face bunched in fear. "E-e-e-k," he screeched. Suddenly he was gone.

"Where'd he go?" asked Elma Mae, twisting around on her branch. The hanging scroll rolled up and swept through the air, following Elo.

"I see his wings," squealed Chalmers, pointing toward another tree. "They shakin'."

Tobias burst out laughing. "Yep, he's behind that tree. That's him, all right." He cupped his hands around his mouth and called out, "Elo, come back! You just saw *yourself* in the teachin' scroll. You cain't—uh—cannot be afraid of yer—your—own face."

"You mean he seed … uh … seen himself in that teachin' thing hangin' in the air?" Elma Mae asked doubtfully.

"Yesterday he seen his own finger right in front of him, and that scared him," Tobias said, chuckling and shaking his head.

Elma Mae pondered for a moment, gnawing on her fingernail. "Well, that scroll do look kinda like the lookin' glass by my bed," she said. "Sometimes when I see myself in that thing, it gives me a start."

"He be back. Just wait," said Tobias calmly.

Minutes passed. Chalmers and Elma Mae grew restless. "Guess he not comin' back," said Chalmers sadly.

"Mebbe not." Tobias swung lower to the ground, offering Chalmers a hand. Just then a tiny purple butterfly lit on the top of Chalmers's left ear, its wings caressing his cheek. He brushed at it lightly, and it fluttered away as a high musical note broke through the forest. Tobias watched it and turned to Chalmers.

"That was him. He was on your ear."

Chalmers's eyes were full of joy. "He be … *is* … my teacher too, ain't … *isn't he*, Tobias?"

"He your teacher too." Tobias smiled and helped the little boy climb down from the tree.

Elma Mae passed them on the way down, clinging to each limb as she left her high perch in the glass tree. Masses of leaves tinkled around her. Tobias gently coaxed Chalmers from one branch to the next. "Just plant your foot solid and keep hold of my hand," he told him patiently.

"It not *jest*, Tobias! It *just*. 'Member what Elo said!" shouted Elma Mae. "Whoop-da-dee!" She swung past and called out to Tobias. "I loves these tinklin' leaves! They just like my old music box." She stopped suddenly beside him. "Someone comin' up outa the bushes!"

The three of them looked down and watched a lone figure struggling over dead logs and brambles, plucking at his clothes and muttering to himself. He emerged in the clearing beneath the glass tree, swinging a rifle and dragging his deformed foot. Sweat glistened on his sallow face as he paused and looked around.

"He that meanie at Mr. Ricketts's store," whispered Elma Mae viciously from behind her hand.

Tobias nodded soberly. "I know."

Uncle Pete emerged from the bushes and began to bark, baring his teeth and emitting low growls.

"What in tarnation a damned dog doin' out here?" Ledyard kicked at Uncle Pete. "Pesky critter!" He scratched at his neck and leaned down, speaking softly to the little dog. "C'mere, boy. Mebbe I'll take you along with me," he crooned.

Uncle Pete lunged at him, growling as the hair on the back of his neck stood straight up. Ledyard swiped the butt of his rifle at him. "You porky-eatin' mongrel!"

Elma Mae let out a small cry from the glass tree as Tobias grabbed one of her pigtails and clapped his hand over her mouth. "Don't! We keep quiet, mebbe he won't see us." He pushed his face close to hers. "Anyway, we safe here. This tree different from the rest, 'member?"

"He scary-lookin'!" whispered Chalmers.

Tobias placed his finger on his lips. "Shh."

"Quit that damned yappin'! I got enough pain in my head without listenin' to some yelpin' hound," yelled Ledyard, swinging his rifle again at Uncle Pete. He picked up a rock and hurled it at the dog, sending him whimpering into the bushes. "Git away from me!" he roared.

Ledyard turned toward the tree, cocking his rifle. "Somethin' strange goin' on here," he muttered. "Some kinda tinkle bells around here." He stepped closer to the tree and peered upward. "Well, well, lookee what we got here." His face split in a wide-mouthed grin, his small eyes narrowed. "This is my lucky day after all," he said, his voice slithering and smooth. "I just out here to go coon-huntin' on this fine day, and what do ya know? Three of 'em waitin' in a tree!" Chuckling, he leaned closer to the trunk. "And one of 'em be that queer purple boy, that bottom-run weasel. Ain't that what you are, boy?"

"Ya hurt my dog, and ya sayin' bad things about my friend," yelled Elma Mae, leaning down from her branch, her face flushed. "What ya doin' out here? This be our fishin' hole!"

"You s'posed to say *you*, Elma Mae," murmured Chalmers.

"It is, huh?" Ledyard cackled. "Your friend—he ain't one of you, ya know."

"You ain't ... uh ... *are not* talkin' right," Chalmers piped up.

Ledyard moved closer to the tree, his rifle aimed at the children. "Gonna git me three coons without even huntin' for 'em." He stopped suddenly. "Y'all doin' some kinda voodoo up there? 'Course you is. Might of known, considerin' the company you keepin'." He reached up to part the low-hanging boughs, his hand brushing the leaves. "Barney sakes!" He was knocked off his feet, rolling on the ground and grasping his hand in pain. "Them ain't real leaves, all tinklin' 'n' such." He attempted to stand, lurching against the tree trunk. Again he was thrown to the ground, tossed against the blackberry bushes.

"You should just leave us alone, mister. It ain't ... uh ... *is not* no use," Tobias stated calmly from up on his branch.

"*Is not* no use, huh? Where'd ya come by that high-fallutin' talk, boy? I leave when I leaves." Ledyard rose to his feet with difficulty, clawing at the dirt, his twisted foot throwing him off balance. He stood heaving and panting against a couple of old logs, his eyes bulging. Leaning over, he picked up a small piece of polished wood that lay near his boot. "Looks like this here a real treasure," he sneered, studying the object. His voice sang out, high and mocking: "To my son Tobias, born to Myron and Jewell, this be to member yer folks who loves ya—1934."

"Musta fell outa my pocket," said Tobias quietly, searching his overalls. "Better give it back to me!" he shouted. "That from my daddy!"

"Your daddy, huh? He dead, your daddy."

"That don't belong to you!" Tobias exploded.

"It do now," said Ledyard. "You seen the last of it. Just an old splinter anyway. I'll be tossin' it in the fire tonight. Get rid of it just like we got rid o' that no-good—" Ledyard stopped in midsentence, smirking. He slipped the treasured gift into his pocket.

"You nasty old meanie," screamed Elma Mae. "I gonna tell my daddy."

Tobias sat quietly, tears running down his cheeks. Elma Mae squeezed his hand. "Daddy'll get it back for you, Tobias."

Ledyard raised his arm, his finger jutting upward, trembling. "Don't go makin' cracks like that about me, girl. Y'all smart-mouth me again', I can have that daddy of yours follow along same way—reclinin' in the swamp."

"I tells my daddy too, ya mean man!" squeaked Chalmers boldly.

Ledyard raised his rifle, taking aim at Uncle Pete as he leaped from the bushes, snarling at him. "Gonna shoot that cussed animal," he announced, backing toward the high bank above the fishing hole.

Tobias spoke out from his tree limb, his voice tearful but clear. "I sees a sudden current. It beyond yer control. This very hour yer ...

yer heart, it same as yer mouth. Yer foot be waverin' on the verge. There be no escape. You be shoutin', but it fall on hollow ears."

"We can go now," said Tobias, and the three of them dropped to the ground. A horde of butterflies enveloped the tree, their purple wings creating distant music and drowning out Ledyard's cries as the bank he was standing on gave way. Struggling with his rifle, he slipped from view.

Elma Mae wrapped her arms around Uncle Pete. "Oh." She nuzzled her face in the dog's scraggly coat, giggling as Uncle Pete covered her face with kisses. "You scared that old meanie away with all your barkin' 'n' growlin'."

"He won't be hurtin' us, will he?" Chalmers asked as he grabbed Tobias's hand.

"No, not ever, Chalmers." He swung his fishing pole over his shoulder, and the three of them headed down the path toward home.

Beyond the woods, Ledyard clutched at tree roots and clumps of weeds as the muddy bank carried him slowly to the pond below. The more he struggled, the farther he slipped. Looking down fearfully at the still and murky water, his eyes bulging in fright, he desperately tried to regain a foothold on the slimy bank. In the distance he could see the children setting off through the field, only their heads visible in the tall grass.

"Help! Help!" he called out. "A hand is all I need! Please!"

The three bobbing heads disappeared, and he was alone, helpless to prevent a headlong plunge into the pond below. "I can't even swim," he panted. He spied a low-slung branch within his reach. Thrusting his arm out, he grabbed for it. But he missed and was carried swiftly into the pond, the water up to his chin. A great swarm of butterflies dipped low over the pond and flew off. A strange current began to flow across the usually still and tranquil fishing pond, forming a strong, swift-flowing circular movement that pulled Ledyard into its depths. Coughing and choking, he struggled to keep his head above water, but the circle tightened. He was swept into the center of the whirlpool and disappeared. There was a roar of rushing water and a loud sucking noise, and then all was still. The pond was peaceful, its surface like shimmering glass.

"Those butterflies, they followin' us, Tobias?" said Chalmers. "They was in the tree too. Some were settin' on the glass leaves."

"They *the Enriching*, Chalmers," Tobias said. "They is … uh … *are* like Elo. Very wise."

CHAPTER 11

It's a Live One

PERCY SPRAWLED ACROSS THE trunk of the Snaught brothers' car, his arms folded across his chest. He had wakened this morning to find himself alone at Hazer's field, the ground churned up around the car, and dead insects scattered in clumps here and there. Thinking back to the night before, he remembered the comforting warmth of a swig of rum as dark had closed in. He'd been bored and was sorry he'd come out here. The whole point had been to find that spooked horse. Orville and Ledyard had worked themselves into a lather talking about it and wouldn't let up. So he'd finished off his pint of rum and whiled away his time, and before long he'd been dead to the world.

Now the morning sun seized his head, and a blazing red light on top of the sheriff's car jolted against his eyeballs. He sat up, his head throbbing, and watched the car ramble off the mountain road onto the grass of Hazer's field. He watched as Neil climbed out of the car, hitching up his trousers, glaring across the field with its mounds of churned earth.

Orville emerged from the other side of the car, slammed the door, and ambled casually across the field toward Percy, who was staring in horror out over the damaged field. "See you slept off your imbibin' last night," he observed. "Missed the nightmare! Didja have sweet dreams?" said Orville sarcastically, eyeing him with disgust.

"Didn't appreciate bein' left out here, Orville," said Percy, his voice trembling. "You coulda left the keys, or---that make-belief spooked horse---did it---?"

"Did it what?" interrupted Orville. "You couldn't have made it into town anyway. You were tippin' that bottle till you was cross-eyed." He turned away. "Wasn't no party, Percy," he said. "Lucky you passed into dreamland. Wouldn't of lasted five minutes seein' what we were seein'." Orville turned and started across the field.

"Well, if that old critter showed up after all, an' got you fellas scared an' yer brains addled, 1 didn't want no part of it!" Percy shouted after him.

"Found it over here, Neil," Orville yelled at the sheriff. He kicked at the ground on the far side of the clearing, squatting down, his head bent low, as Neil and Percy joined him. In front of them was a long spear stuck in the ground at an angle, carved with odd symbols of winged creatures. The shaft was fashioned out of exquisite ivory bearing tendrils of purple leaves. As they inspected it closely, the ground around it appeared to shift slightly, the dirt moving on its own. Occasional muffled sounds rose up around them.

"What the hell! What do y'all make of that, Sheriff?" Percy asked.

"B'longs to those fellers, Neil. I told you, didn't I?" Orville said proudly.

"Uh-huh," said Neil. "Heard you and the boys had yourselves a high ol' time up here last night. Didn't hear that you found that horse, though. So can't say, Orville, no more'n you can."

They watched as the ground around the strange spear began to undulate, pitch, roll, and spit dirt. A moaning sound came from deep in the earth around it. Neil prodded it with his toe. "Must be a nest of some kind, movin' all that dirt around," he muttered. "But where that sound comin' from?" Crouching down, he sighed heavily, spitting a stream of tobacco juice. "By the way, where all those moths ya been tellin' me about, Orville?" he asked. "Purple, did you say ... or was they red? Caused you boys to shriek and carry on, according to what I heard. And of course there was some sort of sword fightin', now, wasn't there, Orville? Wanna tell me some more about that?" Orville didn't answer. "Still," he mused, "this thing stuck in the dirt is mighty strange."

Percy tossed his head, laughing. He ambled back to the car.

Just then another police car appeared and came to a stop in the clearing. Deputy Shelly Bowles stepped out, sliding his sunglasses into his pressed uniform pocket and staring over at the men hunched around the long spear.

"What's goin' on here, Neil?" he shouted across the clearing. Shelly was Neil's top deputy, imparting quiet orders of his own. He knew well of Neil's vanity and his need for a high profile. He considered Neil ineffective, generally avoiding him and keeping to himself. It was easier that way. Leaving his regular Sunday morning church service, he had heard through Soddy that there had been riotous behavior the night before up at Hazer's field, that some of the men at Ricketts General Store had spent the night up there looking for a ghost horse, with some of them carryin' on in "sword fights." Talk about the critter had been all over Anker for years, but he'd ignored it, knowing that stories spread through this town like wildfire and became larger than life. Soddy, though, had seemed unusually disturbed, aside from his normal brash rambling. After due consideration, Shelly had decided to take the trip up to Hazer's Field.

Shelly joined the group, which appeared to be inspecting what looked like a long spear stuck in the ground. "What we got here, Neil?" he inquired briskly.

"Well, Shelly, seems Orville and his pals ran into some night riders last night," Neil said. "My guess is they mistook our boys for some drunken Negras out drinkin' up batter piss. They musta hauled off and tossed this fancy carved stick at 'em." He mopped his sweaty face with a large handkerchief.

"What'd they look like, Orville?" asked Shelly. "Heard you was one of the party."

"Hell, I barely seen 'em, Deputy," answered Orville. "Hopped in the truck to get away from all the fellers' jumpin' an jivin'. We all heard gallopin' from far off, and then outa nowhere, rompin' and whoopin' they was, horses and fellers. The ground under the truck was tremblin'. Didn't see nothin' but a blur. Jay and Ledyard, they got whomped bad with a big ol' sword." Orville's eyes widened, his face flushed.

"Did you see 'em?" Shelly shouted at Percy.

"Nope. I was takin' a nap," Percy called out from the car. "Just a rowdy party up here, Deputy, that's all."

Shelly leaned forward and grabbed hold of the spear. He suddenly shrieked and flew backward and sprawled on the ground. His neatly parted hair sprang straight up from his head, and he clutched at his throat. The men stood dumbfounded as Shelly writhed in the dirt, the spear muttering a garble of foreign sounds.

Percy turned at the sound of the commotion and headed back to the men. "Did the spear do that to you, Deputy? Or are ya havin' some kinda fit?"

Shelly reached for Orville's extended hand and struggled to his feet. "Gawda-mighty! Some kinda spell on that thing. Can't hardly breathe, either." He coughed and leaned over, looking closely at the spear. "What in God's name? It's some kind of lance, like somethin' old-time, maybe from a palace. Orville, head back to my car and grab my work gloves out of my trunk. We gonna bag this stick before it causes our boys here to wanna give another party!"

"Now y'all stand back," said Neil importantly, grabbing the gloves. "I'll take care of this." He slipped them on, squaring his shoulders and gingerly reached for the lance. It garbled a line of strange-sounding noises and shimmied at their feet.

"Shelly," said Neil, "this thing got some engine of its own. Feels like a live one." He leaned down, grabbed it by both gloved hands, and held it at arm's length. The strange spear wobbled back and forth like a bent arrow, making tiny sighs and screams.

"For gawd's sake, man, what happened up here last night?" Shelly spun around to confront Orville.

"How do I know, Deputy?" Orville shrugged. "Been tellin' all of you 'bout this creature ridin' through these woods so fast it just a blur. Rode through last night ... lots of 'em, with fellers on 'em, like I said! Prob'ly threwed this thing."

Shelly raised an eyebrow. You're seein' things, Orville," he said.

"Then what's that spooked spear doin' up here?" shouted Orville defensively.

Shelly didn't answer. He stood back and watched Neil place it cautiously in the trunk of his car.

"Someone's gotta take charge," Neil commented over his shoulder as the spear sprang upward out of the trunk. He jumped back and tried to slam the trunk lid, only to have it leap upward again.

"Grab the damned thing!" he shouted at Shelly as they both pounced on the shivering spear. But Shelly was knocked off his feet again, and Neil finally managed to cram it into the trunk and get the lid closed. Shelly struggled to his feet, and both men stood listening to the strange sounds coming from the trunk. "What the hell we got here, Shelly?" Neil's voice seemed to tremble.

"Like you said, Neil, it's a live one," said Shelly,

Neil stood back and removed the gloves. He spit a long stream of tobacco juice and continued to chew, his jaw moving slowly. Odd spears don't come outa nowhere, he thought. That thing couldn't have come from night riders either. These fellas had walked into a mighty strange fray last night—a real skirmish of some kind—like time had moved backward. Fast-movin' horses, swords, and strange insects all over the ground. Might hafta get hold of the crime unit over in Biloxi and have them send out some special investigators.

"What you thinkin', Shelly?" Neil leaned his ear to the trunk.

"Tell ya, Neil, either someone's makin' a real fool out of us, or this could be mighty serious. That thing had notches on it, swirls and such. Makes sounds, like some kinda secret message. Stuff like that is taboo here in Anker County, you know. I'm not allowing it. That's how I see it."

"Intendin' to tell anybody about this, Shelly?"

"Nope," said Shelly. "Keepin' it shut tight. And by the way, I stumbled across Hoedig this mornin' before I went off for my Sunday kneelin'. Seems that old boy can't stop ravin', Neil. Says he came across some prehistoric miscreation in his aeroplane, and it caused him to take a nosedive. Keeps mumblin' and cryin' about it. Walked around the woods of Old Stone Road for nearly a week."

Neil turned in surprise. "You sayin' Hoedig, Shelly? Out near Old Stone Road?"

"Yeah, you know he takes that old crop duster up over those hills right along. Why you askin'? That old crank probably tipped too many pints. Seein' things."

Neil shook his head and stared at the ground. "He was seein' things, all right."

CHAPTER 12

Take Courage, Elo, Take Courage

HEADING TOWARD THE HOUSE, Jewell looked over her shoulder at the sound of a car approaching down the narrow lane. The police car moved slowly into the barnyard and came to a stop. Neil stepped out, placed his hat on his head, and sauntered to the front of his car. He leaned back on the hood, his arms folded as he watched her silently make her way toward the barn.

Jewell slowly lowered Tawny's feed bucket to the ground, feeling suddenly afraid and trapped by his presence. "What brings y'all out this way, Mr. Neil?" she asked, keeping her tone casual. She mentally took note of Tobias's whereabouts and remembered with a feeling of relief that he and Elma Mae had gone to town with Tom.

"Mighty hot today," commented Neil, ignoring her question.

Jewell said nothing, her eyes riveted on him. She watched as he sauntered toward the barn, his hand resting on his pistol, whistling to himself. He peered into the barn, stepping just inside.

"What can I do for you, Mr. Neil?" asked Jewell quietly.

"That's 'sheriff' to y'all, hear?" said Neil without looking at her. "Don't go askin' me questions, gal. I got a powerful position in this town. I'll ask the questions." He stepped closer to her, his eyes narrowed. Jewell stared back at him, her eyes wary. She felt a sinking realization that she was totally isolated with Sheriff Swanny. Even though Grampa Perry was doing his usual porch-setting, he could neither see nor hear anything that happened out near the barn. Her instincts told her she was in danger.

"Sheriff," she said boldly, swallowing hard, "y'all has no right to come lookin' for what ain't here."

"You got guts tellin' me about my rights." Neil's voice was patronizing, and a strange smile broke across his face. "Come on in here." He looked around quickly and then took her firmly by the arm and pushed her into the barn. He shoved her up against a wall and leaned close. "I just sniffin' around. Gotta do that when you're sheriff. See that things are peaceful-like. I believe I like what I see out here." Neil stood back, his eyes roaming up and down her body.

Jewell ducked around him and headed for the barn door. "I'd appreciate it if y'all would go now."

Neil laughed and lunged for her, jerking her face up to his. "I'm not ready to go yet, gal." Neil paused, his grip on her arm like a vise. He stared down at her, his tongue flickering across his lips. "By the way, awful bad news about Myron and your boy. Just terrible. You know, 'course, that man of yours was always sassin' me. Disrespectful of my position." He gave her a shake. "You knew that, didn't you? I can't allow that."

"My Myron were a good man, always took care to ..." Jewell heard her voice beginning to shake and freeze. *Dear God*, she thought, *don't let Tobias come back up that road yet.*

"Uh-huh," Neil drawled, letting loose of her arm. He picked up a piece of straw and clenched it between his teeth, his eyes glittering. Folding his arms, he stood in front of her, blocking passage to the barn door. "Would I say he were sassin' me if he weren't? That man was headin' for an early grave, Jewell. You might as well face up to it. It was just meant to be. Prob'ly miss havin' a man around here, though, don't you?" He locked his eyes on hers, the bit of straw rolling around his lips.

"My husband and my boy, they be killed by—"

"Go get me a cool drink now, gal!" interrupted Neil. "Some shady water, hear? And be quick about it." His voice roared in her ear as he flung her out the barn door.

Jewell hurried toward the house, stifling the wish to cry out, praying that Grampa Perry wouldn't question her as she filled a water glass. He always knew when she was upset, for his uncanny instincts were sharp.

Neil strolled around the barn, kicking at bundles of hay and chuckling to himself. A tiny purple butterfly landed on his neck. He absent-mindedly swiped it away, scratching at his open collar as he sauntered around the barn, ran his finger along a rusty saw blade, and fidgeted with other tools. From up in the rafters above him came the soft sound of whiffling, as if feathers were being ruffled. Curious, he looked up but saw nothing. Barn swallows, he thought idly. He moved closer to the barn door, glancing toward the house. Uppity woman takin' her time, he thought. Takin' big chances speakin' out like that. He saw Jewell step out onto the porch and lean down to the old blind man. She pretty damned good-lookin' ... real beauty far as Negras go, he mused. She knows, though, no doubt about it. That husband of hers, and that tall boy—they didn't just get slopped up to the eyeballs in that old swamp on their own. Told the boys not to tie 'em up. Looked too suspicious.

Reaching up, he pulled a curious-looking set of reins from a hook. They were embellished with intricate adornments and purple tassels. Mighty fine trappings for a poor colored family, he thought, studying the finely chiseled leather as it lay across his palm. He turned abruptly, looking closely at Tawny in her stall. The chestnut horse was draped in a purple-colored tunic. Intricate designs of butterflies, knights in armor charging on horses, and an odd-shaped winged ship covered the silken fabric. This was the same design as on that spear, he thought as he ran his hand over the silken cloth. Impulsively, he kicked a bucket aside, knocking it over, and the contents spilled out on the barn floor. Neil froze and stared down at the heap of horse feed that lay at his feet. Slowly he wiped his sweaty forehead and scooped up a handful, examining the golden feed that covered the bottom of the bucket. Turning it upside down, he spilled the remaining oats into his palm. Shimmering gold kernels filled his hand, their brilliance making his eyes water.

Jewell slipped back into the barn, a glass of water in her hand, but she stayed close by the door. She held the glass out to him, but he ignored it, his hand full of golden kernels. Angrily he swiped the glass from her hand and backhanded her hard across her face. She screamed, her hand covering her cheek, as he pointed his finger at her, his voice menacing.

"I comin' out here all polite, and all I hearin' is Devil lies!"

"What ... what you talkin' about?" said Jewell, backing away from him.

He pointed over at Tawny. "Your son is of a kind no livin' folk in this town ever seen before, and you just keep your mouth shut about it, thinkin' you're high 'n' mighty. Your man ain't here, you live in a fallin'-down shack with a ragged old blind man, and now I starin' at a horse covered with some kinda fancy blanket, expensive trappings, and tassels that cost more than my county budget. I got me two men in serious ruin, fellers that seems like they was cut up with a sword—some kinda spear, swirls 'n' twirls on it, just like on this horse blanket. What do you make of all this now, gal? I ain't leavin' here till I has some answers!"

Jewell held her hand to her cheek, her eyes enormous. She pushed past him and ran toward Tawny, and then she backed up, shaking her head, her face aghast. "I never seen this blanket before, Sheriff," she whispered. Sliding her hand over the silken tunic, she turned and faced him. "I swear to ya, Tawny never had a coverin' like this. An' I don't know nothin' about your men gettin' hurt. It's the truth, Sheriff. Y'all come out here lookin' for reasons to take back to town with you—peerin' for reasons just to kill a colored." She shook her head over and over, gingerly touching the beautiful reins and Tawny's tunic.

"What? What y'all say? Did I hear a long-tailed cat whistle?" shouted Neil.

Jewell set out running toward the barn door. Neil grabbed her by the wrist and pulled her back, and she fell to the barn floor.

"This is what happens when there no man to keep you in line! Gettin' all smart, all uppity." He leaned over her, raging. "You lyin' to me, Jewell. That mangy horse over there, you tryin' to make me believe why its wearin' that king robe, why it got that fancy purple harness and eatin' gold corn outa that bucket—y'all tellin' me you don't know nothin' about it?"

Jewell crouched in terror at his feet, her mind swirling with fear that Tobias would appear in the lane any minute now. She struggled to her feet and faced him, trying to keep her voice calm.

"Sheriff, I told y'all the truth. That blanket on Tawny ain't knowed to me."

Neil swiped his wrist along his mouth. " Prob'ly got somethin' to do with that purple boy you keep out here with you. Talk in town about voodoo and spells. Witchcraft maybe. Where'd you get him anyway, Jewell? You never says, that I heard of."

"He mine, Sheriff," she said, meeting his eyes with defiance. "He all mine. Has been since he was borned."

Neil met her gaze but said nothing. He began to unbuckle his belt as he moved toward her. "Gal, y'all leave me with no other recourse. You been sassin' your sheriff ever since I came out here. I don't take lip from nobody, 'specially a colored. You oughta know that. My daddy taught me ... hell, his daddy taught him ... just the way it is."

Jewell caught her breath and leaped for the barn door, but Neil caught her midway and dragged her back toward Tawny's stall.

"No!" Jewell screamed, but he clapped his hand over her mouth. She struggled against him but was helpless as he locked her head in his arm. "You a real looker, Jewell, a real prize. Just lettin' ya know that before I teach you not to back-talk. After that we'll have an understandin', you 'n' me." His raspy whisper was against her ear, his forearm beginning to cut off her breathing. She heard the whip of his belt as he yanked it off, saw him raise his arm above her head.

There was a loud whiffling sound as a cascade of blinding colors streaked past the two of them. Neil twisted his head, looking up into the rafters. Immediately another fleeting ray of colors swept by them as all the tools along the wall fell to the floor of the barn with a crash.

"Who's there?" shouted Neil. "That old blind fellow? C'mon in here. Got somethin' for you, boy."

"Daddy? Daddy, don't come here," Jewell called out desperately.

"Y'all be interferin' with your sheriff's police duty!" yelled Neil, pushing Jewell over to the barn door and shouting toward the house.

Elo sat unmoving on a high rafter above the floor of the barn, breathing in whiffles and ruffles. He reached into a pocket and pulled out his tiny white gloves, carefully fitting them onto his hands. "I must call forth great courage at this moment," he said, his reedy voice sounding like the tuning of a finely stretched wire. "Jewell is in trouble. Take courage, Elo, take courage. Perhaps I should call forth the Trumpeter," he muttered to himself. He began to pace, smoothing his little gloves. Tiny tears began to fall from his eyes, and he sniffled as he extracted a patch of handkerchief from behind one wing. Dabbing at his tiny wrinkled head, he became stern with himself. "I must overcome my fear! The sheriff is going to hurt Jewell! This calls for extreme fortitude and grace to fool this evil one. Onward, Elo!" He darted from the rafter and suddenly appeared, tall and majestic, in front of Neil, towering over him. Rainbow colors shot from his huge, revolving eyes.

"How many fingers do you see?" Elo asked Neil pleasantly. He held up one white gloved finger for a moment, and then he was gone like a flash of lightning through the dark barn.

Neil staggered backward, releasing his hold on Jewell. She fell to the floor, trembling. She had just seen Elo, the curious creature Tobias had talked of—his "teacher," he had told her.

"Jeez-us! What in the name of Colonel Lee … What was that?" Neil yelped. He turned in all directions, stumbling and holding his stomach as if he was about to be sick. The whiffle sounds returned, vibrating through the barn, their echo bouncing from one corner to the next. Elo reappeared in front of him, so close now that Neil backed up in horror. He held up three gloved fingers. "How many do you see now?" came the scratchy voice assaulting Neil's ears. Elo towered over him as he bellowed in fright and fell to his knees. He began to crawl frantically out of the barn on all fours.

Elo turned to Jewell and bowed low, his huge wings sweeping through the sawdust on the floor. "You will be safe now." Then he was gone.

Outside, Neil lurched toward his car, gasping and attempting to run. But suddenly Elo was back again, hanging upside down in front of him, asking him the same pleasant question, with four fingers held in front of Neil's face. "Argh-h-h" he yelled, gaining a foothold and stumbling to his car. He scrambled inside and backed the car up, the tires skidding. He drove out of the barnyard, raising plumes of dust, his eyes on the rearview mirror as the narrow lane appeared before him in a blur. Whipping out his handkerchief and swabbing at his sticky neck, he turned onto the main road to Anker. Breathing a sigh of relief, he glanced once more in the rearview mirror.

Elo sat placidly on the backseat, tall and solemn, his huge eyes trained on Neil's in the mirror. Neil slammed on the brakes, and the car jerked to a stop. He turned around, staring at Elo with his mouth gaping open. The face like a walnut opened in a strange smile, and he rubbed his gloved hands together. "How many fingers?" His voice was a series of tiny squeaks as he held up both hands.

"T-t-ten," stammered Neil.

"Ten what?" asked Elo, nodding at him.

"F-F-Fingers," came the answer.

"Why, yes, there are ten," Elo said politely, his voice pulsing like electric shocks. "You are correct. What color is my left eye?" He lifted the rolling eyes upward in their sockets, a mischievous expression on his face.

"P-p-pink!" wailed Neil. He slumped over in the front seat, his hands covering his head.

"Speech, mountains, and splendor, I call forth the Queen Trumpeter," Elo proclaimed from the backseat. High-pitched trumpet notes in clashing minor chords rang out, rippling in waves through the car.

Elo held up one finger. "Now there is one, and blind you will run." Elo's wings began to whirr and buzz. In an instant he was no longer in the backseat. Only a tiny butterfly was there, and its delicate wings fluttered lazily out the car window.

Neil tried to open his eyes. "I can't see! I can't open my eyes!" He held his head in his hands, sobbing uncontrollably. "I'm losin' my mind. I'm goin' insane. That thing is after me! Same damned creature I saw on the bridge." He blubbered into his shirt and slowly dragged his eyes open. They were red and watery, heavy, as if they had been glued shut. He smacked the steering wheel and picked up his police radio but then threw it down on the seat beside him. "No use callin' anybody. Nobody'd believe me anyway." Suddenly he began to laugh hysterically as he peered into the backseat. "Can't even tell Soddy I been conversin' with a butterfly who wears gloves."

CHAPTER 13

Daddy Didn't Raise No Kitten Fox

GINGER LEE PULLED INTO her driveway, turned off the motor, and sat quietly for a moment, her thoughts still lingering on her recent visits to the Valentine farm. She thought about the beauty of the purple child, Tobias— his unusual eyes, a kind of power she sensed from him whenever he turned his gaze upon her, and his unfailing politeness, though he was just a boy. And how he loved his mama! Ever since the day she had arrived with a beautiful peach pie—and on a later visit when Grampa Perry had given her hand a lingering squeeze when she'd said good-bye—Tobias had whooped with joy when she drove into the barnyard. She smiled at the thought of him. During her years in Anker, she had never had friends like this little family. She stared now at her front door, not looking forward to encountering her husband. She climbed out of her car and headed into the house.

Neil stood in the front hall, a phone to his ear. He briefly looked over his shoulder as she walked past him into the kitchen. The sight of him—and even the sound of his voice—caused her a brief moment of distaste. She noticed his eyes, red and puffy as he stood in the hallway, with unshaven stubble on his chin. She dropped her keys into her purse and entered the kitchen, busying herself at the sink. Probably just my imagination, she thought, but he sounded odd, agitated. She shuddered for a moment, listening.

"Now y'all listen to me, Coates ... Uh-huh, y'all want respect? Well, it sounds to me like you got to be coaxed. Why is that? ... Uh-huh. You bein' difficult." Neil's voice boomed down the hallway. There was a pause, and then his voice began again—oily, patronizing. "Tha-a-t's right, mister," he drawled. "Uh-huh. That Negra is deep 'neath the coals of hell, Coates. I don't want no more mention of this Valentine feller—no more, hear?"

Ginger Lee turned off the faucet and froze. Valentine! That was Jewell's name, the only Valentine she'd heard of in this entire county.

Her husband's voice continued, demanding and rude. "He been stomped on just like I told you. Now you git that paperwork readied, send it on up here, and in no time at all we'll be swimmin' in oil."

Ginger Lee reached for a cigarette and quietly moved closer to the hall. Neil's tone suddenly became hushed. "Now listen, Charlie. I don't know how y'all do things down there in Texas, but you listen to me! This gal is good as gone, an' I'm not gonna repeat this again. And that old man, that rickety old man. And the boy—he's purple. Yeah, you heard what I sayin', Coates—purple!" Neil chuckled into the phone. "We got our ways, Charlie, me and the boys. You hearin' me?" He paused and turned to see Ginger Lee stubbing out her cigarette. "Yeah, well, wife's home now. Gonna have me some supper. Get them deeds up here, and if you know what's healthy for you, don't call me here anymore. Got it?" He slammed the phone down and sighed heavily. Avoiding his wife's stare, he shouldered past her and slumped into a chair to remove his boots.

"Well, you dressed up mighty fancy today," he commented, gesturing toward her shoes. "Totterin' heels an' all. Where you been? I'm thinkin' it way past time to be gettin' some supper on the table. I got me important business to take care of this afternoon, Ginger Lee, so I'm just settin' here waitin'." He shot her a look of warning.

Ginger Lee reached into the cupboard, picked up plates and glasses, and set them on the table. She turned to the stove, ignoring him. What had she just heard? Was he was talking about Jewell and her family? It was dangerous talk. And Jewell's husband—did Neil have a hand in that man's murder? Was he the one who—

"I asked you where you been," Neil said loudly. "Do I have to keep repeatin' myself? Pour me a beer, will you? And get a move on. I'm starvin'."

"Out doin' errands," Ginger Lee said briefly. She scooped some greens and potato salad onto his plate, set a glass of beer in front of him, and turned back to the stove, flipping some pork chops into a skillet.

"Uh-huh," said Neil. He tipped his chair back and ran his fingers through his hair, watching her stab at the skillet. "There's some real peculiar happenings around this county. Big old creature lurkin' down by Old Stone Road, looks like from over million years back. Couldn't believe what I was seein'. Had a real live encounter with the thing just yesterday." He swung around, reaching for his beer. "You listenin' to me, Ginger Lee?" He rubbed his eyes viciously.

"I'm listenin'," said Ginger Lee briefly, her back to him.

"Big ... and tall as a house. Had wings all orange and ... and purple, I guess," he stammered. He seemed agitated and rubbed his eyes again. "Creature talked—talkin' an' talkin' to itself, pacin' up and down. By gawd, I just blinked once, and it was gone!" Neil sat rigid in his chair, staring into space. The only sound was the ticking of the kitchen clock.

Ginger Lee slipped into a chair across the table and sipped at a cup of coffee. "That right, Neil?" She stared at him, half smiling.

"Don't go mockin' me, gal. Don't believe me, do you? Well, I've a mind to get the army boys down here and look into this matter. Creature come outa nowhere! And that ain't all. Me 'n' Shelly found a spear up at Hazer's field, stuck in the ground. It babbles 'n' cries. Damnedest thing. Hell, before you know it, I gonna be gettin' calls from up at Ratfill Cliffs and down in Cudlow Flats and all over the state, sayin', 'Sheriff, Sheriff! I got me a live one up here. Space varmints is courtin' my wife'!" He suddenly giggled hysterically, filling his mouth with potato salad, his jaw working as he rambled on. "And another thing. Old Hoedig rantin' and ravin' over his radio up in that crop duster of his. I heard his engine sputter, and it went dead just over Old Stone Road. And then there was nothin' but a lull. Shelly, he came across him this morning and says the old boy seen the same creature. Boy's near gone insane." Neil pushed his plate away, rose from the table, and grabbed his hat.

Ginger Lee sat quietly, occasionally raising an eyebrow. "You and Soddy—the two of you—y'all can take care of that creature in no time, Neil. You always get rid of what you don't want. That's your job, isn't it?" Her voice was soft and calm.

"Is there an air in your tone, Ginger Lee? You're actin' strange. Where exactly have you been today? What kind of errands?" Neil demanded as he headed for the back door.

Ginger Lee reached for the bowl of potato salad and carefully arranged a spoonful on her plate. "I been out to visit Jewell at her farm, Neil. Jewell Valentine."

Neil's face was incredulous. "You … did … what?" he thundered at her. "You sayin' you visitin' that purple boy and his—"

"That's right," she interrupted calmly. She sat back in her chair, inspecting her nails. "Took her some of my finest magnolias."

Neil grabbed a chair from the table and straddled it, leaning over the back.

She stared at him defiantly. "I visit Jewell right along these days, Neil. Couple weeks ago I came close to runnin' her over ... her and the child. They were crossin' the street and—"

"You mean that purple boy?" asked Neil, his voice rising.

"Tobias. His name is Tobias."

Neil stood and kicked the chair over. "Oh, now you callin' them Negras real friendly-like—first names and such!" He grabbed his beer glass from the table and flung it on the floor. It shattered across the kitchen. "So you takes yourself out to that Negra woman's shack these days and has tea and biscuits with 'Jew-ell' and 'To-bi-as'," he drawled, his voice biting and sarcastic. "Don't say another word, girl! Y'all just ruined yourself in this town, and maybe me too. 'Has himself a Negra-lovin' wife'—that's what folks gonna say about this sheriff. 'Oh, didja know? Ginger Lee Swanny havin' herself afternoons with that purple boy and his mama, takin' 'em pies and posies, havin' Sunday sunshine!" Neil jeered at her.

Ginger Lee leaped around the table at him, her face inches away from his, her eyes blazing. "You never gonna talk that way to me again, Neil Swanny," she snarled at him. "If I decide to travel out of Anker for a visit, you got nothin' to say about it. You and your mealy-mouthed gang that works for you, just mind your own business."

Neil backed away, flabbergasted as she shook her finger in his face. "My daddy didn't raise no kitten fox, Neil. I knew it was the right thing to do, and I will keep on doin' it. They are good folks. Jewell, she's my friend! They live honest and don't wish harm to anyone!"

Ginger Lee grabbed his arm, digging her long nails into his flesh. He winced and wrenched loose. "Can't say the same about you, Sheriff!"

Turning his back on her, he headed for the door again, kicking the splinters of glass out of his way. "You creatin' nothin' but trouble,

Ginger Lee. Gonna be sorry you mouthed off to your husband in that manner." Stomping out the door, he disappeared just as the telephone rang.

Ginger Lee dashed into the front hall and furiously grabbed the receiver, breathing hard. "Hello," she snapped. "Yes, Pearl … yes, he just stepped out. Yes, I'm all right. Just a little out of breath." She hung up and watched Neil's car roar down the street and disappear.

CHAPTER 14

The Luminous Stones

TOBIAS SAT CROSS-LEGGED NEAR the barn, the cluster of glowing stones spread out on the ground before him. He had awakened several times just before dawn and opened the golden bag to peek inside. His excitement had risen as he'd hopped out of bed early this morning, stuffed his new treasures into his pocket, gobbled down the cornmeal mush Jewell had placed before him, and dashed across the barnyard.

Now he sat quietly watching the sunlight create vivid colors on the stones as he passed his hand over them as Elo had instructed him. One by one, they rose in midair and made curious sounds, some of them humming or giggling or whistling, and all shooting off tiny darts of rainbow colors. He began to rearrange them, frowning in concentration. They shivered in front of his eyes, changing places as if searching for a permanent pocket of air.

Tobias stared at them, enraptured, changing his fixed gaze from one to another. Slowly he reached up to pick one out of the air, but it buzzed and shot off toward the barn. "You not s'posed to do that. C'mon back!" he called out softly. But the rest of them followed the first, shooting around inside the barn. He could hear the commotion of noises they were making, and he chuckled to himself. Suddenly he remembered what Elo had told him: "Close your eyes tight and hold out your hand, Tobias. They will come if you think hard."

He shut his eyes, squeezing them hard, and held out his open palm. With a clamor of noises, the cluster of stones arrived back on his outstretched palm. He carefully placed each one back into the bag. "I think I gettin' it," he said to himself. "I'm practicin' like you said, Elo."

He looked up at the sound of his name. "Tobias! Daddy takin' me an' Chalmers to town. You gotta come! Ask your mama." Elma Mae ran across the barnyard. "I gets to buy us lollipops with my nickel that the fairy left." She arrived at his side, breathless, her eyes shining, and squatted down beside him. "Are ya practicin' to embark? I 'member Elo said it."

Tobias nodded. "I s'posed to every day till I get the positionin' right."

"I told Daddy about the magic balls, how they rises up and all. He looked at me real funny. Didn't say a word."

"Don't go sayin' nothin' about it, Elma Mae. Folks don't understand."

"Okay. Now go ask your mama if you can go. Daddy and Chalmers waitin' on the road." Elma Mae skipped across the barnyard. "The Tooth Fairy, the Tooth Fairy, got me a nickel from the Tooth Fairy," she sang loudly, her blue hair bows bobbing up and down.

Tom had agreed to let her wear her favorite overalls today, the ones he'd ordered from the Sears catalog. They were patterned with tiny pink flowers. She had begged to wear her T-strap Sunday school shoes with white anklets, and he had braided her red pigtails with extra care, tying blue ribbons around each one. Feeling encouraged that perhaps his daughter was beginning to enjoy dressing up now and then as a real girl, he'd smiled as she stood in front of her looking glass, admiring herself—and astonished to see the wide gap between her front teeth.

"Will it grow back, Daddy?" she had asked Tom. "Will the Tooth Fairy bring me a new one?" Tom had chuckled, assuring her she would soon have her front teeth back in place. The visit from the Tooth Fairy had sparked her excitement, and she had polished her shiny new nickel as least six times since Tom had dropped it into a glass of water beside her bed.

"Howdy, Tobias," said Tom as the two children clambered into the backseat.

Chalmers's small head was barely visible in the front seat as he peeked back at his two best friends. "You have the nickel that the fairy bringed ya, Elma Mae?"

"Yep, she does," said Tobias. "She singin' about it too." He let out a peal of laughter, and they both broke into song.

Tom chuckled from behind the wheel. "Got to have you sit straight in the seat, Chalmers," he said, reaching out to place his hand on the knobby little knee. "I hear y'all had yourselves a real good time at the fishin' hole a couple days ago."

"We climbed up in a glass tree," announced Elma Mae. Suddenly she clapped her hand over her mouth and looked at Tobias. He nudged her and frowned.

"And Uncle Pete, he chased a bad man!" reported Chalmers from the front seat.

"Just pretendin'," Tobias whispered in Tom's ear as he leaned forward. "Mama, she said to ask you when you're comin' over to check on Tawny."

"Soon, Tobias," said Tom. "You tell her." He glanced at the boy in the rearview mirror. He was constantly puzzled by Elma Mae's strange stories—marbles rising in the air, a tree with glass leaves, her insistence that her little friend had special powers. But then there was the curious event of several weeks ago when a butterfly had escaped out of a drawing. He himself had sat and listened, enraptured, as Tobias had carefully explained it to him. He adored the sweet little boy, but he was mystified. There was something about Tobias that he couldn't explain.

He shook his head and turned his attention to Chalmers, who was sitting quietly next to him. "You're gettin' to be a growed boy, Chalmers," he said, looking over at him.

"I almost six," said Chalmers, sitting taller. "Soon I be big as Tobias."

The children scrambled out of the car in front of Mr. Ricketts's general store.

"Can I see your nickel?" asked Chalmers. "Are you sure you don't wanna just keep it? I got me two smoots."

"Yeah, Elma Mae," said Tobias. "You could just keep it in your treasure pile."

"Nope," said Elma Mae. "We gonna have lollipops. Besides, the Tooth Fairy, she'll be comin' back next time I start wigglin' my tooth—won't she, Daddy?"

"Betcha! You wait around Mr. Ricketts's, hear? Got some business to tend to, gonna be a few hours. Walk around a bit if you want to," he said, pulling gently on Elma Mae's pigtail. "But behave now."

Elma Mae nodded and headed down the boardwalk, skipping to the screen door of Mr. Ricketts's store.

"I wants cherry," called out Tobias.

"Me too," echoed Chalmers.

The little girl squinted in the dimness of the old store, empty except for one man leaning lazily against the counter, in low conversation with Herbert Ricketts. At the sight of her, Herbert brightened.

"Well, if it ain't Tom's girl, and lookin' mighty fine in them flowered overalls. And lookee here! Fancy shoes! What can I do for you?" Herbert Ricketts leaned over the counter, peering at Elma

Mae through thick glasses, his eyes kind. She carefully placed her nickel in front of him. Herbert beamed down at her, jumping back in mock surprise. "Well, that about the shiniest nickel I ever seen! Your daddy give that to ya?"

"Nope," said Elma Mae firmly. "The Tooth Fairy bringed it cuz o' this." She displayed the gap in her front teeth. "And I come for some lollipops."

"Well, 'course," came a voice from just inside the screen door. Jimmy Snaught slouched against the door frame. "Them Tooth Fairies, they always good 'fer nickels. I once heard that a feller pulled out all his own teeth. Tooth Fairy didn't pay no attention— just brought him a nickel like always." He snickered, his shoulders shaking.

"Don't see nothin' funny about that, Jimmy," Herbert remarked, selecting some shiny lollipops from the candy case. "Sure it gotta be lollipops, Elma Mae? I have me some mighty fine peppermint sticks."

"Oh, I sure, Mr. Ricketts."

"Well, then, which one be your pleasure, gal?"

Elma Mae reached up on tiptoe to select three lollipops from Herbert's jar.

Jimmy leaned on the counter, his chin in his hand. "Three!" he exploded. "Hell, y'all be rottin' out all your teeth. You real greedy, ain't ya?" He slowly shifted a wad of tobacco to the other cheek, chewing slowly and eyeing Elma Mae.

"Mind your own, Jimmy," said Herbert, putting two pennies into Elma Mae's palm. "This here is Tom's girl. Don't go shootin' your mouth off at her."

"They for my friends too, Mr. Ricketts. One for me, and one for Tobias, and one for Chalmers. They waitin' outside." Elma Mae slipped the pennies into her pocket and turned toward the door.

"That's real nice of you, Elma Mae," said Herbert.

"Tobias an' who?" inquired Jimmy. "Outside, huh? How come they didn't come in here so they could pick their own?"

Elma Mae turned back as she opened the screen door. "Prob'ly cuz yer in here!" she shouted over her shoulder.

The three children ambled slowly across the street, licking their lollipops. "One of them mean mens was in there, Tobias," Elma Mae grumbled, "the one who always with his kin that looks just like him."

"I know which ones you mean, Elma Mae. I seen 'em."

"Do he be real icky, with bumps on his face like a frog got?" asked Chalmers, listening closely.

"Yeah," Elma Mae flared back. "He sure was in a bad mood. But Mr. Ricketts ... I like him. He's kind and wears those funny eyeglasses."

Chalmers skipped alongside Tobias and took his hand, while Elma Mae dashed ahead and peered into store windows. A tiny purple butterfly lit on one of her pigtails.

Chalmers gasped. "Look, Tobias! Elo ridin' on Elma Mae."

"Yeah," said Tobias. "There he is. He never very far away from me. Next thing you know, he might be hitchin' a gallop on your ear."

Chalmers squealed with delight as they made their way down Main Street, paying no attention to the stares from the few folks who had come to town this Saturday morning. Tobias was used to the eyes riveted on him. All of his short eight years, he had endured comments and rude behavior from the people of Anker. Only when he was with Tom was he aware that no one made snide remarks, for Tom would not allow it. When striding through town with Tobias and Elma Mae, Tom's eyes blazed if he sensed an insolent observation from anyone about his daughter's beloved friend, almost daring folks they passed to open their mouths. Today, without Tom, they soon encountered trouble.

Turning down a side street, they passed a playground—hard dirt with a few swings, a slide, and a teeter-totter. The Anker Elementary

School loomed nearby—two stories of schoolrooms with an old, rusty fire escape angling up to the roof. Three white boys were playing Cops and Robbers up and down the fire escape stairs, their shrieks of "pop-pop," "gotcha," and "yer dead" ringing out over the neighborhood. They aimed at each other with wooden guns.

"Lookee here, fellers! Look at what lost its way home!" called out Monty, the tallest of the three. They all scrambled across the dirt yard, advancing toward the children. Monty, his friend George Henry, and the third boy, a chubby child named Darci, began to skip in circles around the children, chanting at them.

"Nigger, nigger, pants on fire," taunted George Henry, a ten-year-old with unkempt blond hair. He stepped forward and pushed Chalmers. Instinctively Tobias moved in front of his little friend, and Elma Mae stuck her lollipop into her overalls pocket and bunched up her fist to swing at him.

"He didn't do nothin' to you. Leave him be!"

Tobias stared hard at George Henry. "He just little. Don't go pushin' him!"

"Didn't hafta do anything," the boy said, laughing. "He's just a little runt. This our school ground. Ours, ya hear? We busy playin' and don't want y'all here—'specially you." He twirled his wooden pistol and sneered at Tobias. "I seen you around town before. How'd ya get that purple color? I'd be hidin' if I was you."

"He been dipped in a can of purple paint!" said Darci, laughing. "Or mebbe his folks colored him all over with a crayon."

The three boys bellowed in laughter, doubling over and nudging each other with their elbows. Tobias stood silently, his hand on Chalmers's shoulder.

"I oughta show ya my whistlin' pete," scolded Elma Mae, stepping in front of Tobias.

"Whistlin' pete? You gonna call the cops or somethin'?" Monty tossed the hair out of his eyes, poking his toy rifle at Elma Mae.

"It my knuckle in your lip," Elma Mae pronounced loudly. She glared at Monty. The boy inched close to Elma Mae, grinning down at her. "Git, you hear? Y'all botherin' us just lookin' at ya. Besides, why you goin' around with this ugly-lookin' Negra anyway, carrot top?" He took a swing at Elma Mae, but his fist was stopped in midair as Tobias grabbed his wrist, his small hand clutching it tightly.

"Let go of me! Git yer paws off me!" shouted Monty, easily releasing himself from Tobias's grip. He spat at Elma Mae's feet.

"C'mon, Monty." George Henry grabbed his friend's arm. "Let's go play." He pulled a slingshot from his pocket and scooped up a pebble from the ground. "If y'all don't git outa here, I'm gonna aim this at your ugly purple head, hear me, boy?"

"C'mon," shouted Darci as he ran up the fire escape and climbed out on the ledge. He pointed his wooden gun at the children down below.

Tobias faced Monty calmly and began to speak. "When the trees blow, it be the invisible that stirs them. The song of victory is sung before the battle been fought. It be I who singin' the song. It be I who doin' battle. I doesn't fear what I already won."

Monty stepped back, his face puzzled. Elma Mae looked down at her shoes, scuffing the dirt and drawing Chalmers closer.

"Would y'all announce yer victory, mister, if your enemy were gatherin' together in front of you?" Tobias asked.

Monty scowled at Tobias, shaking off George Henry, who had grabbed his arm again.

"Y'all ain't gonna let him talk that way to you, is you, Monty?"

"Shut up, George Henry." He looked fiercely at Tobias. "Would *you*, ya purple freak?" he sneered.

"I have just done so, Mister Monty."

Monty pushed his face close to Tobias, his mouth twisted. "I ain't never heard no colored talk that way. Where you learn that?"

The two boys turned and walked off, Monty looking over his shoulder now and then to stare back at Tobias.

"Did you say Elo never far away, Tobias?" asked Chalmers in a tiny, frightened voice. "Them boys make me 'fraid."

"They gone now, Chalmers. Elma Mae and I here. No need to be afraid."

Chalmers continued. "But y'all say Elo, he—"

"Never you mind now," Tobias said firmly, his small face in a frown. "They gone." They watched silently as the boys played guns with each other across the school yard, running and shouting, flailing their arms from the top of the fire escape.

"You did well, Tobias," said a wee voice from the top of his shoulder. "You are making great progress."

Tobias smiled. "Thankee, Elo," he whispered.

"It is not *thankee*, Majesty. It is *thank you*," came the reedy voice.

Tobias rolled his eyes and sighed. "*Thank you*, Elo."

Past the school yard, the children turned back toward town, quieter now, but savoring the remnants of their lollipops. Suddenly a high scream pierced the air from behind them. They turned around to see Darci, who had been balancing at the top of the fire escape, plunge to the ground. His body lay crumpled and still on the hard dirt. Monty and George Henry pranced frantically around him, crying and pulling at his shirt.

"C'mon!" yelled Tobias. He raced back down the road toward the school building with Elma Mae and Chalmers behind him.

"Why we goin' back there, Tobias?" panted Elma Mae.

"Gotta help him. He falled off the fire escape, didn't ya see?"

"But dang, Tobias, he ... he wasn't nice to you." She dragged Chalmers along with her.

"Don't matter. He's hurt," Tobias shouted over his shoulder.

Darci lay on the ground, still and pale, his right arm flung awkwardly to the side, bone protruding from the flesh. Blood soaked the ground beneath him.

The three children ran to his side, panting and out of breath. "Wow!" breathed Elma Mae. She looked down at Darci, squinting in disgust. "Serves ya right."

"Git that nigger outa here," screamed George Henry, jumping up and down in front of Darci.

Monty shoved Tobias, knocking him to the ground. "I can help him," said Tobias, jumping to his feet. "He hurt real bad."

"What do you know, ya purple toad?" Monty bent over his friend, sobbing and plucking at his bloody shirt.

Tobias dug in his pocket, his fist closing around the small bag. Saying nothing, he stepped around George Henry and Monty and moved in closer. Opening his palm, a brilliant small stone rose above Darci, purring and whistling. Tobias raised his hand, directing its path above the unconscious boy. It rose and fell, dipping down to the injured arm. Soft billows of light appeared around him ... green, lavender, and scarlet.

Monty and George Henry stood aside, their faces frozen. "George Henry, get on over to your aunt's house *now*, hear? Tell her to go get your Uncle Orville. Beat it!" Monty's voice rose to a hysterical pitch. The boy turned and stumbled across the school yard, half sobbing and hollering incoherently.

Chalmers and Elma Mae watched him go, standing apart from the commotion in front of them. "Chalmers," whispered Elma Mae, "that boy gonna bring one of them old meanies back with him. The one called Orville."

Tobias knelt beside Darci, extending his hand out and holding it motionless above the shattered arm. "No, no, don't touch me. I don't want no Negra puttin' his ... it burnin', it burnin'," Darci moaned. His eyes were open now, his gaze terrified. Tobias remained motionless, watching the injured boy. The murmuring stone lay still in his open palm. Slowly the broken arm regained a normal shape, the flesh folding softly over the protruding bone. The translucent stone hovered above him, darting back and forth. Darci slowly closed his eyes and lay still. There was no sign of injury.

"What's goin' on here?" a harsh voice boomed out over the playground. "George Henry just a-pantin' and a-cryin'. What's all the fuss about?" Orville stood there, confronting the children.

Tobias stood silent as Orville approached. He slipped the glowing stone into his mesh bag. "He all right now," he said. "He be just fine."

An immense swarm of purple butterflies swirled around the playground. Monty stood there looking confused and frightened as Darci sat up, rubbed his eyes, and got to his feet. The other three children slipped away.

"What y'all doin' starin' at me for? Ain't we playin' no more, George Henry?" Darci asked.

Orville turned angrily to George Henry. "Thinkin' up tales, are you? What'd I tell you about that?"

"But Darci, he fall from up there, his arm—it broke, bone stickin' out, blood all over, like I told you!"

"What you talkin' about, George Henry? Ain't nothin' wrong with my arm," Darci said. "Y'all is just playin'." Orville gazed at him, narrowing his eyes.

"Honest!" shrieked Monty. "George Henry sayin' the truth! Then that purple boy, he came and he … he had a marble that made funny sounds, and Darci—he just healed up!"

Orville stared hard at Monty. "You tellin' me that purple Negra boy, the one who live out by Bunny Bayou … that he was here … right here on this play yard—an' all these things happened?" Orville spoke slowly, deliberately. "Boy, I got a sign around my neck that say 'stupid'?"

"If I ain't tellin' you the truth, how come that dry blood be on Darci's shirt?" asked George Henry defiantly.

Orville leaned closer to Darci. "Well … stand up, boy." They all stood staring at the streaks of dirt and dried blood smeared on his shirt.

"Go on back and play, now, hear?" Orville spoke quietly. He started slowly back across the school yard.

Old Cottonseed limped slowly toward him, his left leg dragging. "Really hurtin', ain't ya." Orville squatted down, caressing the dog's head. "Poor ol' Cottonseed." He nuzzled his face against the dog. "Strange happenings around here lately. Mighty strange."

CHAPTER 15

The Cupbearers

NEIL DROVE SLOWLY DOWN Main Street in his newly polished car, adding to his usual sense of superiority and awareness of high visibility to the citizens of Anker. Today he wore sunglasses, which he felt were necessary for his image but also for his blinding headaches, which had recently come upon him since the "creature" had appeared in the backseat of his car.

He waved casually to a few women standing on the boardwalk near Marabelle's Beauty Parlor, and several of them began to fluff their hair as they followed his car with their eyes.

"Howdy, ladies. How are ya?" he called out. He passed three old Negro men in patchy pants and worn shirts sitting on a bench in front of the hardware store. The three merely stared as Neil drove past. He ignored them.

A man in a pink seersucker suit crossed the street in front of him. Neil slowed the car, raising his hand to blot out the glare of the sun. He noticed that Judge Pinky Forrest was wearing his usual attire of seersucker pants, complete with flowered suspenders, white socks tucked into shiny black oxfords, and a flat-brimmed hat. He carried his expensive gold-knobbed cane with style.

"Howdy, Pinky," Neil called out to him. "What brings y'all out in this afternoon heat? Drummin' up court business, or just out to eye the ladies?"

Judge Pinky Forrest stepped over to Neil's car, clearing his throat as his eyes darted up and down the street. His neatly trimmed goatee seemed lost in the folds of his chin, and his wispy white hair hung limp from beneath his hat. Resting both hands on the top of his cane and leaning into the car, he growled, "Neil, got a call from Charlie Coates today. His timin' for this oil speculation really upset my stomach!" Pinky Forest scowled, his flabby jowls shaking as he peered into the car.

"I told that harebrain not to call you, Judge! Seems I gonna have to give him the round side of my billybob when he gets on down here."

The judge stared at Neil with pained tolerance. He was used to whiners like this sheriff, but there was something about Neil Swanny that especially rankled him. Maybe it was his arrogance, his smug, self-satisfied bearing.

Pinky Forrest had been Anker's municipal judge since 1920. For fifteen years he had held the court as his own. His reputation as a shrewd man and a landowner of extreme wealth was well known all over Anker county. The people gossiped and whispered about him, as they did everyone else, for he was not above shady dealings, and the townsfolk knew it. Some people believed it was Neil's father, Panther Swanny—Anker's last sheriff who was married to Pinky Forrest's half sister—who had placed Pinky in the position as Anker's municipal judge.

Pinky shook his head distastefully. He turned to walk away and then swung around, pointing his finger back at Neil. A large, gaudy diamond ring glittered on his forefinger. "Y'all need to talk to Orville!"

"What in the name of tarnation did that blockhead do now, Judge?"

"He hasn't done anything, Neil. Why're you always lookin' to blame that boy for doin' his duty? Unkind rumors floatin' around when he just passin' time talkin' to his friends and restin' a bit," said the Judge. "My assistant, Leota Claypole, tells me she had a real scare with her nephew playin' at the school yard this mornin'. Seems that purple child, that strange Negra boy, come to town causin' a whirlwind of voodoo, and George Henry—him bein' her nephew—came runnin' and fallin' at the mouth about that boy. She lives next door to Orville, ya know, across from the school. Had tears runnin' down his chin, Neil. Him and his friend Darci been playin' there in the school yard, mindin' their own business, and along comes the purple boy, stirs things up. Before you know it, the little purple Negra pushed Darci off the fire escape and broke his arm real bad." Pinky lowered his voice to a whisper. "Then that strange child stirred up the air with secret hand signals. Scared the pants off poor George Henry. He went howlin' over to Orville's house, and by the time they get back to the school yard, Darci playin' on the fire escape again, good as new, and the purple boy was gone, nowhere to be seen. Orville walked over there and took charge. Just the kind of responsibility we all lookin' for—fella like him." Pinky pulled out a handkerchief from inside his seersucker jacket and mopped his jowls, breathing hard.

"Where is Orville, Judge?" asked Neil impatiently.

"Don't know. But y'all listen here! I want you to look into this situation, and I don't mean next week! I'm growin' old, Neil. Probably couple years before they put me in the ground, and I'm thinkin' about this town and how to help good white folks to make this a place where people feel safe and want to visit. You hear me, boy? You're wearin' that star for outcome, for gettin' things done, not for how your hair is combed. Am I makin' myself heard here?" Judge

Pinky Forrest turned and continued on across the street, tipping his finger to his hat as three women walked by.

Old gobble-chin, thought Neil. *Who does he think he's talkin' to? Oughta rid this town of him and his fancy suits, paradin' around.*

The car radio stuttered with static, and Soddy's voice crackled off and on. Neil shook his head. Boy always badgerin' me, he thought, always callin' me—Neil this, Neil that! Fella just doesn't understand I got important work to do. He picked up the mic and said in a monotone, "Yeah, Soddy, what is it now? Over."

"Neil, I got me a pretty strange call just now. Thought you should know."

Neil rolled his eyes and heaved a sigh. He motioned urgently to Orville who had just emerged from Ricketts General Store with Cottonseed lagging behind.

"Seems Punchy Green went out huntin' early this mornin' up near Cudlow Flats." Soddy's garbled voice came through the radio. "Said there's a big slack-water Huxley up there in those woods. His whinin' turned to downright 'mad as hell', callin' me all kinds of names, Neil, and he sounded scared outa his wits. Says he sneaked over and kicked the odd-lookin' thing, and damned if it didn't start whistlin' like a kettle, flashin' a color he never seen in all his days. Over."

Orville stopped beside the car, gnawing on a toothpick, and rubbing Cottonseed's grizzled head. "Go on now, boy, jump up in there," he said, opening the back door and sliding the old dog onto the seat. He stood listening to Neil, resting his elbows on top of the car door.

"Now hold on, Soddy! Stop botherin' me with Punchy's fancy yarns. Don't you think I got anything better to do? Prob'ly just run across some old gin still. Over."

Orville slid into the car beside Cottonseed. He leaned toward Neil, flipping a toothpick back and forth between his teeth. "Mebbe I should ride along with you. Some things ya need to know."

"Yeah?"

"Seems your purple bird of heaven came to town this mornin'. He keeping company with Tom Clausen's gal and another little colored. I told you weeks ago that girl of his, called Elma Mae, been pickin' up some kinda witchcraft, actin' and talkin' all sassy over at Ricketts's store, threatenin' old Ledyard. But you had nothin' to say to me then. 'Mind yer own, Orville,' you said."

The radio crackled again, and Neil grabbed it, turning his back on Orville.

"Soddy, can you hear me? You tell Punchy to go home and get some sleep. Stay away from that moonshine. Stop botherin' me! Over."

"Neil, Punchy's dead sober. Says he happened on this big old thing up in the trees, looked like made of tin or somethin' and making belchin' noises, moanin' and hummin'. Had big eyes all around. Punchy half outa his wits now. Says he's leavin' Mississippi and never comin' back. He seems to think it's the end times that old preacher Leroy Byrd rantin' about on Sunday mornin', scarin' the church folks. Neil, I'm tellin' ya—"

"Hell's bells, Soddy," interrupted Neil, letting out a big laugh, "most of 'em needin' repentance. Leroy just helpin' 'em along. Over."

"Ain't ya gonna look into this story Punchy's tellin' me? Over."

"No! Probably just some army boys up there playin' war. I might be notifyin' the gov'nor's office, but that's all. Over and out."

Neil slammed down the radio. He started the engine and headed out of town. "What was that story you were tellin' me, Orville?" Neil shifted gears. "Pinky Forrest fixin' to bust outa his damned suspenders. He's tellin' me there was some kind of hocus-pocus goin' on over at the school with Tom's gal and her two friends. One of 'em was the strange purple—"

"That's right, Neil," stated Orville. "Tom must have turned those three loose to roam about town. They jostled my nephew and his friends right off the playground, rude an' pushy. Caused one of 'em to run up the fire escape, he was so scared. Then he got pushed off. Coulda killed him. George Henry was cryin' and not makin' sense when Leota brought him to my front door. Said the purple boy done some kinda strange dance right in front of those poor scared kids. I went over there to help. Least I could talk gentle to them. But it was too late. Purple boy was gone, just evap-or-ated. So were the other two.

"I ambled on down to town, and guess what! Seems that boy was seen walkin' on Mrs. Pearl Wiggins' roof. Prob'ly flew up there on a witch's broom, snagged her cat, flew around town for a spell, and dropped the poor critter in a flour sack. Caused Pearl to cry and shout for marchin' Christian folks to rise up and hailstorm that purple child to hell." Orville's voice rose higher and higher as he continued his narrative. "Got that story from Henry Hicks across the street from Pearl. Why, Henry says she so undone she threw away her crutches and was seen stumblin' around without 'em." Orville grew quiet, exhausted from telling his tale.

Neil kept driving. "I tendin' to believe Pinky, Orville, but not you. You're a lung tosser, always got a mouthful and gettin' folks worked up over those make-believe stories of yours. Like that ghost horse you been talkin' about for years."

"Old Cottonseed believes me, don't you, boy?" Orville said, leaning back to nuzzle the old dog.

The two men rode in silence, heading out of town.

"Where those three now, do ya s'pose," asked Neil quietly, "the little purple feller and his friends?"

"Gone home," said Orville sullenly. "Saw 'em headin' outa town with Tom Clausen about an hour back."

The car swerved, kicking up dust.

Neil slammed on the brakes and came to a sudden halt. They had arrived on the road leading past the cornfields.

"Where we goin'?" Orville demanded.

"We're gonna find that boy. Gonna put a stop to all this monkeyshine. I'm bettin' he still on the road, headed home."

"What you got in mind, Neil?"

"We—you and me—we're gonna find him and rid this planet of that goblin." Neil stared intensely over at Orville. "You've got that look," he said.

"What? What look?"

"The look that says you don't want to hear what I've got in mind."

Orville sighed. "I got no taste for hurtin' no child, Neil. My hands be washed of a child bein' pained while I on this earth. God talk mighty powerful about layin' hands on them little ones in the Holy Book. I ain't killin' no child—not colored, not white, and not purple."

Neil brought the car to a sudden stop and grabbed Orville by his shirt collar, jerking his face inches from his own.

"We playin' hopscotch, Orville? This is serious police business, are we clear? I don't want no whinin'!" He pushed Orville aside and crammed a wad of tobacco into his mouth as the car picked up speed again. "I see 'em. Right up ahead. Might I remind you, Orville, that you're my deputy? Get that think-box of yours straightened out!"

Approaching the crest of the hill ahead, they saw Tobias and Chalmers trotting along together, holding hands, their small heads bobbing up and down. Neil hummed quietly to himself, pleased and smug. Orville sat scowling out the window.

Suddenly Neil slammed on the brakes again, and dirt and gravel swirled around the car. The two men slowly leaned forward, peering through the windshield.

"God's sakes, Neil. What—must be some kinda emergency from over at Tuscaloosa." Orville started to climb out of the car.

"Stay where you are!" exploded Neil. "I'm in charge here! Don't you move a hair till I say so!" He stared bug-eyed out the window.

Standing directly in front of the car, blocking the road, were two
tall figures on horseback, draped in purple tunics with white tassels.
They wore silver armor and held reins of gold. In the iron-gloved
hand of one, a tall banner whipped and snapped, its colors vivid
with purple, orange, and black spots. They appeared to be knights
of battle. They sat perfectly still, the facets of their armor adorned
in scrolls of lavender. At their waists were massive sheathed swords.

Neil slowly emerged from the car, placing his boots carefully on
the gravel. Orville stepped out from his side, looking cautiously at
Neil. He cradled his shotgun in his arms. "Damn! Look at the size
of 'em, Neil," he muttered, choking on his words.

There was no sound as the two men stood on either side of the
car, squinting up at the massive figures in front of them. Curiously,
the banners whipped and snapped as if in a high wind, but the air
was still and hot, with only the sound of crickets chirping from the
cornfields.

Neil took a step forward and cleared his throat, carefully placing
his hat on his head. He rolled his shoulders importantly and glanced
over at Orville. Hitching up his trousers, he spit out brown goo
from his tobacco plug and called in a loud voice, "Now, I don't know
who y'all is, or what town you from, but I'm fixin' to call over to
Tuscaloosa and find out!"

"Neil, you hear that?" said Orville nervously, looking down. The
ground beneath their feet began to tremble and rumble, the dirt
shifting beneath their shoes. The two men were thrown off balance
and clutched at the car doors as the gravel whirled in tight circles
around them.

Suddenly from over the horizon, two more knights appeared,
their tunics billowing to the stride of their great horses galloping
in perfect rhythm. They stopped next to the first two knights and
remained still. Riding across a distant field, there came another
pair of knights advancing toward them like a mighty wind, with the

same colorful banner whipping as they approached. They stopped alongside the other four knights, facing Neil and Orville in silence.

"Why don't I shoot a couple a' warning shots, Neil."

"Boy, them swords are as long as you is tall. Now shut up!" Neil took a step forward. "We the county law, fellas! That's right. We got official police business to take care of, and y'all is blockin' the road. That carries a fine—about five hundred dollars—not to mention you're gonna have to stand before Judge Pinky Forrest. If you gentlemen understand what I'm tellin' you, just nod your ... uh ... helmets!"

There was no response. Neil adjusted his tie and tried again. "Those flags is whippin' a snappy crackle, and there ain't no wind! I gotta suspect some kind of witchcraft. No place for that behavior in *my* county, fellas."

The strange rumble began again as Neil squinted up at the huge figures sitting like statues in front of him. "Get in the car, Orville," he commanded. "We're headin' back to town."

Orville slid into the car and reached back to scratch Cottonseed behind the ears. "Damn, boy! How could you sleep through all that? In your younger days, you woulda been out there a-barkin to beat hell, houndin' them horsemen right outa the state of Mississippi!" Cottonseed lifted his drowsy eyelids for a moment and looked sadly at Orville.

"Oughta toss that old good-for-nothin' hound out there with them metal fellas, Orville," said Neil as the car screeched into reverse gear. He took off toward Anker at high speed.

"You can't talk about my Cottonseed like that—no, sir!"

"Orville, just keep your mouth shut now! I'm suspectin' them boys was out celebratin' some party or such. Looked real au-then-tic to me. Places in Tuscaloosa that dresses you up like the real thing. On the other hand, could be that purple boy again. Maybe his kin got a hand in this!"

"Betcha that's it, Neil. Could be y'all will never get that boy now!"

CHAPTER 16

Pearl Wiggins

ELMA MAE PLANTED HER feet in front of Tobias, her hands on her hips. They were suddenly back in town near the boardwalk. She grinned at him, her eyes sparkling. "First we in the school yard, you helpin' that Darci. Then we walkin' on the road. It's all to do with that bag of little rocks Elo gave you. And the whistlin' they do."

Chalmers rubbed his eyes with his small fists. "I feels like I just waked up."

"They wasn't takin' kindly to us bein' there," said Tobias, grabbing Chalmers's hand and starting down the boardwalk.

"Do you remember much, us leavin' the school yard and all?" asked Chalmers.

"Nope," answered Tobias. "We was there, and now we here."

"And that rhyme you said about singin' the song? Wow!" crowed Elma Mae. "That Monty, he looked real scared when he heard you say that."

Tobias and Chalmers skipped past her. "It be what I learnin' from Elo. It's part of bein' King of the Cripons," Tobias shouted back.

"What's a Cripon? I wanna be a Cripon too!" Chalmers was panting, his skinny legs pumping.

"I gonna tell Daddy about this," Elma Mae said gaily, "but I just know he won't believe me."

"*Going to,*" corrected Chalmers.

Tobias laughed. "He prob'ly won't."

"Why'd we have to go back there anyway, Tobias? Darci, he say ugly words, and then you makes him heal up."

"They just words," Tobias said. "Words can't hurt ya. Helpin' him with his hurt arm—that called love."

They walked farther down the street, hand in hand, jumping over cracks, squatting down to examine tiny spider webs, poking their fingers at the silken webs hidden along window ledges and under boardwalk benches.

Elma Mae leaped out of sight for a moment and then scampered back to join them, holding two pale-violet magnolia blossoms. "These was hangin' down from a tree. They're real pretty." She buried her nose in the petals.

"Yeah, but they not yours. You shouldn't be a-pickin' 'em just cuz they smells good," Tobias scolded.

They passed the magnolia tree, heavy-laden with blooms. Elma Mae cupped her hand to her mouth and whispered loudly in Tobias's ear. "That lady in her yard doin' the snippin' ... she the same lady told me about old Hoedig washin' his face!"

Tobias raised on tiptoe and peeked over the fence. "That the town lady! She the one who comes in that big white car to visit Mama! Those flowers you picked belongs to her, Elma Mae. Better give 'em back."

Chalmers crouched down and peeked through the slats. "I think she sees us." He pulled at Tobias's overalls. "Hide!"

Ginger Lee peeled off her garden gloves and wiped perspiration from her forehead. She tucked her clippers into her apron pocket and turned to examine her famous Royal Crown magnolias. Glancing up, she saw two small faces staring at her through the fence, one with a wide grin missing a front tooth, the other a rich purple face, eyes round and serious.

"Tobias!" exclaimed Ginger Lee, striding over to the fence. She looked quickly up and down the street. "Why, what are you children doing here? I thought I was seeing things!" She laughed nervously as she stuffed her gloves into her pocket.

Chalmers's head suddenly appeared beside them, and Ginger Lee stepped back, her hand to her mouth. "Lawdy sakes, now who in the world is this?"

"Howdy, missus," said Tobias. "We waitin' for Mr. Tom to finish town business. This be Chalmers."

"I almost six!" announced the little boy.

Tobias slung an arm over Chalmers's shoulder. "We been at the playground and just happened to—"

"They mean boys over there," interrupted Chalmers.

"And I bought us lollipops with my nickel from the Tooth Fairy," Elma Mae chimed in.

Ginger Lee glanced from one face to the other, listening to each one.

"I seen you before," said Elma Mae, "kneelin' at my Sunday school church and talkin' with the Bible folks. 'Member the time you told me about Hoedig washin' his face in his aeroplane?"

Ginger Lee laughed. "Well, my, my, I certainly did! And I never expected to have such interesting visitors pop over my fence just as I was about to pour myself some cool lemonade." Her eyes moved quickly from house to house across the street. Turning her head for a moment, she looked toward her neighbor's yard and then leaned over the fence. "Would y'all like some?" she whispered.

"Wow!" Elma Mae jumped up and down. "We sure would!" The magnolia blossoms fell at her feet, and she scrambled to pick them up. "These was so pretty ... but I just picked two."

"She stealed 'em from your tree!" said Chalmers, looking somberly at Ginger Lee.

Ginger Lee opened her front gate and ushered the children into her yard. She stepped out onto the sidewalk for a moment, her eyes darting up the street. "I don't mind, child," she said. "That old tree has plenty of blossoms to give away. Don't you go fretting about it now." The children followed her through the yard and up the stairs to her kitchen door.

"Can I look in your fish pond, missus?" asked Tobias. "I seen it when we passed by."

"Me too?" echoed Chalmers.

"Of course," said Ginger Lee. "Y'all just take a quick peek, and then we'll have us a lemonade party. Hurry, though, or the ice will melt." She looked quickly through her kitchen window toward Mrs. Wiggins' house next door.

The three of them trooped back outside and dashed to the fish pond. Ginger Lee set out three glasses and three plates, pondering her sudden invitation. There was liable to be "talk" if anyone saw the two Negra boys in her yard—especially Tobias. His deep-purple color would set folks' mouths a-waggin'. This part of town where she and Neil lived was considered "genteel." No coloreds came here except for occasional delivery of goods. If Neil found out, it could be downright dangerous for her—and for the three children. But let him rant and rave, she thought. She was getting sick and tired of his bad temper. He had become sullen lately, quicker than usual to anger, belittling her and accusing her of shirking her duties. And the hushed telephone call about the Valentine family ... what had he become? She turned her attention to her young visitors.

Soon the three children dashed up the steps and back into the kitchen. They were in high spirits, and Ginger Lee refilled their lemonade glasses twice, feeling relaxed as she listened to their laughter and clear, childish voices.

"Sure was good cake you brought me on my birthday," remarked Tobias, taking a last gulp of lemonade.

"I was honored, Tobias," said Ginger Lee, setting a cookie jar in the middle of the table. She sat down beside him. "You know, when I turned eight years old, my mama gave me a dancing party." She reached into the jar and handed each of them a cookie.

"Wow!" chortled Elma Mae. "Did ya dance in a fancy, long dress with music—fiddles an' all?"

Ginger Lee chuckled. "I most certainly did. Fiddles and all."

"My daddy gave me a fishin' pole when I seven," said Tobias. "And then me and Josh went fishin' for the whole day."

"That sounds mighty lovely. Is Josh your brother?"

"Yep," said Tobias, concentrating on his cookie. "But he dead now, drownded down in Bunny Bayou. My daddy too. I think that mean man we seen at our fishin' hole was the—"

"A meany!" interrupted Elma Mae with a scowl. "Had him a wooden foot draggin' like a skunk with no socks."

"Yeah," said Chalmers, swinging his legs back and forth, "he scared me. I didn't see him wearin' no socks."

"He said bad words about my daddy. I think he kilt my daddy and Josh," said Tobias quietly.

The children grew silent. Ginger Lee moved around the table, refilling their glasses.

"Did yer mama cry, Tobias?" inquired Chalmers at last, his voice small.

"Uh-huh. She cry lots." Tobias fidgeted in his chair.

"I'm mighty sorry, Tobias," said Ginger Lee softly. She placed her hand on his cheek for a moment.

"That's okay," he said, lifting his eyes to meet hers. She saw his sorrow.

A telephone jangled noisily. "Back in a jiff." Ginger Lee dashed from the table and disappeared down the hall. The voice on the other end of the telephone was loud and abrasive, an assault to her ears. "Yes, Pearl. No, Neil is not at home, but I expect ..." She paused as the peevish voice continued.

"Land sakes, Pearl," said Ginger Lee firmly, "y'all is getting yourself mighty steamed up. They're just children. Yes ... yes, the boys are colored, but Pearl ... I don't believe I appreciate you talking like this, and you're not duty bound to be spying out your window. My advice to you is—"

Ginger Lee slowly placed the receiver back in the cradle. Pearl Wiggins had hung up on her. The nerve of that woman, she thought, looking back at the three children. She felt sorry for Pearl, trapped in those terrible braces all these years. Polio had struck her down almost twenty years ago, and since her husband had died, she was confined to the big house next door, virtually alone. But she was a bitter woman, meddlesome and narrow-minded. Since Pearl had nothing better to do than spy on her neighbors, Ginger Lee had expected that she would be watching her little visitors as they frolicked around the fish pond. And of course the presence of Tobias and Chalmers would have caused her to erupt with anger. She could picture Pearl now, peering out the window, her flickering eyes narrowed, thinking about who she could call to report on the children's presence in the neighborhood. She was always seeking out trouble.

Now she'd be calling Henry Hicks across the street. No telling what he'd make of her story. It was beyond necessity in Ginger Lee's opinion. Most white folks dealt kindly with the coloreds, but people like Pearl and Henry Hicks built their pipelines of vicious gossip on lies that became exaggerated and eventually passed on to the next generations. Her own husband, Neil, was a good example, a man whose ugly opinions were rooted in his own background. Spiteful gossip spread a sinister evil of hate, and merciless people like Pearl Wiggins and Henry Hicks gloried in such feelings.

Ginger Lee walked slowly back through the swinging door. The children were chattering happily now, and she found herself wishing they could stay.

"Y'all need to be running along now," she told them. "I still have my roses to tend." She joined them at the table for a moment as Elma Mae slid down from her chair. "Don't want to worry your daddy, Elma Mae. He's probably waiting for you now."

"Can we come back for cookies again?" asked Chalmers as he and Tobias headed for the door. His small face was scattered with crumbs.

"Why, I do believe y'all ate every single cookie!" Ginger Lee covered her mouth in mock horror, her eyes wide. "Next time I'll bake a whole batch, and I'll need you to help me eat them all up!" She laughed and rose from the table. "Now y'all skeedaddle!" she said, softly stroking Tobias's head. She watched them from the back porch, amused by their chatter and high spirits.

Heading for the gate, their way was suddenly blocked by a strange looking woman who let loose with a high-pitched string of words that seemed to hang like evil spirits in the still air. Her voice rose higher as she lashed out at the frightened children.

"So, now we can all expect you to be entertaining the coloreds, that right, Ginger Lee?" Her words hung in the air. "I just won't have it! Shame on you for letting them frolic in your yard and inviting them into your house! Won't be long before you'll be having all kinds of coloreds from the shanties over for supper, dancing, and praying—and shouting like they do."

Ginger Lee ran down her back steps and approached the woman. The children were wide-eyed and silent, their eyes riveted on Pearl Wiggins, who brazenly stood before them, leaning on a pair of crutches. Both her legs were encased in heavy steel braces. She wore a long, shapeless dress and square-toed black shoes laced tightly beneath the steel supports. Her gray hair was pulled back in a tight bun, and her eyes glinted with fury.

"It is my responsibility to report this to your husband, Ginger Lee, and I intend to do just that. All the good citizens of this town will soon be hearing that the wife of their sheriff is not only a nigger-lover, but she's entertaining them as well!" She hurled her words high-handedly, her loose lips trembling.

"Pearl, you're losing control of yourself," Ginger Lee said. "These children were just drinking some lemonade, and—"

"I don't care what they were drinking! This purple boy—why, folks have been talking about him all over Anker, and you ... you invite him to your home! Disgraceful!" She stared hatefully at the children. Chalmers started to sniffle, and Elma Mae pulled him closer to her.

Somewhere there was the insistent meowing of a cat as Pearl Wiggins stood panting with anger. Ginger Lee returned her stare wordlessly, her hand on Tobias's shoulder.

"Do that be your cat, missus?" Tobias's small voice cut through the silence. He pointed toward Pearl's house, and all of them turned to look. High up on the eave of her roof, a big gray cat paced back and forth, yowling in distress.

"He stuck up there!" yelled Elma Mae, breaking away from Chalmers and jumping up and down. "He can't get down!"

Pearl leaned down to Tobias, her hands gripping her crutches, her eyes gleaming wickedly. "Furthermore," she said, "I do not intend to have a conversation with a peculiar-lookin' colored who has been sittin' around the kitchen table with the sheriff's—"

"I'll git him!" shouted Tobias, ignoring her. In a split second, he dashed past Pearl and into her yard. "I'm a-comin' up to git ya!" he shouted up at the cat. Looking around, he quickly spied a ladder and dragged it to the side of the house. Elma Mae dashed behind him, with Chalmers taking up the rear.

"Tobias, no!" called out Ginger Lee.

"Get out of my yard," shouted Pearl.

But Tobias was already high up on the ladder, his hands gripping each rung. "My mama lets me help scrape the barn like this all the time. I be all right," he yelled back over his shoulder.

"My Lordy!" breathed Ginger Lee. "The child has no fear. He could fall and kill himself!" She stared coldly at Pearl. "Isn't that the cat you love so much, Pearl? The one you're always talking about?"

Pearl stood motionless, gazing at the ground, seeming unsure how to answer. The purple boy was quite obviously going to attempt to rescue Delilah, her beloved companion. Tobias reached the top of the ladder and began to crawl precariously along the steep-pitched roof.

"O-o-h," let out Ginger Lee with her hand over her heart, breathing rapidly. "That's a long way from the ground. Real risky just to rescue a cat."

Pearl turned to her. "I believe I have told you many times about Delilah, Ginger Lee," she said, "but I'll tell you again. She is my only comfort, my only friend. Y'all know I can't go gadding about like you, driving your fancy car, getting your nails polished at the beauty parlor, dressing up like—

Ginger Lee interrupted, shaking her finger at Pearl. "Then you'd better be regretting that talk of yours," she advised. "It just might be a Negra boy will bring back the joy of your life!"

"Well, I still say …" said Pearl, her words fading.

"Don't say anything more, Pearl," Ginger Lee said sharply.

Tobias was descending the ladder now, very slowly, leaning carefully into each step. He held the big cat over his shoulder, its paws draped gracefully down his back, its yellow eyes glowing. Elma Mae had held fast to the ladder, yelling encouragements. "Wow, Tobias, you real brave!" She turned back to Ginger Lee and Pearl, calling over her shoulder. "He saved your cat, missus."

"Yeah, Tobias did! He saved yer cat!" called Chalmers.

The children surged around the big gray animal, who set up a loud purring, rubbing against their legs.

"Yer cat be real scared, missus. Now it saved!" Chalmers nuzzled his face in the cat's fur.

"What do you call your cat, missus?" Tobias asked, kneeling beside Chalmers.

"Delilah. She's all I got," Pearl said quietly.

Tobias looked up at her and saw her eyes brimming with tears. "It be all right now. Delilah safe."

Ginger Lee stepped forward and leaned close to Tobias. "There is a beautiful lavender butterfly on your shoulder, Tobias," she whispered.

"What be laven—lavender, missus?"

"Like purple. It's just sitting there. Probably came out of my magnolia tree, maybe because you were such a brave boy."

"Oh, yes, missus, I know it be there. I never heard nobody call Elo lavender before." Tobias smiled at her and dug into his overalls pocket. "Can I show ya somethin'?" He pulled out the small bag, untying the purple string.

"Oh, I thought you wasn't s'posed to show 'em to nobody else, Tobias!" wailed Elma Mae, jumping up to see the shiny stones emptying into his hand.

Pearl stood rigid, her eyes on Chalmers, who was cuddling her beloved Delilah. "Does you want to hold your cat, missus, now that she safe?" the little boy asked.

"You can see I can't hold her, boy," Pearl shot back stiffly.

"My, my, child. Why, those are just beautiful! My heavens! Where on earth did you get them?" Ginger Lee held her hands high as one of the brilliant stones shot up from Tobias's open palm. She watched, flabbergasted, her mouth slowly falling open. Another one rose from his open hand, swooping around the garden, tinkling in front of Ginger Lee's eyes. The stones swept past them, a flash of rainbow colors swirling around Pearl and then disappearing. Pearl tottered forward on her crutches, trying to maintain her balance. Suddenly she cried out, her voice a high croak.

"Lord God ... oh, Lordy, what is happening to me?"

There was a crackling sound of steel breaking apart as a glowing stone hovered near her legs and crutches. A flash of radiance engulfed the frightened woman. Ginger Lee screamed, grabbing Pearl just as the heavy steel braces began to fall away—first one leg and then the other. Her crutches twisted out of her gnarled hands and clattered to the ground. The two women stood frozen, clutching each other.

"I'm having a dream," Pearl wheezed, her breath coming in short spasms.

"I knows who did it! I knows who did it!" Elma Mae called out in a singsong.

Chalmers mimicked her, prancing behind.

"Pearl ... your braces—they're gone," said Ginger Lee. "And your crutches. Did you know you're standing on your own? Why, this just isn't natural. Pearl, something happened here, and I don't know what." Ginger Lee's voice drifted off, and she looked up as the brilliant stones began to land softly in Tobias's hand. She stood gaping at him, trembling, as Delilah purred noisily around her skirt.

"Betcha kin walk now, missus," screeched Elma Mae. "Dang! I wish Daddy could see this."

"Yeah, me too." Chalmers grinned and ran after Delilah.

Pearl didn't hear them. She raised her eyes to Ginger Lee, tears streaming down her cheeks. "Help me," she pleaded.

"Help yourself! Take a step!" advised Elma Mae loudly, placing her hands on her hips.

Ginger Lee, crying softly, managed to gently steer Pearl forward. The crippled woman took a halting step, and then another, her legs free of the steel braces.

Tobias watched her as he gathered Delilah in his arms. "Your sorrows be made better if there be joy in the middle of 'em. And them things that propped you up ... you don't need 'em no more," he announced soberly.

Leaning on Ginger Lee, Pearl walked haltingly toward her front door. She stood tall and straight now, weeping softly, with Ginger Lee murmuring to her.

"What happened to me?" Pearl asked in wonderment. "You were standing right there, Ginger Lee. I ... I can walk now, and I feel a kind of softness, different from ... it's a joy in my heart, like I was happy ... or something. I can't explain it, but I ... I think I need to go and rest now."

"I'll take you in the house." Ginger Lee opened Pearl's front door and guided her inside. Pearl looked back over her shoulder for a moment. "That purple child, the strange one, ... did you hear what he said about joy being in the middle of sorrow? Have you ever heard such words from a Negra? Or from anyone? What's going on here, Ginger Lee? He looked at me with such ... such love! I don't understand." She shook her head and looked down at her legs, which were suddenly free of the heavy braces.

"I know. The child's words were ..."

"Oh-h-h," moaned Pearl, clutching Ginger Lee's hand. She began to go limp, and Ginger Lee stopped her fall.

"C'mon now, Pearl, just lean on me."

Pearl turned around, gasping, her eyes enormous as she stared out the open door.

Elma Mae could be heard from the yard, shouting gleefully. "Tobias, the window on her door got eyes just like Elo! Whoopee!"

Pearl stretched her hand out, cautiously touching the window. The glass was turning slowly and continuously, revolving in wondrous, sparkling colors.

"Oh, my ... Lordy, Lordy! Am I seeing things, Ginger Lee?"

"No, Pearl. You're not seeing things." She stood transfixed, listening to the three lively children, looking around in disbelief.

The children ran off, whooping and carousing with each other, out of the yard and onto the sidewalk. Soon they were gone.

"Tobias, I apologize for what I—" Pearl stared blankly out on the empty lawn and turned slowly to Ginger Lee.

"Let me help you lie down, Pearl," said Ginger Lee, her voice soothing. "We'll see him again."

The three children ambled slowly back to the general store, Tobias listening quietly to Elo on his shoulder.

"You brought love to Pearl Wiggins today, Tobias. She has learned from you that hate can only destroy. Your progress continues, my Royal One. You did well."

"Thankee, Elo."

"Sire, that is *thank you*. You must remember."

"Okay. *Thank you*, Elo," answered Tobias. "Sometimes it hard."

"As is life," said Elo.

CHAPTER 17

The Aftermath

A SMALL GROUP OF TOWNSPEOPLE gathered outside the fence at Pearl Wiggins's house. They peered impatiently at her front door, the undertone of their talk a constant low buzz. Ginger Lee stared out her window at them, shook her head, stepped back, and continued to apply her lipstick.

Things were going to get out of hand now, she thought. She could only imagine what all this was going to cause. Pearl had been locked up in that old house now for over twenty years, stuck in those awful braces, and now she stood alone as a completely healed woman. Talk would take hold in this town where stories grew and got misshapen until you didn't even recognize them. Folks from the newspapers would come. Probably Henry Hicks had been the first to spread the word about Pearl.

Ginger Lee looked over at Pearl's house again and watched as Delilah appeared on top of the fence and then leaped off into the shade of her magnolias. The big cat curled up gracefully on the warm soil, languidly licking her paws, her yellow eyes half closed. In her mind she saw Tobias again, never hesitating as he seemed to climb forever to the top of Pearl's high gabled roof, and then scooping up the distressed animal and descending again with such ease. The look on Pearl's face as she'd watched in astonishment was forever etched in Ginger Lee's memory. Now, her reaction to the miracle of Pearl—after the initial shock—was to protect Tobias. "I've got to get to Jewell," she thought.

Pearl Wiggins moved quickly around her house, placing things in order, dusting, tidying. Her energy was endless nowadays, and she never stopped hurrying—testing the stairs, up and down, walking rapidly from her kitchen to the front porch and back again. Frequently she stood in front of her mirror and saw a figure she hardly recognized. Her mind was unable to fully comprehend what had happened to her. That recent afternoon seemed hazy and dream-like, as if she'd been watching someone else.

The boy, Tobias, wove in and out of her thoughts—the humming silver stones, the hated steel braces clattering to the ground. Was he magic? Did he have special powers? Just a Negra child ... odd color and unusual, piercing eyes. Nevertheless, she regretted the words she had said to him, the hate and scorn she had heaped upon him and the other little boy. Perhaps she would be able to tell him. Ginger Lee would help her to do that, she was sure of it.

The telephone rang now for the tenth time that morning. Pearl was not accustomed to any kind of attention. Her normally reclusive life had seldom included telephone calls unless she herself had made them. Now the whole town wanted to get a glimpse of her and hear her story about the purple child and his healing powers. She was trying to dress with a little more flair since her leg braces had disappeared, and today she wore a pale-blue dress with gold buttons and a lace collar, which she had laid away in a trunk years ago. She'd put pink powder dots on her wrinkled cheeks and had applied a special pomade to her hair, which was pulled back softly in a knot. She picked up the receiver.

"Yes, this is Pearl Wiggins. Yes, Mr. Buell ... yes, I am. Oh, how sweet of y'all to say so, sir. It's been three days now. His name is Tobias Valentine, and he was just visiting my neighbor, Miz Ginger Lee Swanny, when ... yes, sir ... yes, sir, he is a Negra boy and a bit odd, I grant you, sir." There was a long pause as Pearl looked toward her front door. "Well, you will just have to see him for yourself."

Pearl set the telephone down and parted the curtains. The low rumbling of many voices suddenly confronted her as she looked out to see the faces of dozens of citizens from the town pressing against her front fence. They seemed to be moving forward, jostling each other, several holding box cameras. She straightened, whisking her hand down her dress as the doorbell jangled insistently. Opening the front door, she found Doctor Babbit, her trusted physician of many years, standing on the porch. Tipping his fingers to the brim of his hat, he regarded her with astonishment.

"Good mornin' to you, Pearl," the doctor intoned, smiling kindly at her. "Don't believe I've ever had the pleasure of seein' you standin' so tall and upright!"

"My gracious, Doctor Babbit," Pearl said as her hand flew to her heart. "The misery been lifted off my legs, and my heart is so full of joy and ... and happiness! Come on in now, before that crowd out there swallows you up." Pearl laughed lightly as she stepped easily around the foyer.

"God in heaven, Pearl, this is a true miracle. Never believed in such things, but this ... I'm seein' it with my own eyes! You know those hounds out there are a-clamorin' to get your story. Gonna be told all over the country. Can you tell me how it happened?" Doctor Babbit removed his hat politely. "Heard it was some kinda curious Negra boy who's s'posed to be so dark he is actually a purple color. He healed ya. Some is sayin' voodoo, but voodoo don't heal dread diseases like your polio." He adjusted his glasses and looked more closely at her.

Pearl looked down at her shoes as the two of them stood quietly by the front door, ignoring the hum of voices that persisted beyond the fence. "I know it's just downright unbelievable, Doctor, but I swear, as God is my witness, the braces just broke apart, fell off my legs, and I was walking again like I was twenty years old. I told Ginger Lee to take me in the house. Then the boy, the little purple one ... he was gone. I don't know what he did, but there were beautiful glowing stones floating in the air like a storm of colors— after he got my Delilah from the roof. I can't remember any more, Doctor Babbit. My mind was in confusion and swirling for a day or two. I get out of bed now, the sun is shining, and I'm the old Pearl like I was before the polio, walking around just as natural as can be."

Doc Babbit listened intently to his old patient, the Pearl Wiggins he had treated for years as a bitter, elderly woman blaming the Almighty and anyone else she could think of for her misfortune. He had always felt a certain amount of compassion for her plight, but usually he was glad to see her leave after her monthly cranky visit to his office. The change in her now was downright remarkable, a phenomenon he had never witnessed in his long years of medical practice.

"Who is this boy, Pearl? I heard a story over at the barbershop that he is kin to that Myron Valentine who lived out on Bunny Bayou—Myron, the Negra who was found dead in the swamp a year ago."

Pearl cleared her throat and fingered the lace on her collar. "Well, that must be him, Doctor. He got unusual courage too, climbing up that ladder to rescue my Delilah. Did that after I said terrible things to him ... how I felt about colored folks." Pearl lowered her gaze, frowning down at the floor.

Dr. Babbit touched her arm gently. "Well, someday you might have a chance to see this purple child again. You've changed, Pearl. Even this old doc can see it. Now, the reason I came is to walk you on down to my office and have a look at those legs ... legs that have been well nigh useless all these years. Tryin' to get some medical answers from that miracle you experienced."

"You are a good-hearted gentleman, Doctor Babbit. I've probably never told you that before."

"No, you never have." The doctor chuckled and turned to the window. He reached up and ran his hand over the exquisite faceted glass. "This window glass and your front door ... I've never seen anything so beautiful, Pearl. Seems like it never stays the same, keeps changin' colors."

"Happened after the miracle. Up till then this old house had plain old windows with old weathered glass."

"I mean, this window glass is like from a palace or somethin'." Doctor Babbit stepped from window to window.

"Maybe it is, Doctor. Maybe it is," said Pearl quietly.

The telephone jangled again, and Pearl picked up the receiver. "Yes, sir, this is Pearl Wiggins. Yes, I've been crippled for twenty years." She cupped her hand over the receiver and whispered to Doctor Babbit. "It's a reporter from New Orleans. Wants to put my picture on the front page! And he's sending down more newspaper folks to look into the healing miracle. Says there's a big outcry to know about it up there in Louisiana."

Ginger Lee opened her front door and held up her hands defensively as she faced a throng of townspeople.

"What is all this nonsense about the Negra boy, Miz Swanny?" one man shouted. "Did he really heal Pearl Wiggins? What does the sheriff think about all this?"

"Can you send that little pickaninny over to my house, Miz Swanny?" someone else yelled out. "My wife keeps gettin' such bad headaches she can't clean the house!" The crowd laughed and whistled.

Ginger Lee backed up, distressed and frustrated. "Please, just go on home now," she pleaded, her voice lost among the clamor

of the crowd. She turned as Neil drove up and parked in front of
the house. He slowly stepped out of the car, adjusting his hat and
tie, his eyes sweeping the crowd. A newspaperman moved close to
him, the camera aimed at his face. His expression took on an air of
authority as he moved toward the crowd of local folks standing in
front of his house.

"What about the purple boy, Sheriff?" a woman called out.
"Your wife isn't willin' to talk to us. Did he really have somethin'
to do with Miz Wiggins walkin' an' all? And is it true the boy been
taught all his polite ways by you and your missus?"

"Now, look here, folks," Neil shouted. "I believe y'all should go
on back home now. You're gettin' all steamed up and tramplin' on
my lawn. I'm the law in this town, and I won't tolerate trespassin'!"
He tossed his head and headed up the steps.

A stout woman stepped in front of the crowd, her dimpled
arms pummeling in anger, her voice hoarse. "As county sheriff, you
should be goin' on out to Bunny Bayou! Arrest that boy! We don't
feel safe, havin' some colored runnin' around puttin' spells on folks
and comin' into our backyards." Neil tried to step around her, but
she blocked his path and raged at him with her hands on her hips.
"I heard Henry Hicks sayin' that Negra boy workin' with the Devil!
What y'all gonna do about it?"

Neil ignored her and shouldered his way through the crowd as
he tried to reach his front door. "Get off my property!" he roared.

Suddenly Herbert Ricketts stepped out of the crowd and
confronted the indignant woman. "You got no right to tell Sheriff
Swanny what to do, missus! That child and his mama been comin'
into my store since he was barely walkin', and they always mannerly
and no trouble at all. You just whippin' up hysterics, ma'am." Herbert
edged away from the woman as the crowd moved closer, eager to
hear her next words.

Neil disappeared inside, slamming his front door. Ginger Lee
stood aside as he strode past her, shouting obscenities. She glanced

out the window as the crowd dispersed. Then she picked up her purse and her car keys and headed down the hallway.

"See what y'all has caused?" Neil spoke slowly, seething with anger. "I warned you, didn't I? Goin' out to that Valentine farm for a tea party, then havin' one of your own with the little Negras. Who is that boy anyway, Ginger Lee? You know somethin' I don't?" Neil stepped closer to her, his eyes menacing. "Huh? You do, don't ya!" He grabbed her wrist and twisted her arm.

"Take your hands off me!" she said, wrenching her arm out of his grasp. "That child got a kind heart, that I do know !" Her eyes were blazing now. "But you don't know anything about kind hearts, do you, Neil? And I believe he's got unusual gifts, helping people and bringing love. That's somethin' you don't understand either."

"What kind of unusual gifts, Ginger Lee? You mean he just puts his itty-bitty purple hand on that old crank next door, and next thing you know she's good as new!" Neil laughed bitterly.

"That's right, Neil. You could use some of that yourself!" Ginger Lee snapped her purse shut and headed for the back door.

"Where do you think you're goin'? I came home for my supper!" Neil pushed his hand against the door.

"Driving out to Jewell's farm, Neil," she said calmly, "and I'll thank you to get out of my way."

"C'mon now, honey. You know I can't fix my supper. Mama never taught me," he whined, his tone beseeching.

But Ginger Lee was gone, had already started the engine and was looking at him with contempt. "Then go hungry, Sheriff!" she shouted as she drove off.

Neil stood unmoving by the back door, unsure of what to do next. The hostile woman next door, crippled in mind and body ... did the purple boy really have something to do with what people were now saying—that she was healed? And Orville's crazed account of the boy with the broken arm—talk was that the Valentine boy had been at that scene too. He felt overwhelmed, like he had lost control of his town, his position as sheriff, and now his wife. Staring morosely at the house next door, he watched in disbelief as Pearl Wiggins and Doctor Babbit emerged from her house and strolled out through the front gate, Pearl's arm linked gracefully through his. Grabbing his hat, he hurried out the door.

"Miz Wiggins! Doc Babbit!" he called out. "Just home for supper and wanted to extend my greetins' to ya."

They both turned, smiling pleasantly. "Why, thank you, Sheriff," said Pearl. "Lovely day, isn't it?"

Neil stared at her. She stood tall and graceful beside the doctor, her face open and content. The ill-humored old recluse was gone, and in her place was a new Pearl, cordial and warm.

"Hard to believe, isn't it, Neil?" she said softly. "The little purple Negra boy gave me back my life."

"That so?" croaked Neil. "How did he—"

"It's love, Sheriff. That's what it is."

Doctor Babbit doffed his hat. The two of them turned and continued up the street. "Good day, Sheriff," he called back.

I've got to get to Jewell, thought Ginger Lee as she headed out of town, her white DeSoto picking up speed along the back road. She passed the golden cornfields, still ripe with fat, healthy stalks, thinking again of the old man Birdie Foy and Jewell's whispered account of the dead fields coming to life. Tobias had done it. She must warn Jewell about Pearl's miracle. Word was getting around now, and it was dangerous for Tobias. The child with such a lovely heart could never cope with this onslaught, nor could his mother.

And there were those who wanted to do him harm, her own husband being one of them. It had not taken her long to realize the evil he carried in his heart, and she had now come to terms with it. Through the afternoon haze, she saw the Valentine farm in the distance, and she turned down the narrow lane that led to Jewell.

CHAPTER 18

The Queen Trumpeter of Zinfoneth

T HE THIN CURTAINS IN Jewell's small house moved gently in the warm night air. Drooping cypress and pines whispered softly under a full moon, casting shadows over the quiet little farm. Grampa Perry slept soundly, his old, delicate hands resting lightly on the worn cotton blanket. Through his open window a river of butterflies swept in, swirling around the room and landing on his shelf of faded, cracked family photographs that were dear to him from decades past: Jewell as a child and as a grown woman with tiny Tobias, and his wife, dead now for thirty years. As the delicate creatures lifted off the old photographs, the pictures now appeared new, as if the camera had taken them only yesterday. The curtains along his window whipped as another swarm of butterflies fluttered into his room and flew around his bed.

Grampa Perry opened his eyes, seeing only darkness but sensing a strange need to leave his warm bed. Slowly he eased his feet into a pair of worn slippers placed at the side of his bed and instinctively reached for his cane. Shuffling across the dark room, he felt a gentle whirring of wings around him as the butterflies guided his hand to the doorknob.

"Umph," he grumbled, swiping his hand into the darkness. "Somethin' goin' on! Gotta find out what." Clad only in his long white nightshirt, he tapped his cane in front of him and made his way to the front door of the house. He felt his way down the creaking old porch steps, unaware that he was encircled by the butterflies, some perched on top of his head, others on his shoulder, their wings whispering.

Elo floated in through Tobias's window and hovered above his bed. Then he stood at the end of his bed, looking at him with adoration. Tobias opened his eyes, a slow smile spreading on his lips.

"Hello, Elo. I was dreamin' about ya."

Elo's walnut face glowed as he heard the words. He glided around the side of the bed, drawing back the blanket.

"It still night time!" Tobias said. "Does I have ta git up?"

"It is *to* and *get*, not *ta* and *git*, Majesty. You must remember to pronounce the *o*. Make a circle of your lips. The word is *to*. And yes, you must arise. We have much to do, and your grandfather awaits you in the barn. He is not aware of what is to transpire, but you must now step forward, have courage, and believe in your powers."

"Should I bring my Royal Stones?"

"No, sire. Tonight you shall use the growth that the stones have ingrained in you. It shall all come from your command."

"Will Mama know, Elo? Us goin' out so late at night?" asked Tobias in a sleepy voice.

"Come, come, sire ... soon to be king and liberator."

Tobias climbed into his overalls and slipped into his shoes. He sat down on the floor, his tongue at the edge of his lip as he concentrated on tying his shoelaces.

"A lib'rator, Elo? Like the one who sings the song before the battle? Am I right, Elo?" asked Tobias drowsily.

Elo began to pace back and forth as he waited, watching Tobias carefully tying his shoes. He rubbed his tiny hands together, the moonlight capturing the lovely gossamer of his wings. He stopped, his antennae waving back and forth as he pondered the question.

"Yes, being a liberator is part of being a king."

Grampa Perry made his way into the dark night, his cane probing ahead of him with each step. He was familiar with the pathway that led to the barn, night being no different from day for him. He knew every bump, every small root that blocked his way. Something was drawing him to the barn, and he followed along the path, the strange whirring noises still surrounding him. Inside the barn the bright light of the moon shed streaks of silver across his face. He stopped and turned his head from side to side, sensing another presence.

"Tobias, where you be, boy?" asked Grampa Perry. "Your mama ain't gonna take a likin' to y'all bein' out this time of night."

It was silent in the barn. He grunted, poking his cane into the darkness. Tawny whinnied, restless in her stall.

"Nope, I ain't talkin' to you, you ol' rug of manure and flies!"

"That is not a proper way to speak to Tawny, Sir Perry," came a squeaky voice from high in the rafters.

"Who that? Who up there? Ain't never heard no voice like that ... like scratchin' nails on a rusty tin can!" Grampa Perry twisted his head upward, his sightless eyes staring into the blackness.

"Tawny has trod many years to your voice and followed your command as she plowed your fields, placing food upon your table," continued the scratchy voice. "And this wondrous creature has always stayed obedient to your choice of lodging. And since I have been here, I cannot say that this house of care is the most alluring."

Grampa Perry jabbed his cane into the dark. "Who ya be, boy? What y'all doin' on my property in the middle of the night with all them fancy words?" he said, his tone defiant.

Elo floated from the rafters and came to stand tall in front of Grampa Perry. The big creature bowed to the sightless old man.

"Sir Perry, revered grandfather of Tobias, I am Elo," he stated grandly.

"Elo, huh! You that big bug my grandson been drawin', the one I been hearin' about since he no taller than the patch on my knee?"

"I am he, but I, sir, am not a bug—not as this world sees my ancestors. I am a Cripon."

"What y'all look like, Mr. Elo? Does ya live in that swallows' nest over yonder? Fer all I know, y'all could be one of them Snaught brothers I used to hear over at Ricketts's years ago, talkin' sophisticated an' all. I heard them ugly boys talkin' all kinda languages." Grampa Perry turned his head back and forth as he spoke.

"I know of the Snaught Brothers—which is not their true name, by the way. A horrible choice, Snaught. I know of their true intent as well." Elo sniffed. "But I, sir, am Elo. I have been with Tobias since his birth, even though I have never made myself known to you."

Elo fluttered upward as Tobias appeared beside the old man, grabbed his hand, and looked up at him.

"Hi, Grampa."

Grampa Perry's face creased in a warm smile. "I was wonderin' ta myself where ya was," he said. "There I was, sleepin', and for some reason I just crawled outa bed like I was wantin' ta taste me some honeycombs. Had a flutterin' feelin' all around my head, and next thing I knowed …"

Tobias giggled playfully, swinging his hand with Grampa Perry's. "That was the Enriching, Grampa. They helped ya come out here."

Jewell walked into the barn holding her lantern and cradling her shotgun. Its glow cast over Grampa Perry, Tobias, and Elo. Her face grew alarmed as she stared in astonishment at the huge butterfly. He bowed to her, his wings sweeping the barn floor.

"We have met briefly, Jewell. Do not be frightened. I am Elo."

Tobias laid his small hand on his mother's wrist. "Don't be afraid, Mama. Elo the one I been drawin', and he the one brought you the fine dishes for cake with the town lady, 'member?" he said softly.

Jewell swallowed hard and looked around the barn.

"Do you want to touch his wings, Mama? He'll let ya."

Elo stepped forward, nodding his tiny head, his mouth pursed in a smile. "Take a deep breath, Jewell. I am real. I briefly introduced myself to you here in the barn. There was a dangerous occurrence that day, a man whose words toward you were foul and evil. Do you remember?"

Jewell nodded. "Oh, yes ... and I thank you, Elo ... and for the beautiful china dishes." She drew Tobias close to her. "But what we all out here for? I not wantin' to have a secret talk in the middle of the night. Grampa Perry, he needs his sleep."

Her eyes were riveted on Elo, who began to pace back and forth, his tiny head bowed. He stared down at the barn floor.

"Tobias is now of age, and I believe you know of this." Elo turned his gaze directly on Jewell.

Grampa Perry stepped forward. "Don't mind comin' out here, Mr. Elo," he declared loudly, "'specially if you havin' a friendly time passin' with Tobias. Even if it be during sleepin' hours, but what you want me to do? I cain't see even if a firefly were perched on my nose."

Elo rested his chin in his tiny hand. "Sir Perry, tonight the reflection of yourself will change. Even a firefly will see himself in your eyes. It is the newfound power of Tobias."

Jewell sighed. "I have seen all you did, and I knows you is a special creature."

"I am not a creature, Jewell. I am Elo, a Cripon. With time, you will understand that."

Jewell closed her eyes for a moment, regretting her bad choice of words. What was she to say to him, to this strange Elo. He has proven to be kind—and very wise in keeping things simple for her child. But Tobias was only eight years old! She couldn't allow this. With Josh gone now, Tobias was her only child. What was she to do? He was still just a little one. He needed to be with his mama and his grampa, not floating off in those dark stars she'd seen flying in the night!

Elo spoke solemnly. "Jewell, on Elios he is fully grown and soon to be released as an ambassador. And as the 'chosen one,' he will in time be king."

Jewell moved past Elo and walked across the barn, the lantern in her hand casting long shadows. She sat down on a barrel, holding her bowed head in her hands.

Grampa Perry stood leaning on his cane, sensing the tension around him. "Tobias, your mama, she ain't one to have this conversation with, boy. Talk between her and this Elo. It's not makin' sense ta her."

"Elo knows best, Grampa. He is very wise. He kind too." Tobias looked up at his Grampa, still holding tight to his hand. Grampa Perry slowly bent down and passed his hands over the boy's face. "This here Elo, how do he talk, bein' a bug an' all, Tobias?"

"He not … I mean, he is not a bug, Grampa. He is a Cripon. On the planet of Elios, he is an Ancient, old and wise. He sent to earth as my teacher. One day I will be given the throne as king."

The old man rested his gnarled hand on the little boy's head. "I always knowed you was not of this world. Somethin' about ya was unlike peoples here on earth. Your mama knowed too, but she carried ya in her belly, she borned ya. You understand what your Grampa is sayin' to ya?"

Tobias looked down, his face sad. "Yes, Grampa, I know."

Elo floated up to a rafter, his head bowed low, and closed his huge eyes. He squeezed his tiny lips together and raised his head. "Speech, mountain, and splendor ... I call forth the Queen Trumpeter of Zinfoneth!" His voice screeched out, the rasping tones floating out of the barn.

Tobias clapped his hands over his ears. Grampa Perry stood still, his eyes shut tight, his face crinkled. "Sounds like a buncha tin cans fallin' from the sky, boy! That yer Elo?"

Jewell whirled around in alarm. "What's that screamin' mean?"

"Elo been doin' that for a long time now," said Tobias, "tryin' to call the Fairy Queen Trumpeter. I never seen her, but Elo say she very powerful, that she'll be comin' if he keeps callin'. She pretty too, Elo says, and—"

"Speech, mountain, and splendor! I call forth the Queen Trumpeter of Zinfoneth," Elo screeched again.

A brilliant spotlight began to swirl around the barn and then suddenly faded to dark. Another spot of light, more brilliant than the first, circled around the inside of the barn. Like a cascading water fountain, ignited arrows fell from the high wooden ceiling planks, bouncing off the rafters, and gracefully formed themselves into a beautiful, young, female butterfly, her wings adorned with glittering gold. Her head was like Elo's, small and wizened. A radiant purple blush surrounded her eyes, and from each eyelid sprang long curved lashes shaped like triangular wings. Upon her forehead were three brilliant-yellow antennae. Her gown was deep purple, and she wore a helmet-like headpiece with silver bands looping around her neck. Intricate lace lapels were tucked in at her waist and cascaded down into a long train behind her. Silver cuffs were on her wrists, and at the ends of her wiry hands were long, curved, lavender fingernails. Folded across her shoulder was a slender silver trumpet that twisted upward into a large bell alongside her head.

She bowed gracefully to Tobias and remained motionless as Elo floated down from the rafters. Jewell stepped out of the shadows, her eyes wide and staring.

"Queen Zinfoneth! Where ... where have you been?" rasped Elo anxiously. "I have called you many times but received no response."

Queen Zinfoneth slowly unfolded her wings, a soft purring sound filling the barn with a quiet vibration.

"Thank you, Elo, for calling me," came the musical voice.

"Thanking me does not explain why you have not answered. You have caused me to worry incessantly about your whereabouts, your—"

"I apologize for not coming upon command," came the lilting voice. "The atmosphere of this planet has caused me serious damage. My wings have not taken flight. But I have blown the horn in answer to your call many times. Did the Cupbearers not come?"

"Yes, they heard your horn, which brought them forth when required," said Elo. "I am perplexed, however, to hear about this trouble with your wings, my queen. I myself find my own wings often laden with strange dust. This is most distressing." Elo bent close to her wings and placed his spectacles on his tiny wrinkled face, murmuring to himself.

Queen Zinfoneth watched Tobias as he tiptoed toward her, bringing Grandpa Perry with him. She floated toward him, her movements graceful and giving off distant musical notes.

"This is my Grampa Perry, Missus Queen," said Tobias politely, still clutching the old man's hand. "And this be my mama. Her name is Jewell." Jewell stood staring, unable to respond.

"Greetings, Sir Perry." Queen Zinfoneth gazed down at Tobias. "I know of your grandfather, sire, and your mother is known throughout the Ninth Wheel of Og."

"What y'all sayin' about me?" Grampa Perry brayed into the darkness. "Who that talkin' like some pretty tune?"

Queen Zinfoneth leaned close to Grampa Perry. "I am the Queen Trumpeter of Zinfoneth, Sir Perry. I carry the Silver Trumpet and heed the calls of Elo. On my planet I am called simply Queen Z."

"Then can I call you that, Queen Zin-fo-neth?" asked Tobias, his voice excited. "Queen Z be easier."

"Whichever suits you," she said, her laugh tinkling through the barn. "And you, my child, you are a joy to look upon, as befits a king. On our planet, King Suryes foretold that the child born on Earth who would come to us would be very beautiful and would lead the Cripons to heights of splendor not yet revealed."

Grampa Perry smiled grandly, gesturing with his cane. "He is, ain't he! That be my boy, my grandson—the most beautiful chile in all Mississippi, the stars above, and beyond. Cain't see him, but I sure knows him just by the feel of him!"

Tobias lowered his eyes, embarrassed by all the attention.

Queen Zinfoneth brushed Grampa Perry's face with the tip of one wing, causing him to jump back. "Sir Perry, this is a very special night." Her words hung in the air, riding up a musical scale.

Jewell moved to her son's side, her hand cupping Tobias's head.

"Aside from our introduction," she continued, "we have gathered here to give you back your sight."

The old man stumbled backward, his hand covering his eyes. Jewell reached out to him as his balance gave way and called out to Tobias. "Grab that old crate over there, Tobias! Grampa gonna fall!"

"I ... I gotta sit down for a minute," he said, panting. "Cain't seem ta breathe no more. I ... I don't believe I heard right." He slumped over on top of the wooden crate, holding his head. "Did y'all say somethin' about givin' me back my eyes? You mean, bein' able to see?" He began to cry softly.

Jewell knelt at his feet, stroking his hand. Tobias stood near them, watching quietly.

"Being able to see. Yes, Sir Perry, that is what I have placed before you." Queen Zinfoneth's yellow antennae curved toward him.

Grampa Perry sat quietly, tears running down his furrowed cheeks, his frail body trembling.

"Are you saddened by this, Sir Perry?" asked Elo. He turned his gaze on Tobias, waiting for the old man to respond. "Is he sad, Tobias?"

"No, Elo," said Tobias quietly. "He just havin' a hard time believin' what you said. He's never seen us—me and Mama—for about eight years."

Queen Zinfoneth knelt before Grampa Perry, her purple gown swirling around him like fine gauze. She opened a small, carved silver box. A mist floated from it, followed by a stream of white butterflies, each glowing with tiny gold droplets. Like raindrops they fluttered above the old man.

"Now, Tobias, you must cup your hands out in front of you and stand here."

Tobias turned from Grampa Perry and extended his small purple hands outward. The tiny white butterflies swept around the barn and gathered one by one in his open palms. Queen Zinfoneth and Elo bowed deeply and stepped back. Droplets of gold liquid dripped from Tobias's hands. Each droplet ignited into a tiny flame as it landed on the barn floor and then extinguished itself with a puff of smoke. Tobias watched in wonder as the butterflies lifted off from his palms and began to swirl around him. Tobias giggled. "They ticklin' me," he said.

Elo stood by, tall and solemn. "Now, sire, place your hands on your grandfather's eyes. This is the process of being a Lord of Fire."

Tobias looked up at Queen Zinfoneth, who was watching him closely.

"A Lord of Fire?" Tobias asked. "I am going to be an ambassador and then a king. What be a Lord of Fire, Queen Z?"

"Sire, as foretold by King Suryes, you will have many powers," she said, leaning down to him. "Each is a stepping stone to being a king—powers seen and powers imagined."

Tobias turned toward Grampa Perry and held his hands out toward the old man.

"You must seek the words of your command, Tobias," said Elo.

"Grampa, lift up your head. It will be okay. An' keep your eyes closed."

Grampa Perry slowly lifted his head upward, his breath coming in huffs and puffs. Tobias carefully placed his hands over his grandfather's sightless eyes.

"Use your heart, Tobias. Seek true meaning in what you say, and trust your words," said Elo.

There was silence in the barn. Tobias glanced briefly at Jewell, who gave him a small smile of encouragement and nodded her head. "Is you afraid, Mama?" he whispered to her.

"No, Tobias. I am not afraid."

Tobias swallowed hard, closed his eyes, and then spoke out, loud and clear.

"I seeks ... *seek* truth. Each morning I sweep my broom in the grip of darkness and woes. I command sunshine bringed by ... *brought* by the light. There be ... *will be* no more darkness hid in the night."

Grampa Perry moaned and placed his hands to his eyes. "Is you hurtin', Grampa?" asked Tobias in a small voice.

"Nope, I just a little warm," he answered. "My toes is a-wigglin', and by golly, I got me a sense of bees squirmin' through my kneecaps." Grampa Perry fell backward onto the hay-strewn floor, his hands covering his eyes, groaning softly. Jewell flung herself down beside him, stroking his face as Tobias looked up at Elo, his eyes filled with tears. Queen Zinfoneth bowed before him as Elo placed a wiry hand on his shiny bald head.

Grampa Perry whooped. "And I swear by mud coats an' Sam Puddle, I got a taste of lollypop mint swellin' on my tongue."

"You did well, Majesty," announced Elo. "Your words were well chosen. Remember, your grandfather is not of Elios; he is of this planet Earth. But because of your powers, when he opens his eyes, all that he sees will be brighter and more colorful than what he saw before he lost his eyesight. He will see as it is on our planet. Do you understand, sire?"

"Yes, Elo," said Tobias in a low voice. "But what did the mint candy mean?"

Elo reached into his purple, pin-striped vest, took out his small spectacles, and placed them on his nose. "Sire, on Elios—the origin of the Cripon and all inhabited planets in the Ninth Wheel of Og— it is like climbing the glass tree. It is all about belief. Life is very different there: thousands of colors, wonderful tastes such as your grandfather is experiencing—mint and strawberry, lemons and limes. And beyond that is belief ... belief and love that will bring change, such as new eyes for your grandpa."

"I think I understand," said Tobias, his brow wrinkled in confusion, "but what about Nuc-tem-er ..." He stumbled over the name. "You said he needs ta be—"

"Yes, Tobias. I have warned you of difficulties, which in time you will come to understand. On Elios, although there are great pleasures as I have just explained, it is not always as it seems in the glass tree. As I have told you, Nuctemeron is very treacherous. But even though he says he is loved in the hearts of the inhabitants of Elios, he is the snare of evil. He seeks power, and with that comes jealousy and wickedness. All these things you will learn as time passes and your knowledge increases. You will learn how to negotiate with Nuctemeron. Unfortunately, he is not our only adversary."

There was a pause as Tobias considered Elo's words. "What is an ad-adversary, Elo?" he asked, pronouncing the word slowly.

"That was a very good question, sire. An adversary is your enemy, one who does not believe what you believe."

"Then with Mr. Nuctemeron, we must tell him to stand in the middle and listen!"

Elo stood back, his wizened face twisted in a smile. He stretched his wiry arms wide, his wings whipping. Tobias regarded him with delight, realizing suddenly that Elo was excited and pleased.

"Very good, sire, very good indeed! That is most correct. Your wisdom is growing!"

Jewell sat cradling Grampa Perry in her arms as Tobias leaned down to him. "Open your eyes, Grampa. You can see my face now, me 'n' Mama. Are you still feelin' afraid?"

Grampa Perry's hands trembled as he lifted them from his eyes, which were still squeezed shut. "I afraid, boy. That old dark night prob'ly still gonna be there."

"Trust me, Grampa," pleaded Tobias. "It my new powers."

Jewell wrapped her arms around him, laughing softly. "Try it, Daddy. We all here with ya."

Queen Zinfoneth floated above him, her wings moving in slow motion. Elo stood before him, his gloved hands folded sedately across his purple vest. They all waited.

"By Gawd, gal, I seein' wings! Ya sure I ain't in heaven?" asked Grampa Perry, his eyes wide open.

Queen Zinfoneth laughed. "You are seeing my wings, sir. Your heaven is right here in this barn with your family who loves you." Her musical voice filled the air. "If you like, I can take you for a night flight. That way you can see your own beautiful planet."

Grampa Perry stared around at them, his gnarled hands reaching out. "I gotta touch everything! Jewell, darlin', I can see, I can see ... your face, them dried tears, yer sparklin' eyes. Where that big ol' bug? Tobias, where are ya, child? Ol' Grampa can see, boy. I can see!"

Tobias stood before him as Grampa Perry's eyes filled with tears. For a long moment he stared at the little boy and then held out his arms to him. "You be just as beautiful as I imagined all these years. Such a wee babe last time I saw ya, sleepin' in yer mama's arms." Tobias stepped into his embrace, and the two of them stood together as Grampa Perry stroked his head, chuckling softly. Presently he reached down and picked up his cane, tossed it across the barn, and wandered over to Tawny, his steps slow and halting as he held on to Tobias.

"Why, you ol' patch of grass hair, I can see! Imagine that! Ol' Grampa Perry can see ya." He reached up and stroked the sleek nose. "I've always loved you, old friend, an' I apologize for talkin' to you like I did." Tawny whinnied softly as Grampa Perry whispered in her ear. "Know what? Tobias, he healed my eyes. I can see now!"

"Grampa! You can see! You can see!" Tobias skipped around the barn in delight. "Elo, can I go tell Elma Mae and Chalmers?"

Elo removed his spectacles and tucked them back inside his vest. "In time they will know, Tobias. At this moment you must begin to guide your grandfather back into the seeing world. There are undoubtedly many things he has forgotten."

Grampa Perry took a step toward Elo, who bowed to him, Queen Zinfoneth at his side. "You ain't no bug in my eyes, Mr. Elo and Missus ... er ... Zinfo. My eyes be open now, and I beginnin' to understand better my Tobias ... his treasure 'n' callin'.'"

"Can you really see me, Daddy?" asked Jewell quietly. She had hung back in the shadows as her daddy's sight was restored, still unable to accept her son's powers.

Grampa Perry walked toward her. "Darlin', I sees so clearly. Your face ... I can even see the fear lurkin' in your eyes."

Jewell raised her hands. "Stop!" she said firmly. Her delight was still there, for her daddy could quite obviously see again, but she was having trouble comprehending. Tobias had restored his sight in front of her own eyes. The meaning of this was beginning to seem ominous, something to be dreaded rather than celebrated.

"Tobias, do you understand what you was able to do with your hands ... 'n' all them butterflies?" she asked.

"The proper grammar," Elo chirped, "is 'those butterflies,' not—"

Jewell turned angrily toward him. "Be quiet, Elo," she interrupted. "Y'all and this other creature have brought all this on my family. Daddy can see now, but what my boy doin'? Leave him outa this!"

"We are not creatures, madam, and ..." Elo began. He stopped, his face puckered with concern.

Jewell stared out of the barn door, her eyes hard. She paid no attention as Tobias took her hand, whispering, "Mama?" She was barely aware of the whiffling of Elo's wings and the soft musical notes as Queen Zinfoneth spoke to them all.

Oh, what am I to do? she thought. What about the stories Ginger Lee had told her yesterday? Folks had grown wary of her boy, and he was in danger. There was a story about a white lady in town who was now walkin'. Folks always noticed Tobias being so different. And now all this magic. She couldn't have this goin' on no more. They needed to leave. She'd take Tobias and Grampa Perry, and they'd slip away. Her daddy could see—oh, it was an answer to her prayers. But could her son really have done this? Her daddy had been blind for eight or nine years now, eyes useless, livin' in a dark world. Did Tobias understand what this meant, with the creatures guidin' him and all, and talkin' about powers and bein' royal? Now they were sayin' he was gettin' ready to go somewhere far away, and that meant he'd be leavin' his mama.

"Be quiet!" shouted Jewell. "I want you to leave, leave this land of mine. Do not come here anymore! I will not allow you to take my only boy. I don't care about no other peoples wantin' him!" She whisked her hair back, breathing hard. The barn was silent.

"Jewell, my gal ... y'all can't be sayin' these kind of things." Grampa Perry stepped close to her and laid his hand on her shoulder. "You knowed about his birthplace, and it ain't here."

Jewell shrugged away from him and grabbed Tobias by his arm, dragging him out of the barn.

"Mama, Mama, please don't do this," he whimpered. "It what I s'posed to do."

Queen Zinfoneth watched them go, her beautiful face troubled. "I do not understand," she said.

Elo called out gently as the two left the barn. "We must discuss this, Jewell. You have to understand exactly what it is you are stating. Tobias is not an earthly child, my dear. He is to be a king. If he does not leave here, he will …" Elo's voice faded to a tiny scratch.

"He will what?" flung back Jewell angrily.

"He will not survive, Jewell."

Jewell ignored him and hurried down the path toward the house, firmly grasping Tobias by his arm. The barn echoed with his pleading to his mother as they disappeared inside the house.

Grampa Perry stood silent and then turned to Elo. He stopped for a moment, searching for words. He walked to the other end of the barn, stared out at the moonlit night in wonder, and saw the Milky Way again. Elo moved up behind him.

"What are you thinking of, Sir Perry?" asked Elo.

Grampa Perry slowly looked back at Elo. "I be amazed at the beauty of that big ol' scatterin' of stars I ain't seen in so many years. An' I feels lost in this sight that I now sees, with my gal actin' this way. I be talkin' to her, Elo," he said. "She very upset with the thought of losin' Tobias. He only a chile, a baby in her eyes."

Elo frowned, gazing seriously at Grampa Perry. He reached out and carefully placed his tiny twig hands on the old man's cheeks. "Sadness has achieved its victory today with Jewell," he said. "We haven't much time."

CHAPTER 19

A Broken Heart

J EWELL OPENED THE BEDROOM door and stood looking down at Tobias. The cotton blanket was tucked neatly beneath his chin, and he lay in a deep sleep.

"Tobias, you need to be gettin' outa bed now. It's growin' late." She leaned over him, laughing softly. "Not like you to be lettin' your chores go."

Tobias stirred and turned his face into his pillow. "Mmm ... don't want to, Mama," he said, his voice muffled.

"Son, it's time to get up! Sun peekin' in your window long time ago. Ain't never slept this long in the mornin'," said Jewell firmly.

He rose slowly and sat on the edge of the bed, unmoving and silent. Jewell stooped down in front of him and lifted his chin. "What's the matter with you, Tobias? You not yourself this mornin'." The child's face was ashen, his deep-brown eyes dull-looking.

"Nothin', Mama. I comin'." He shuffled into the kitchen and with effort climbed into the chair in front of his cornmeal mush. "I not very hungry," he said, pushing the bowl away.

Jewell watched him, a frown of concern on her face. "Is Chalmers and Elma Mae goin' with you to Birdie Foy's place today, Tobias? He was plannin' on lettin' you play on that old tractor, 'member?"

Tobias stared down at the table, his small shoulders hunched. "I dunno," he said briefly, sliding down from the chair. Slowly he headed back toward his bedroom as Grampa Perry came through the door, carrying a grain bucket.

"Where you off to this mornin', boy? Just finished feedin' Tawny," announced the old man cheerfully. "Gobble down that mush. Then you 'n' me, we gotta go fishin' today! Can't wait to see them fish jumpin' on my hook! These old eyes o' mine got a good notion to jump outa my sockets, everything be so beautiful!" Grampa Perry stepped inside the bedroom, wrapped his arm around Tobias, and gazed down at the little boy. "Lookin' like you might be feelin' poorly this mornin', Tobias. Mebbe you 'n' me can just set on the porch for a spell."

Tobias only nodded. He turned to reach for Grampa Perry's hand—and all at once he sank to the floor and lay still.

"Tobias!" screamed Jewell, hearing him fall. She knelt down beside him, lifting his head in her arms. "Daddy! What wrong with him? What wrong? He ain't never fell sick before." The two of them lifted him gently up onto the bed.

"I know that, gal. We need to lay him down for a while and then get some food in his belly. Prob'ly just needin' more sleep after last night. Child be pulled this way 'n' that by Mr. Elo 'n' you." He glanced quickly at Jewell, who looked back at him, her face stern.

"Never mind, Daddy," she said shortly. "We not concerned about last night, just about now. Go get me a damp cloth 'n' bring the blanket off my bed." She leaned down, stroking Tobias's face. "Talk to Mama, son. You need to open your eyes!"

Tobias seemed far away in a deep sleep. Dark circles had appeared beneath his eyes, and his small chest was barely rising and falling. Jewell lifted him with one arm and unbuttoned his nightshirt.

Gently she wiped his forehead with a cool cloth, murmuring to him. "Tobias ... Mama worried. Just open your eyes, even a little bit," she begged. Slowly he lifted his eyelids, and with a tiny sigh closed them again, seeming to slip off to another place where his mother couldn't reach him. Jewell lifted one of his hands, enclosing it in her own, but it fell heavily back onto the blanket.

"Daddy! Y'all come in here!" she shouted over her shoulder.

Elo appeared outside the window, fluttering up and down, his eyes rolling in distress. "Jewell, you must allow me to—"

Jewell whirled around, slammed the bedroom window shut, and turned back to the bed.

"Gal, that ain't a proper way to be treatin' Mr. Elo. Mebbe he know why this child fallin' down with a strange ailment." Grampa Perry bent over the little boy, his old hand shaking as he stroked the boy's face.

"I his mama, Daddy! What do he know about my child?"

Grampa Perry lifted Tobias's hand, holding it in his own. "They is from the same place, Jewell. You can't change that. Slammin' the window ... well, he know to come, like he know Tobias be poorly."

"Let me set awhile with him, Daddy." She lowered her head, avoiding his eyes. "I be callin' you if I needs to." She carefully spread a patched quilt over the still child.

"Maybe he got some kind o' typhoid, gal, or that fever used to be around when you was just a babe. Swamp fever, they used to call it." Grampa Perry's voice was trembling. "I growin' mighty worried, Jewell. Think I'll have me a walk over to Birdie Foy and see if him or Jumper got any potions for ailin' folks. Boy sweatin' now. It not good."

Jewell spread a wet cloth on Tobias's forehead and wiped his small purple chest and arms. "I don't want you walkin' nowhere, Daddy. You need to give your eyes time to get used to seein', hear? I'll take care of my boy. I borned him. I'll nurse him.

Grampa Perry sighed and headed to the front porch, easing himself into his old rocker. Boy under some kinda spell, he thought to himself. 'Course, mebbe gettin' my eyes back, and Mr. Elo and Jewell a-quarrelin'—mebbe it all too much for the child. He stared out at the cornfields, aware for the first time that he was seeing with his own eyes the elegance of the golden cornstalks that stretched to the horizon. He nodded to himself. Yep, that the work of Tobias, just like I thought.

Suddenly he heard a whirring overhead as Elo and the Queen Trumpeter landed on the high eave of the barn. Keepin' watch over Tobias—that what they there for, Grampa Perry mused.

Chalmers skipped into the barnyard, stopping at the bottom of the stairs and looking up at Grampa Perry.

"Is you Chalmers?" asked Grampa Perry, smiling down at him. Chalmers hung on the railing, swinging his feet back and forth and peeking over at Grampa Perry.

"Yep. 'Course I is. Tobias, he my best friend! Didn't ya know?"

"Well, Chalmers, I ain't ever really seed ya before, not with my eyes. See, I not blind anymore. Your best friend give me back my seein'."

Chalmers stopped swinging and stared at the old man. "Ya mean you won't never have to tap the ground with that old stick no more?" His eyes grew large and round. "Can ya see the fish I be catchin', me 'n' Tobias?"

"Yep. And I'll be helpin' you count 'em, Chalmers," Grampa Perry said with a chuckle.

Chalmers continued to stare at him curiously. "Did you say Tobias got ya some new eyes? How'd he do that?"

Grampa Perry reached into his pocket and took out his old pipe, turning it over and over in his hands. "Love, Chalmers ... 'cause of love."

"Did he tell you about our glass tree out by the creek? Elo say we gets ta play in it ... that we always be safe there."

Grampa Perry raised an eyebrow. So many things he didn't know about his grandson. He had no idea what the little one was talkin' about, but it was somethin' unusual.

Chalmers jumped off the porch railing, scuffing his bare feet in the dirt. "When Tobias gonna come out 'n' play?" he asked. "We gonna do skippin' rope today, an' then we gonna have us a race across them fields to visit Mr. Foy an' swing on his tire. We gets to stand on top of it and swing back an' forth all day if we wants to … and play on his old tractor." Chalmers skipped around in circles, humming to himself.

"Tobias is sick, Chalmers—real sick, I 'fraid," said Grampa Perry in a low tone.

Chalmers stopped and frowned at Grandpa Perry. "Tobias can't be sick," he announced. "He a Cripon, and … and he gonna em-embark. He got another glass tree where he goin', ah'll betcha. We gots all kinds o' smoots too. They hangs on the tree. I got some under my pillow, an' I blowed me six bubbles with mine. Taste like strawberries."

Chalmers pointed toward the roof of the barn. "Hey! Ain't that Elo up there?" He began to run, shouting as he scampered across the barnyard. "Hi, Elo! Are we gonna learn some more words?"

Elma Mae came bounding up the lane, her jump rope looped over her shoulder. "What y'all lookin' at, Chalmers?" she called out. "Brought me some lemon smoots. We can eat 'em after we done jumpin' rope." She stopped, eyeing Chalmers suspiciously. He seemed sad and serious, his head drooping.

"I already blewed bubbles with mine," he mumbled. He stood with his hands in his overall pockets, staring dejectedly at the ground.

"Whatsa matter, Chalmers?" Elma Mae asked. She draped one arm around his thin shoulders.

"That were Elo up on the barn. He prob'ly here to see Tobias. Grampa Perry say he real sick."

Elma Mae covered her mouth with her hand and ran to the porch. "Chalmers say Tobias feelin' poorly! Is it true? He ain't never sick! Can I go talk to him?" The words poured out of her mouth as her eyes brimmed with tears.

"Slow down, gal. Don't do no good gettin' yerself in a state before we knows what wrong with him." Grampa Perry removed his pipe and stared at Elma Mae. "Come on up on the porch, child, so I can look at ya."

Elma Mae regarded him seriously, absently fiddling with a pigtail.

"Last time I seen them beautiful blue eyes o' yers, you was a babe ridin' in yer daddy's arms. Now I sees ya wearin' a whole head o' hair, redder'n a sunset!"

"How you know my hair red? You blind, Grampa Perry." She squinted up at the old man, moving up on the porch, and stood in front of him. "How many fingers I holdin' up?" she asked, stretching out two.

"Grampa Perry put his pipe back in his mouth. "Two!" he chortled between clenched teeth.

Elma Mae stood dumbfounded. "How come you can see again, Grampa Perry?" she whispered loudly. "Wow! Does Tobias know?"

"He knows. Boy healed my eyes last night, gal. Right over there in the barn with his teacher, Mr. Elo, and Missus Zinfo, the one who blows on that horn. She sittin' all pretty on top of that ol' rickety barn right now. See her? What y'all think about that?" asked Grampa Perry.

Elma Mae looked up at the top of the barn, but the Queen Trumpeter and Elo had disappeared.

"They gone," said Chalmers mournfully, dragging himself up on the porch. He sat down on the step, his chin in his hands.

"Me 'n' Chalmers, we met Elo too. He got big ol' eyes like windows. But I never seen nobody named Zinfo." Elma Mae turned and peered through the screen door. "Where Tobias's mama? Is she makin' him feel better? We s'posed ta go play on Birdie's tractor."

Grampa Perry reached out, encircling her with his arms, pulling her close. "Tobias can't play today, Elma Mae. I gettin' a morsel worried. It ain't some usual turn o' temperature. Mr. Elo, he come by to check on Tobias, but his mama ain't lettin' Elo near him no more."

"I wanna see him, Grampa Perry. I wanna see him," wailed Elma Mae, her voice teary.

Grampa Perry held her close, stroking her bright-red hair. Chalmers came and stood beside them, wiping his eyes with his fists. "I wanna see him too," he sniffled.

"I knows, children, but we gotta wait and see what his mama gonna say. She mighty upset with all these goings-on, an' her mood ain't one ta have a smilin' chatter. She ain't intendin' to let Tobias go."

"You means to embark?" asked Chalmers in a small voice.

Grampa Perry lifted his head at the word. "Where y'all hear a word like that?" he asked.

"Elo, he teached me and Elma Mae too," said Chalmers. "We had a word lesson in the glass tree, an'—"

"An' he told us Tobias gettin' ready ta embark," interrupted Elma Mae. She grabbed Chalmers's hand and pulled him down from the porch. The two began to run toward the lane. "We gonna go to the glass tree and maybe find Elo there! He's gotta know about Tobias!"

Grampa Perry rose from his rocker and watched the children disappear in the distance. He shook his head sadly, wiping a tear from his cheek.

Ginger Lee's big white DeSoto came to a stop in the Valentine barnyard. Several days had passed since Tobias had taken sick. Ginger Lee and Pearl Wiggins emerged from the car, followed by Doc Babbit. They walked together up to the porch where Jewell sat alone in Grampa Perry's rocker, looking off toward the cornfields, her face drowned in sorrow. "I brought Doctor Babbit with me, Jewell," Ginger Lee said softly. "You need to let him look after Tobias.

And Pearl Wiggins is here too. She my next door neighbor. Tobias, he ... changed her life. She asked me if she could come along."

Jewell glanced up at the tall man who stood regarding her kindly at the foot of the steps, holding his black medical bag.

"It's a privilege to meet you, Mrs. Valentine," he said, removing his hat. He glanced past her and through the screen door. "With your permission, I'd like to take a look at Tobias. Chances are I might be able to help him. If it's all right with you, I can just slip quietly inside."

Jewell stood and nodded politely, acknowledging Pearl as well. "Thank y'all for comin'," she said. "I'm much obliged. My daddy in there now, settin' with Tobias, but just tell him who you are, and it be all right."

Doc Babbit disappeared into the house as Jewell turned to the two women. Pearl held out her hand. "I'm honored to meet you, Mrs. Valentine. I'm hoping you'll understood why I wanted to come. Your son ... Tobias, well ... he taught me what love is ... that is, my life began again, and I ..."

Jewell took her hand for a moment. "I knows, Missus Wiggins. Ginger Lee has told me. Y'all can set awhile in the porch swing." She resumed her seat in the rocker, and the three of them sat silently.

"Can you help my boy?" asked Jewell as the doctor emerged some time later. He tucked his thumbs under his belt and rocked on his feet, choosing his words carefully.

"The boy got a normal temperature, Miz Valentine. He doesn't seem to have a cold. It isn't influenza or typhoid, and not swamp fever either, from what I can tell. But what's ailin' him isn't normal. It's like he ... well, it's like he got a broken heart, like he lost his will to keep on livin'. He's a healthy boy, but it just seems like he's given up."

"Do all you can, Doctor Babbit, and spare no cost," Pearl said.

"There won't be any cost, Pearl."

"I'd give my life to save his. Truly I would." She sighed, wiping her eyes. "I'm so sorry, Mrs. Valentine ... Jewell." She clutched her handkerchief. "I was so blinded by deeming all colored folks bothersome and inferior to myself. I said terrible things to your child. It is my wish now to speak to him. I just need to tell him, need to say how thankful I am for what he did for me. Your beautiful child healed my legs, and I can walk again. And he rescued my closest companion, my lovely cat, Delilah. And on that day, why, I never got a chance to say thank you. He was there, and then he was gone." Pearl dabbed at her eyes, her cheeks wet with tears.

"He knows he brought joy to you, Pearl," said Jewell, touching her arm. "He just knows these things."

Tom turned into the lane and headed for Jewell's farm. Beside him, Elma Mae sat still and sad, her usual sparkle gone, streaks of dried tears on her cheeks. Chalmers was in the backseat, his arms around a big hound dog who huddled near him. They had come upon Cottonseed out on the road, barely able to walk, making his painful way along the deserted road.

"Daddy!" Elma Mae had cried, "isn't that ol' Orville's dog, the one you said he be lovin' so much?"

Tom screeched to a halt and looked down at the poor creature. "By golly, child, it surely is. He must've wandered off from Orville's place. Looks like he won't be with us much longer. He's old and ailing." He hopped out of the car and gathered the hound in his arms, guiding him into the backseat. "Hold onto him, Chalmers. Can't just leave the old boy out here to die."

They arrived at the farm, and the children tumbled out of the car and raced for the porch. "Is he better, is he better?" they both shouted. Tom followed with the old hound in his arms.

"We bringed Cottonseed with us. He poorly, just like Tobias," called out Chalmers.

"Hi, Missus," said Elma Mae, spotting Ginger Lee. "Whatcha doin' out here?" She turned in surprise to see Pearl sitting in the porch swing. "Aren't you the lady next door, had them shiny sticks on your legs? Tobias, he helped you to ..." Her words faded away as she stared at Pearl's straight legs and stylish shoes.

"Calm down now, gal." Tom strode up behind them and tenderly placed Cottonseed on the floor of the porch. "These ladies don't need to be peppered with your questions."

Ginger Lee drew Elma Mae into her arms, folding the girl's hand into hers. "I'm sorry, Elma Mae. Tobias is not doing so well. We don't know what is wrong with him."

Chalmers huddled near Tom, and both children started to cry. Tom sat holding the little boy close. Pearl watched them silently, her eyes brimming with tears.

"What do y'all think, Doc?" Tom asked quietly.

"Well," said Doctor Babbit, sitting down beside Pearl on the porch swing and tenderly stroking Cottonseed's head. "I been practicin' medicine for thirty years, and I've never seen a child so poorly, yet seems in perfect health. Strong as an ox, he is."

Jewell fell forward from her chair and huddled on the porch, her sobs filling the still air. Suddenly she grew quiet, rose to her feet, and stood tall, her eyes blazing with anger. She tore away from Pearl and barged past Ginger Lee. She leaned over the railing and flung her arms out wide. "You can't have my boy, you hear me? You can't have him!" she shouted hysterically. She stumbled off the porch, running past Tom and the children, looking up at the sky and stretching her arms wide. "You can't have him! I borned him. I his mama, and you have no right! You hear me? You hear me, Elo? You can't take my boy!"

Jewell turned back, facing the sad group on the porch. Grampa Perry appeared at the screen door, his face full of sorrow. She swiped at the tears on her face, her head slowly drooping, and slumped to her knees at Tom's feet, weeping bitterly.

"Elo don't mean no harm," came Elma Mae's small voice from the folds of Tom's shirt. "He just doin' what a teacher s'posed to do. I knows he loves Tobias."

The sun was sinking low on the horizon, casting a rich, golden glow over the tiny farmhouse. Inside, anxious faces stared down at the little boy lying still beneath his thin blanket. Cottonseed wandered in on shaky legs. He sniffed at the blanket and licked Tobias's hand. The boy's glowing purple skin had lost its sheen, and his hands seemed lifeless as they lay on the covers. His eyelids had ceased to flicker as Jewell leaned over him, speaking his name.

Elma Mae lifted one of his hands, resting it in her own. "Tobias, we bringed ya some smoots, me and Chalmers. They sure does taste sweet. When you wakes up, I'll give ya my favorite. It tastes like cherry." The little girl held his hand to her face, her eyes pleading. "Can't ya open your eyes, Tobias? We want ya back, me and Chalmers, and your mama be worried real bad. She loves ya so much. We all loves ya. You're my best friend, Tobias. I can't have you leavin' without sayin' good-bye. You need ta open your eyes and talk ta me."

Chalmers leaned close to Tobias's ear, wiping his teary eyes. "Can ya hear me, Tobias? My daddy, he told me I always s'posed ta listen to you, cause he say that Tobias is one smart alley cat. He say you is the kindest chile he ever met, and he knows how much I like ya. I needs ya to come back." The little boy lay his head next to Tobias, whose breathing now was barely visible.

Elma Mae looked up at Tom as he stood beside the bed, his arm around Jewell. "He not gonna come back, Daddy. He not gonna say nothin' more," she said mournfully. "Why he sick, Daddy? What wrong with him?"

Tom dropped to his knees beside his daughter, his head bowed. Ginger Lee wiped at her eyes, clutching Pearl's hand. Grampa Perry leaned against the wall, apart from the others, his hand absently caressing Cottonseed's ears. His eyes never left the still, small face on the pillow. "I don't know, Elma Mae, but you know he loved ya," said Tom.

Elma Mae flung herself away from Tom, her fists clenched. "Don't say that, Daddy! Don't say he loved me, 'cause you make it sound like he gone!"

Pearl leaned down to the side of the bed and softly stroked Tobias's hand. "Where do I begin, Tobias?" she murmured softly. "I was a silly old woman with no understanding of just how sweet life is. I was angry at myself, not you. I want you to find your way back to us, to all the love that is in this room." Pearl paused, her eyes searching his still face. "Please, dear child, you have so much to live for, such a purpose. Please hear my words."

The chill night air filled the room as the hours passed and the moon rose high in the sky. They stood in silence around Tobias as Doctor Babbit stepped across a patch of moonlight and leaned down, placing a stethoscope on the small chest and listening. After a few minutes, he closed his eyes and shook his head. Jewell cried out, gathering the still body of her little boy in her arms. Grampa Perry fell to his knees, his head in his hands, sobbing quietly.

As dawn approached, they all sat quietly together on the porch. No one spoke. Jewell sat alone, despondent with grief. Tom held Elma Mae in his arms, while Chalmers lay with his head in Ginger Lee's lap. Cottonseed was curled up beside Grampa Perry. Suddenly the old hound struggled to his feet, his eyes appearing curiously alert, his tail wagging. He barked loudly as a rainbow of brilliant colors swooped down on them and then was gone. Jewell sprang from her chair and reached for the railing as Grampa Perry lifted himself from the old rocker, clutching his pipe. The rainbow returned and hung in the air in front of the barn.

Elo appeared before them, standing with his hands clasped behind him, his great wings sweeping the barnyard, raising clouds of golden dust.

"Elo!" screeched the children in one voice. "He here to help Tobias!" Elma Mae ran down the porch steps as Tom leaped up, his eyes staring in disbelief.

"I never thought it was true!" gasped Ginger Lee.

"I didn't either," said Tom, shading his eyes.

Elo turned and faced the group on the porch, who stood frozen with awe. He reached into his vest pocket and brought out his spectacles, balancing them delicately on his nose. Placing his white gloves on his wiry fingers, he began to pace back and forth as he summoned his courage and his words. At last his curious, rasping voice fell upon their ears as they listened, captivated by the majestic figure in front of them.

"I am Elo," he said, his great eyes rolling back and forth at them. "Some of you already know of my presence." His gaze fell upon Jewell and Grandpa Perry. "But I ask all of you to listen." He paused for a moment, fingers intertwined, his spectacles glistening. "I am an Ancient, a teacher sent here from the planet Elios to prepare Tobias. I have been here since his birth, and like most of you, I have watched him become the boy he is today." Elo paused, turning his wizened face from side to side to include all of them. "Let me help you understand this royal child, this boy we love.

"On Elios he is nearly grown, and he is soon to be king of the Cripons, who inhabit our planet. You see, on Elios love, and love alone, prevails. Life there is not as it is for earthlings. Tobias has walked among you and learned many things. Loving others is part of who he is, but as he has progressed, he has come to recognize that evil and hatred also prevail. He is learning how to cope with earthlings who feel these things and wish him harm. On Elios love exists through music and thousands of colors. From one day to the next, from one year to the next, in all seasons, life on Elios is lived surrounded by every color you see on your planet, and by music borne of love. There is no hatred on Elios, for it can only consume and leave its sting. Only Nuctemeron, the seeker of power through evil means, will challenge the significance of Tobias's calling. His agents remain among us on your planet." Elo bowed low and then swirled upward, cupping his gloves to his mouth. "Speech, mountain, and splendor!" His voice croaked like great gusts of wind. "Speech, mountain, and splendor! I call forth the Queen Trumpeter of Zinfoneth."

In the distance was the sound of trumpet notes. A quick streak of color blew across the sky and swept back and forth, swirling around like a tornado, and then suddenly stopped with an explosion of tiny crystal lights falling to the ground. The shower of lights gradually molded and shaped into the figure of the Queen Trumpeter. She stood before them, her long train flowing behind her over the ground, the brilliant silver loops around her neck reflecting the early sunrise.

"Wow," gushed Elma Mae, jumping off the porch and rushing toward the glowing figure. The Queen Trumpeter lifted her hand, gently admonishing the little girl.

"Not now, my child. You see, I have come to speak with the mother of Tobias." As she spoke in her musical tones, she turned toward Jewell and held out her hand. "Come forth that I may speak to you."

Jewell stood, her eyes wary. She smoothed her disheveled hair and wiped her cheeks, glancing quickly at Grampa Perry. The old man nodded but said nothing. Slowly she descended the porch steps and came to stand before Queen Zinfoneth.

"My boy is dead," she declared flatly. "Why has this happened? Elo and … and you, before we ever seen you, he was just a boy, playin' every day, and a-growin'. Now he just laid down and died. I want you to tell me why. You need to tell me!" She crumpled to the ground.

Queen Zinfoneth remained motionless before Jewell, her head bowed. Slowly she moved closer to the distraught mother and took her hand. From out of the mist of the early morning light, twelve Cupbearers on horseback cantered side by side, moving past behind the Queen, their helmets bowed low, purple banners snapping in the windless air. They passed silently and disappeared into the horizon of trees.

Jewell stared after them as Queen Zinfoneth spoke in her musical tone. The words stood in the still air like pieces of fine silver. "You are wondering who they are, Jewell. Great in power, the emblem of authority and birthright, they will always protect your son on his journey and in battles to come."

"But ... but he is dead! You speak as if—"

"Jewell, take my hand. It is not as it seems," said Queen Zinfoneth. "Let me explain. At this time, Tobias will only hear your voice. If he is to awaken, it can only come from your heart. If the words he is to hear are not the truth, he will not awaken. I warn you now. You must speak to him. If you cannot let him go, then he will be lost to you. So you must come to terms with his destiny. I cannot tell you I know how you feel. I am not of this planet. But as the Queen Trumpeter, I know of a child's love, for on Elios we exist because of that love—and the purity and imagination of children." Queen Zinfoneth released Jewell's hand. Her great silver train rose from the ground, snapping in the air, and she soared upward in a brilliant flash of deep reds, emerald green, and brilliant yellow, pink, and lavender. The distant music surrounded the house for a moment, and then she was gone.

Jewell stood for a moment in the silence, her head bowed, her eyes closed, trying to find her breath. Presently she raised her head proudly and walked up the steps, stopping to take Pearl's outstretched hand in her own, to stroke Elma Mae's red hair and touch Tom's shoulder. She laid her hand for a moment on Chalmers's tight black curls and smiled down at Ginger Lee. She turned and looked into Grampa Perry's eyes, delighted again at the thought that he could see her. Then she turned and walked into the house.

"Tobias, this be Mama. Can you hear me?" She knelt beside the still form of her son, who lay in the darkness of a deep sleep. Jewell knew now that only she could reach him, or he would be gone from her forever. "Your queen, the trumpeter lady, she told me you can hear me now." Jewell paused, searching for the right words. She laid her hand gently on Tobias's ashen cheek. "You gonna be a king, a real handsome king, and I … I … well, no mama wants to let go of her child. You only eight years old, and I loves ya so much. Since Josh were taken from me, and your daddy, all I got is you, but I tryin' to understand. I wants you to follow through on what you supposed to do. You will be a strong and gentle king. That be what kind of boy you are. And I knows you will 'member your mama and your grampa. Why, with grampa seein' now and all, we're gonna be fine, just fine. I needs to tell you how much I loves ya, and I learnin' to know now that you supposed to be somewheres else so they can know a real king of love is among 'em. So I releases you, Tobias. I releases you to go to Elios." Jewell buried her head in his bedcovers for a moment. The she slowly rose and leaned down to kiss him on the cheek. She turned then and walked out of the bedroom, slipping into her chair at the kitchen table. She listened as Grampa Perry murmured to the others, barely aware of anything he was saying.

Through the open door, as the sun climbed higher in the sky, she heard Tawny whinny from the barn. Then she felt a light touch on her shoulder and turned to see Tobias beside her, his eyes shining, his skin healthy and glowing.

"Hi, Mama," he said. "I feelin' lots better now. I had me a funny kind o' dream, though. I heard you talkin' to me, and … an' then I just wanted ta wake up. Before that I couldn't!" He slipped his arms around her as Jewell drew him onto her lap, crying softly.

"Oh, I so glad you back, son. I was afraid I'd lost ya." Suddenly the screen door swung open, and Elma Mae dashed in, followed by Chalmers and Tom. Cottonseed pranced in, wagging his tail. Pearl and Ginger Lee rose from the porch, taking Grampa Perry's arm. Soon the small kitchen was buzzing with joy as they all gathered around Tobias.

"Tobias, Tobias!" shouted Elma Mae above everyone else.

"You ain't dead!" Chalmers jumped up and down behind her. "You alive, you alive!" he crowed.

Tobias giggled, flinging his arm around Chalmers. "'Course I alive. I just nappin', that's all. Are we still goin' over ta Birdie Foy's?"

Chalmers looked up at him solemnly. "I'd go anywheres with you, Tobias."

CHAPTER 20

Salt 'Em!

S EVERAL DAYS LATER, IN the dusty gloom of Ricketts
General Store, two men leaned close to each other in deep
conversation, their heads bowed. Jay Snaught hooked the
heel of his boot over the rung of his chair and listened closely to his
brother, nodding emphatically as his eyes darted toward the door
when customers came and went. They sat alone, watchful as hawks.

"We will wait no longer," said Jimmy. "The boy, the Cripon, is
ready now. Nuctemeron awaits his orders, and we do not have much
time." Jimmy's eyes took on a strange glow, and his voice slithered
smoothly, deep and cunning, as he spoke. "Soon he and the teacher,
the one called Elo, will be leaving for Elios."

Jay listened intently, inspecting his hands. If one looked closer,
they appeared to be rough and scaly, the fingernails oddly twisted.
He laughed quietly. "I am utterly disgusted with these clothes
anyway. Wearing this—what do they say? Country bumpkin—outfit
has become tedious." He stretched his neck, fingering his tight
collar. "We will finish our work here soon. These others—this Neil,

and the relative, Orville, and the one they call Percy—are causing me much displeasure. I tire of their insignificance."

Jimmy tipped his chair back, running his hand over his tufts of ragged hair. "Today, then," he said briefly. He glanced with distaste at the whirring ceiling fan above them. "I am weary too of the stagnant air on this planet. The fan only serves to push it here and there. After we annihilate the Cripon, we will disengage ourselves from this nauseating place."

Jay inclined his head and then turned in his chair, draping his arm across the back. "How you doin' this mornin', Herbert?" he called out, his voice taking on a friendly twang. "Got a pile of folks comin' in here! Did ya ring the dinner bell or somethin'?" He poked an elbow at his brother and laughed uproariously.

Herbert looked up from behind the counter but ignored the cackling. Birdie Foy appeared through a door at the far end of the store, dragging a large burlap bag. "Got my tractor out front, Mr. Herbert." Birdie laughed merrily. "Got Jumper sittin' on them three wheels. We hitched us up a cart, and we intendin' ta throw these bags o' flour, beans, and such in it and then git on home." He dropped the heavy bags and adjusted his suspenders over his round belly, leaning closer to the counter. "See you got company," Birdie observed in a low voice. "Them brothers—one lookin' like t'other— give me the heebie-jeebies."

Herbert rolled his eyes in the direction of the Snaught Brothers. "Uh-huh," he said. "Just waitin' for 'em to leave, but never mind. Tell me what you need." Birdie took off his crumpled straw hat, and the two men sauntered to the back of the store, Birdie gesturing toward various barrels. "Yup, couple sacks o' cornmeal, some o' that flour, an' a jug or two of molasses, big ol' bag o' buckwheat, if ya please, Mr. Ricketts. And oh! I almost forgot. I needs me some rock salt." The two of them filled the burlap bags and then dragged them over to the screen door.

As they discussed the price of his purchase, Birdie felt a tap on his shoulder. Turning, he found himself staring up at Jay Snaught, his greasy white face too close for comfort.

"Where y'all goin' with that load? Headin' out over them cornfields?"

"Might be," said Birdie as he tied a knot in a bag of cornmeal. He kept his eyes lowered, suddenly feeling clammy and uncomfortable. These fellas were up to no good, he thought to himself.

"That your tractor outside?" asked Jimmy pleasantly, stepping forward beside Jay. "Sure is a fine piece."

"I keeps it polished," answered Birdie briefly.

Herbert heaved one of the bags out the screen door and glanced over at Jimmy. "If you please ... I doin' business with Mr. Foy here. Mebbe you'd like a nice cold Coca-Cola to pass the time, you and your brother. Be happy to get that for ya." Herbert turned his back on them and continued his transactions with Birdie. "Let's see. You got your cornmeal here, your flour, buckwheat, molasses, an' the rock salt."

Jimmy and Jay leaped backward as if hit by a lightning bolt. "He's got salt!" Jimmy hissed under his breath. They walked quickly to the back of the store again and sank down into their chairs.

Herbert and Birdie looked up in surprise, staring after them. "Ignorant coots." Herbert shrugged his shoulders as if sloughing off a wearisome burden. "I'd just as soon they stayed outa here. One of 'em real rude to Tom Clausen's little gal t'other day. You know how she is about the little purple boy, friendly and all. One of them fellers was real insultin'." Herbert grinned down at Birdie. "She no fraidy-cat, though. Stood up to him."

"That'd be Elma Mae, Herbert. Wonder what spooked them gents just now," whispered Birdie.

"Birdie Foy ... he resides in the vicinity of the boy, the small Cripon," murmured Jay. He ran his fingers over the warts on his chin, grimacing. "Chances are we can ride out that way with him in the cart. I believe it is best if I purchase some things from Herbert, and we will bring them to the woman, Jewell, who calls herself the Cripon's mother. Think I'll buy some … uh … some hickory nuts."

Jimmy spoke in low tones. "The earthlings portray nervousness when dealing with us. We must exert caution—and human ways toward Birdie Foy and the son, Jumper. The old man's eyes tell me he carries dislike and suspicion." He glanced back toward the screen door. "Let us make our purchase and be on our way on foot. They will pass us on the road. There is no way they can avoid us." They looked at each other and uttered muffled snickers.

"Two bags, Mr. Ricketts, if ya please," said Jay grandly. Herbert carefully measured a pound of hickory nuts and placed two bags on the counter.

"You fellas be careful now, eatin' them things. Too many might cause ya to—"

Jimmy interrupted, grabbing the bags of nuts. "Ain't for us, Herbert. Takin' 'em to a friend. Boy is leavin' soon, goin' on a trip. Won't see him again. Jay 'n' me thinkin' these nuts just the thing to take along fer snackin' and such."

Herbert watched them squeeze past Birdie and out onto the wooden boardwalk. What'd they mean, those two? He didn't like to hear 'em mentionin' a boy. They had a lot of hate in their hearts, makin' remarks to Tom's girl about Jewell's little fella. He followed Birdie out to the tractor, his eyes narrowing as he watched the Snaught brothers heading on foot toward the edge of town. They were going in the same direction Birdie had come from—the same direction Jewell went when she headed home, he thought.

"Howdy, Mr. Ricketts," said Jumper as he and Birdie loaded the burlap bags into the cart. "We rigged up a way to get these supplies back to our place."

"I see that. Take care now, Birdie. Keep your eyes peeled for any trouble out your way, hear?" Herbert looked knowingly at the old man.

"Yup. Hear ya," he answered as he climbed up onto the tractor, settling himself beside Jumper.

Jimmy and Jay strolled down the main street and out beyond the town limits, each carrying a bag of hickory nuts. The dirt road led past the cornfields, and they looked impassively out over the golden stalks as they walked in step with each other, occasionally swatting at flies that continually buzzed around their shaved heads.

"These creatures that drone around the earthlings, I feel pleasure in knowing that soon we will be rid of them," commented Jay. He let out a strange, high, jeering sound, and the two men were suddenly free of the torment of flies. The air around them shivered with an unpleasant scent. Wildflowers and leaves of trees curled and turned brown. Jimmy looked back over his shoulder but continued walking, the dust swirling around his overalls. "They have appeared. It won't be long now."

Birdie saw the two men in the distance and knew he would have to pass them. He had a sneakin' feelin' he knew where they were goin'. They sure as shootin' weren't comin' out here to pass the time with him 'n' Jumper. Only other place out in these parts was Jewell's farm. What were they plannin'? Ain't got no business botherin' that gal.

The tractor inched its way down the dirt road out near the cornfields, the two men riding in silence on their high seats, the burlap bags bouncing along behind them. Birdie kept his eyes straight ahead as they overtook the two men and rumbled past them.

"Hiya, Birdie," shouted Jay, running alongside, his voice heard faintly in the noise of the engine. "Sure be obliged to hitch a ride with ya. You can just stuff me 'n' Jimmy in the cart with all them bags!" He laughed, beaming at Jumper, who leaned forward to peer around his daddy.

Birdie slowed the tractor to a crawl. "We're pretty full, fellas. Didn't plan on havin' no one settin' back there."

"We kin make room, Pops," said Jumper, glancing back at the load in the cart. "They's only two of 'em."

Birdie looked warily at the two men, his eyes squinting under his old floppy hat. "Where y'all headed for, anyway?" he asked, glancing at their identical small parcels.

"We goin' on out ta Missus Valentine's place," stated Jay, grinning up at him. "Feels like me and Jimmy ain't been very neighborly, with her losin' her menfolks. Just wantin' to share with her and the boy. Least we can do, now that we fixin' to move on. Packin' up and goin' to Biloxi real soon."

"Well, that's mighty kind of you boys," volunteered Jumper, "real considerate." He climbed down from the tractor and busied himself with shoving the heavy bags into a corner. "Plenty room for ya now," he said.

Birdie cast an angry look at Jumper as the boy hoisted himself back up on the tractor. "Didn't like what ya just did, Jumper," he muttered under his breath. He cast a brief look back at the cart, noting the pompous expressions on the faces of his new passengers.

They rode in silence out past the cornfields. Birdie's usual merry face was grim as he removed his old straw hat and mopped at his sweaty head. Jumper sat beside him, whistling a carefree tune. Them fellas is lyin', he thought. Somethin' wrong here. They don't feel no neighborly need, and they got no reason to come out this way. Jewell alone out here, 'cept for old Perry ... and Tobias. Still, he thought, they would of got out there anyhow, tractor or no tractor. So me 'n' Jumper, we'll just stick around when we gets there.

Grampa Perry sat in his creaking rocker on the porch, warming his old bones in the morning sun, his ears picking up the familiar sound of Birdie Foy's tractor approaching over the fields. He chuckled to himself, pleased at the thought of the old man coming to set awhile. Even without his eyes, he had known when Birdie was on his way. He looked forward to the tubby little farmer dropping by with his stories of the old days, always asking about Tobias, always reminding him that "the little twig, he be a special child, Perry." He rose from his rocker as the tractor made its way past the barn and stopped.

"Jewell!" he called through the screen door, "got any a' that peach juice? Birdie 'n' Jumper just rolled in on that old tractor."

"I'm a-comin', Daddy," she called back. "Just finishing mendin' Tobias's overalls."

Grampa Perry shaded his eyes, watching as the tractor came to a halt and stood silently by the barn. He stared curiously as two men lowered themselves from the back of the cart and stood side by side, looking toward the house. Birdie sat unmoving up on the seat, Jumper beside him.

Gripping the arm of his old rocker, he was suddenly alert, sensing danger. Ol' Birdie not wavin' an' callin' out in his usual way, he thought.

"Jewell!" he called again. "Don't come out here, gal! Keep Tobias in the house! You mind me now!" His old, wavering voice sounded urgent and tense.

Jewell was at the screen door immediately, Tobias behind her. "What's the matter, Daddy? You just said Birdie—"

Before she could stop him, Tobias dashed out onto the porch and leaped off the steps. Clad only in his pajamas, he stopped and looked up at Grampa Perry, his eyes alert and watchful.

"I knows 'em, Grampa, those two mens," he said quietly, watching as the Snaught brothers walked toward the house.

"They ain't aimin' fer no friendly visit," said Grampa Perry, fuming. "I 'member 'em too, from years back. Got a mind ta go meet them fellas halfway. They ain't welcome here."

"Go on back in the house, Tobias," said Jewell, her voice firm. She had joined Grampa Perry on the porch. "Put your overalls on, and stay inside."

"No! They means ya harm, Mama—you and Grampa. I stayin' right here."

"Why ain't Birdie sayin' nothin'?" Jewell said. "Him and Jumper, they just settin' there."

"They watchin' 'em, Mama. They watchin' 'em. Them two mens is not who they say they is."

"Mornin'!" called out Jimmy, sauntering casually toward the porch. He held out a small bag, knotted at the top. "Brought ya'll some hickory nuts, Miz Valentine. Me 'n' Jay, we be leavin' soon and thought you and your boy might ... Well, this be a gift, neighborly-like. Herbert, he said you ordered 'em, so when Mr. Foy offered us a ride out here ..." Jimmy paused, his gleaming eyes slithering toward Tobias. "Like to get to know you—and your boy."

Jay stood behind him, scuffing his feet in the dirt. He peered over Jimmy's shoulder, his pasty-white face creased in a smile. "Mornin'," he echoed, his pale, watery eyes blinking under the hot sun.

"I never ordered no hickory nuts," said Jewell coldly. "You got no call to come out here. We don't need nothin' from you."

Suddenly Jay took a full step forward, shouldering past Jimmy. "We got plenty call to come out here, Miz Valentine. More'n you think." He regarded them with an angry stare, scratching his patchy pale head.

Grampa Perry stepped in front of Jewell. "You gents got a nasty smell about ya. Now get goin'. Get off my property!" A small butterfly landed on his ear for a moment, and the old man whisked it away impatiently. "I won't have you comin' out here causin' words with me and mine, hear?" His voice trembled with rage.

Jimmy's laugh split the air, high and piercing. His eyes suddenly narrowed, and his slack mouth became wide and cavernous. "You know nothing, old man," he thundered. "The boy here has spent his last days among you."

Birdie stepped forward from the shadow of the barn, Jumper behind him. He held his shotgun, aimed straight at the two brothers. "What you sayin'? I got my aim right on ya!"

Jay's head jerked upward, ignoring Birdie's threat. His voice seemed to come from an odd place, the drawl replaced with crisp, well-enunciated words. "So, it is true in the Wheel of Og—King Suryes and his vision, most distasteful to our true leader, Nuctemeron—that a king of the Cripons would appear on the planet Earth," he said, his eyes riveted on Tobias.

Tobias planted his small bare feet firmly in the dust, raised his chin, and squared his shoulders.

"We have known for years that you dwelt here among humans. Our suspicion led us to this place, and we disguised ourselves in order to watch for you. My counterpart and I come from the East Halls of Surtaq, cited by the mouth of Yaboo who speaks for the true ruler of Elios. We have orders to destroy you and all those around you who seek to encourage your quest as king and a royal personage!" Jimmy threw back his head and gave out a long, howling laugh that was so depraved and chilling that Birdie dropped his shotgun and stepped back, shuddering as he fell back against the tractor.

Tobias stepped forward and faced the brothers. "I knows who you are. I am the Chosen One," Tobias announced. "I am to be king. Elo has taught me! Soon I will be leaving for—"

Jimmy's hand shot out in an attempt to grab Tobias. The ugly, twisted fingernails snagged his pajamas, but Tobias stepped back quickly, out of his reach.

"You are an imposter! A small, weak underling, masquerading as a child," snarled Jimmy. "A purple child! You will be eradicated, you and yours, as you hunger to rule on Elios!"

Jumper leaped toward the men, but Birdie snatched him back and regained his feet, his words quick and harsh. "Stay, boy!"

"I never heard no words like that, Daddy," said Jumper loudly. "Who is they? What they gonna do?"

"As the lure and measure are given, my power commands you to—" began Tobias.

"You command nothing! Silence!" shouted Jay. His piercing voice shot through the still air and dropped to a slithering monotone. "It is not your purple color, Cripon. We care little about that. You shall not become the Cripon king. This is a great threat to our planet, to the ruler Nuctemeron. You will not replace him with your mastery and imagination. This we cannot allow." He snorted with a strange sort of glee. "You are to be annihilated."

Grampa Perry stared in disbelief at the two men, while Jewell clutched his hand, squeezing hard on his old, fragile bones.

Tobias turned as the sound of pounding hooves filled the air. Off in the distance beyond the cornfields, the shadowy figures of the Cupbearers could be seen along the tree line. In groups of four, then three, they appeared and reappeared in the mist, the figures tall and silent. "They're here," he stated calmly. "They always at my side."

The Snaught brothers stood back and gazed for a moment toward the horizon and then sent forth a high, shrill scream—a sound so unbearable that it caused everyone to clutch their heads and shield their ears. Jumper fell to his knees. Birdie rocked back and forth in anguish.

"I not afraid of you," Tobias said, raising his head. "You can't come here an' try ta scare us!" He clenched his fists and stared as the brothers began to change in front of them. Their human forms started to peel away, and the slack mouths stretched open beyond the length of their faces. The knobs of noses disappeared into their flesh, and the watery eyes became wrinkled slits. They began to give off howls that stirred the air and created a repulsive stench. Wave upon wave emitted from their disfigured mouths.

"Elo, where are ya?" Tobias wailed, trying to shield himself from the horror of the foul odor that rolled upon him.

"I am beside you, Royal One," came Elo's voice. But Tobias had fallen to his knees, overcome by the howling and the stench, only vaguely aware of his mother's voice, Grampa Perry calling out to him, and Birdie shouting.

He was unable to move, except for his head, and turning, he saw that Elo too had fallen, his eyes nearly closed and his tiny mouth moving piteously. "Speech, mountain, and splendor," he called out, his weak voice unheard in the chaos around him. He lay still finally, his beautiful gauze wings limp and tattered.

A thundering of horses suddenly passed so close that Tobias felt a swirling cape whip by his head. They came on in groups again—three, four—and the earth trembled as the Cupbearers covered the barnyard and then disappeared. There was a strange silence just before a huge sword flashed as it sailed past Tobias's head, grazing his ear, the sunlight flashing off the gleaming metal. Tobias struggled to open his eyes, and he saw the great weapon stabbed into the ground in front of the Snaught brothers, its hilt still trembling from the force of its arrival.

The change came quickly. The horrible stench was gone, the high, jeering cries ceased, and the brothers became shapeless. Their slimy heads sank into their shoulders, and only their mouths still moved as one of them shrieked in an ominous tone. "We come from the East Halls of Surtaq." Their mouths disappeared as their arms became one with their torsos, and they turned from their human form into blobs of white mucus.

A high, silvery trumpet call came from the top of the barn. Grampa Perry looked up to see Queen Zinfoneth on the highest gable, her trumpet held high. The notes seemed to soothe him, and his wavering voice reached her as he called out, "Missus Zinfo, we needs yer help down here." He stood with his arm around Jewell. Birdie slumped against the barn, his rifle cradled in the crook of his arm, Jumper by his side.

"Rise, Elo," she spoke from the barn roof, "and you, Tobias. The evil that engulfed you has turned back to its original form. The Cupbearers surrounded you with their protection. Even though their power was great, I was able to hear Elo's call, although barely. He appears to need some repair to his wings."

Elo's eyes began to roll in the familiar colors. His torn wings, sticking to the dirt, moved slowly as he struggled to regain his posture. Tobias leaned down and took Elo's tiny dirt-smeared, gloved hand into his own. Together they stood and gazed at the fleshy, white creatures in front of them.

"Thank you, sire ... and you, Queen Zinfoneth," said Elo. "A most trying day."

Tobias giggled. "They looks like big ol' slugs, the kind mama doesn't like to find in her garden." He turned to Jewell and Grampa Perry, letting them shelter him in their arms.

"Them slugs was out ta do you harm, boy. Lots more on their minds than chewin' up cabbages!" Grampa Perry chuckled, holding Tobias close.

Jewell bent and kissed the top of his head. "I was proud of you, son. Those, uh, men and their strange talkin'. You didn't let on that you was scared."

"They was gonna kill me, Mama. I *was* scared!"

Grampa Perry suddenly let out a loud whoop and moved closer to the fleshy creatures, who seemed rooted in the earth, long antennae waving, their segmented bodies undulating back and forth. Human-looking hands had suddenly sprouted from the glistening bodies, and the long mouths had appeared again, wailing piteously.

"I knows they not gone yet. Look at 'em! They turnin' back into them smelly fellas!"

From over near the barn, Jumper dashed toward the tractor. "Salt 'em!" he yelled. "Salt them varmints!" He grabbed a bag from the cart and dashed toward the slugs, tearing at the burlap as he ran. Within minutes, the fleshy creatures were covered with salt, and they began to melt, the high, wailing sounds growing dimmer and then ceasing. The barnyard was silent as they all stood watching the white slime disappear.

CHAPTER 21

The Tin Suit

A SMALL FIGURE CLAD IN shiny armor wobbled through the barn at a slow pace. Just ahead of him stood Elo, nodding encouragingly, his gloved hands raised, beckoning him forward. Tobias lurched from side to side, concentrating on his teacher, and eventually came to stand directly in front of him.

Chalmers stood near Elo, watching wide-eyed. "Is you gonna walk around all day in that funny-lookin' suit, Tobias?"

Elo turned to him, placing a gloved finger over his mouth. "Shh," he admonished the child. "We must let Tobias learn to walk upright and not fall over. This is very important."

Elma Mae giggled, fiddling with her pigtails. "He lookin' like a tree trunk or somethin'—with crooked twigs on 'im." She sat down on a bale of hay, whistling noiselessly. "Wish I had one of them tin suits," she said softly to Chalmers.

Tobias continued on past Elo, his slow steps unsure, his balance precarious. Reaching the corn bin, he tilted to the right and fell with a thud into a pile of husks.

"That is to be expected, Royal One," spoke Elo, hearing the whimpers coming from behind the shiny helmet. "Do not let discouragement deter you from your goal." He moved toward the small fallen figure and bent down. "Try again."

Tobias struggled to his feet, the armored suit squeaking as he regained his balance. Elo stood sternly in front of him, his tiny fingers sliding the helmet open. From inside, Tobias looked out at his friends, visibly pouting.

"How am I gonna sit on Tawny wearin' this here suit, Elo? I cain't hardly walk in it!"

Elo folded his arms across his wizened chest, shaking his head in disappointment. "Sire, the correct pronunciation is 'wearing this suit,' not 'wearing this *here* suit.' *Cain't* is *cannot*—as I have stated on other occasions. You will achieve what is set before you. Everything takes time. It is like the wind: eyes look for the direction from which it blows, but to master its direction and the power from which it blows is the key to understanding."

"Them is ... those ... is fancy words!" exclaimed Elma Mae.

Chalmers poked her with his elbow. "Elo said to be quiet!" he whispered. The two of them crept silently out into the barnyard.

"Let's go skip rope, Elma Mae," said Chalmers.

"Okay. Maybe Tobias be finished with his tin suit schoolin' soon, and we can go down to the glass tree. I got a pocket full of smoots that I'll share."

"Tobias, you must concentrate. Hold your head up, eyes straight forward. Watch me." Elo began to walk in front of him, his head held high, his delicate wings moving in and out, whisking the straws of hay along the barn floor. "Breathe as you would if you were walking around in your overalls." He cackled with mirth at his own joke.

"Yeah, I gets it!" shouted Tobias joyfully from inside his helmet. "Just like in my overalls!"

"Simply enjoy your suit of armor, Tobias. It is designed only for you, and you must desire to wear it. As with all things on Elios, the suit will understand your intentions."

"Will I have to wear it all the time, Elo?"

"No, sire. As you grow, you will know when you must wear it, when it is *appropriate* ... and so forth." Elo raised his glove to his tiny chin and nodded to himself in satisfaction. "Now I want you to practice walking to the barn door and back six times."

"A-pro-pree-it," pronounced Tobias carefully. "Okay, here I go!" He clattered toward the bales of hay. With small groans and squeals, he sprawled once again at the entrance to the barn, managing to roll over on his stomach. "Dang!" he uttered, trying to push himself upright.

Elo shook his head and cupped his hands to his mouth. "Speech, mountain, and splendor! Speech, mountain, and splendor!" he called, floating up to the top rafter. "I call forth the Queen Trumpeter."

Chalmers and Elma Mae rushed into the barn again. "You can't keep fallin' over, Tobias," Elma Mae admonished him. "You'll dent yer suit!"

They watched as Tobias dug his toes into the hay, his posterior rising as he balanced on his hands and positioned his feet. Up he came, huffing and puffing.

"I standin', Elo. Gonna do six times across the barn now." Elo watched approvingly as the shiny little figure took cautious steps—slowly at first and then picking up speed and confidence. He passed Elma Mae and Chalmers, who stood breathlessly watching him.

"Yer doin' it! Yer doin' it!" hollered Chalmers.

Six times Tobias walked from the barn door back to the hay bales, with Elo urging him on, his joy and excitement a high wheeze. "Very good, sire, very good. You are mastering your walk with fortitude. You will ride upon Tawny with the skill and courage that befits you." Elo bowed low and then looked anxiously around the barn for Tobias, who had disappeared.

"Thank you, Elo." The response finally came from back near the corn crib.

As dazzling lights showered down across the barn floor, Queen Trumpeter appeared among them. She looked down at the children, her eyes revolving slowly beneath her long, wing-shaped eyelashes. The long silver trumpet was folded across her shoulder.

"I heard your call, Elo," came her musical voice. She moved gracefully toward Tobias as Elo floated down from the rafters.

Elma Mae stood staring up at the beautiful queen. "I wanna have powers and fly around like that, Chalmers. Daddy, he'd sure like to see me in that dress too."

Chalmers rolled his eyes and lifted his fists to his mouth, giggling. "You mean ... you'd wear a dress, Elma Mae? That ain't so."

"Sure is, Chalmers. I'd wear that dress if I could fly around with Tobias and blow on that shiny horn. Don't you want to go with Tobias?"

Chalmers frowned. "I don't like those high places. I might fall, and Tobias is gonna go up high, way past the clouds in the sky." He raised his skinny little arms above his head. "Higher than the highest branch in our glass tree."

Queen Trumpeter bowed her head and knelt in front of Tobias as Elo appeared beside her. "Your wings, My Queen ... are they improved?" came his raspy voice.

"They are indeed, Elo. As I explained to you, the air on this planet causes tears in the fragile gossamer, but I have kept myself protected in the safety of the forest by folding them frequently."

Elo floated around her, nodding his tiny head. "Did you bring the King's Blade?"

Queen Trumpeter slipped a long, carved box from beneath her flowing gown. It was covered with intricate designs of butterflies and tiny precious stones. She held the box in her upturned palms and turned to Tobias, who stood quietly before her. "The time has come, Royal One, to present you with the King's Blade," she said.

Elo lifted an exquisite sword from the carved box, his hands bearing it upward and holding it before Tobias. The blade glowed with a burnished sheen.

Elma Mae clapped both hands to her mouth. "Wow!" she exploded. "Do you get to keep it?"

"What you gonna do with it, Tobias?" asked Chalmers.

Elo rolled his eyes toward Chalmers, his wizened face serious. "Hush now, children. I must speak to Tobias." The elegant sword lay in his hands, balanced perfectly, the gems winking in the sunlight. "You may remove your helmet now, Tobias. You will observe more perfectly without it ... for the moment."

Tobias carefully lifted the helmet, his bald purple head shining like his armor. Gently he lowered the helmet to the hay-strewn floor. "The King's Blade," he stated carefully. "The King's Blade. It ... it so beautiful, Elo. But it lookin' real heavy! I mean ... mebbe it better if I just keeps it in that big pretty box."

"Once your hand has held it, sire, it will form to you ... and only when you wear the suit of the Cupbearer's armor. It was made for you by King Suryes himself, and only he knows of its power. Do you remember the supremacy of the Cupbearer's sword that stabbed the dirt when those two identical vultures ... the ones serving Nuctemeron and cited by Yaboo ... stood prepared to destroy you? That sword brought about the Enriching's power. As the Five Stones of Passage have taught you wisdom, this is your Sword of Alliance."

"What does *alliance* mean?" asked Tobias.

Queen Trumpeter stepped forth, one gossamer wing brushing Chalmers's cheek. He gasped with delight as she swept slowly past.

"Tobias," she said, "*alliance* can mean many things, but on Elios it is a pathway between knowing wisdom and patience, and the deep reflection needed before the need to strike your enemy. We do not seek war as Nuctemeron does. This sword achieves peace rather than destruction. Do you understand?"

"Yes, I think I does ... *do*," stammered Tobias.

"Then it is yours, sire," said Elo, placing the glittering sword in Tobias's outstretched palms. Immediately the boy pitched forward and fell to the floor with a great clattering, his armor dented, the jeweled box upside down beside him.

Queen Trumpeter bent over him, looking perplexed. "Elo, I am afraid we may have expected too much. He needs more time. Elo, where are you?"

"I am observing from above, My Queen," came Elo's faraway voice high in the rafters. "The sudden clattering caused me to seek refuge up here." He paused, clearing his throat with a tiny scraping sound. "In my opinion, we must remove a few of the heavy gems for the time being. It is obvious to both of us that the burden is too great."

Queen Trumpeter nodded, her golden antennae swaying as she spoke. "It is true, Elo." Folding her wings around Tobias, she lifted him to his feet. "Rise now, sire. Elo will soon hand you the King's Blade again, and it will fit you well. We misjudged, I am afraid."

"That's okay," said Tobias, panting as he planted his heavy feet on the straw. "Am I s'posed to practice with it now?"

"Yes," Elo said, appearing at his side. "You must know how to hold it with either hand and utilize its power. As the sun sets tonight, men here on planet Earth ... men who are embracing evil ... seek a way onto your Grampa Perry's land. Tonight is the Test of Shattering Glass."

"Is they all smelly and ugly like those two fellas from Nuctemeron?" asked Tobias, crinkling his nose.

"No, but they have the same purpose of hate, and they desire to destroy you, your mother, and Sir Perry. You will be ready, Royal One. And you will have no fear, as the Cupbearers will be at your side."

CHAPTER 22

Danker's Marsh

NEIL CONCENTRATED ON THE dark road, his car lights barely penetrating ahead into the foggy night. He looked into the rearview mirror. Percy was following close behind, the headlights from his truck glaring into Neil's eyes.

Shelly sat next to Neil, glancing uneasily out the window, while Orville stretched out in the backseat, his hat down over his eyes. He wasn't feeling kindly toward Neil for calling him out in the middle of the night to go up to Danker's Marsh, an eerie place, fog-shrouded and isolated. Folks in Anker County occasionally mentioned it in whispers, but no one had reason to go there. It was a fact that several citizens of the town had ventured into the marsh over the past years and had never returned. The place was full of slimy quicksand and unexpected bogs. No sunlight ever penetrated the thick, twisting vines and the sense of abandonment.

"Most folks stay away from this place, Neil," Shelly said. "You know as well as I do that there's been odd tales, folks passin' on yarns. Nothin' to believe, mind you, but nevertheless ...He took a deep drag on his cigarette and looked over at Neil, whose white knuckles gripped the steering wheel. "What's your reason this time, Neil?" Shelly asked. "Seems like we had us a trip together just recently up to Hazer's Field. Are you lookin' for more jibber-jabberin' spears in the marsh at midnight?"

Neil ignored his question, muttering to himself through stiff lips. "Just damned peculiar. Enough to whip the hair on your head and make your flesh crawl." He looked over at Shelly and said loudly, "There's lots more goin' on than some old jittery stick."

The men rode in silence, Neil's mind racing back through all the bizarre occurrences over the past few weeks. Gotta keep a level head, he thought. His plan tonight was to find a way onto the oil-rich Valentine land through Danker's Marsh. His first attempt had been blocked by the strange horsemen wearing armored suits, dressed up for a costume party, lookin' like knights goin' into battle. But this was like comin' in the backdoor where nobody could see you. The purple boy, he was makin' all this trouble. Neil's eyes blazed at the thought of it. He stroked his chin, his eyes squinting in the darkness.

"Lemme put it this way, Shelly," he said. "Somethin's goin' on here in Anker County that never happened before. Folks around here, they'd never believe what I been experiencin'—not nobody in this town, in this county, or in the entire state of Mississippi!"

"Yeah? Now you know how I felt about seein' Noosemouse mule," quipped Orville from the backseat. "'Course, the purple boy was causin' trouble in the school yard too, doin' voodoo and such."

Neil was silent, peering through the heavy fog as the bumpy road jostled the three men in the car, tension building among them. Suddenly words were spilling out of his mouth as Shelly and Orville sat speechless.

"He was in the backseat of my car again. Didn't have no spectacles, but his eyes still rolled. And big ol' huge wings. And he *talked* again—asked me how many fingers he was holdin' up!"

Neil banged his hand against the steering wheel. "Then that big ol'
bug screamed—or sneezed. I couldn't rightly tell. All I know is he
made my eyes burn an' itch. Been botherin' me from that day on.
Somethin' unnatural. It come out of prehistoric times!" Neil's voice
rose to a fever pitch. "Ever heard of a talkin' bug? Wearin' spectacles
too? Second time I seen it was out at the purple boy's farm! What
does that tell ya?"

Shelly stared at Neil, dumbfounded. "You losin' it, Neil. Gone
plumb out of your mind, makin' up hobgoblin tales."

"No, he ain't!" roared Orville. "By jeez, that little feller that
fell off the fire escape over at the school—his pals say he broke his
arm, bone stickin' out, had blood all over his shirt too. Then got up
off the ground and started scamperin' around again, no sign of a
broken arm, like George Henry said. Purple boy was hangin' around
'em, doin' chants and high-style words, and then just disappeared.
Then me an' Neil was out on Bunny Bayou Road, and these tall
gents showed up, blockin' our way. Looked like they dressed up
in costumes, 'cept they was real. Those fellers weren't goin' to no
party!"

"Okay, okay … just calm down," said Shelly. "In case you've
forgotten, Neil, you haven't said why we're headin' up to Danker's
Marsh in the middle of the night. This have somethin' to do with
your outlandish tales? Huh? No place for God-fearin' folks, if you
don't mind my sayin'."

"They was just sittin' there in the middle of the road!" Orville
continued, ignoring Shelly's comments. "Tall and stiff they was.
Then that sound like a bad violin started a-blowin'. Ain't it so, Neil?"
he said, thrusting his face close to the front seat.

Neil remained silent, the memory vivid in his mind, full of the
fear that he hadn't been able to acknowledge to himself. Shelly said
he'd lost his mind, imagining the talkin' bug. Maybe he had, but
those tall fellas in their shiny suits had horses so big you'd need a
ladder to climb up on 'em. They were real—standin' right in front of

him and Orville, blockin' their way, starin' down at them like they'd come out of some ol' dusty history book."

"Quiet down, Orville, you good-for-nothin'," Neil muttered. "You've said enough. You're cloudin' my thinkin'."

The truck behind Neil's car sped alongside, and Percy leaned out the window. "Why we goin' up through Elwin's Climb?" he shouted.

Neil stepped on the accelerator, roaring ahead of the other car, yelling out the window as he sped by. "We headin' up to Danker's Marsh, takin' a shortcut."

The cars began to slow, inching through the dark forest, the narrow road overhung with cypress and black gum trees. Their branches hung in great masses, slapping at their windshields. The three men rocked back and forth, the headlights casting a shaft of light into the primeval gloom. At last they passed through a small clearing with a creek running across the old road at the bottom of the ravine. Neil stopped the car. A fallen tree lay ahead of them, blocking their way. He smacked the steering wheel and sighed heavily.

"Just our damned luck," he said as he and Shelly got out of the car, followed by Orville.

"You still haven't told me why we're up here in the marsh, Neil," said Shelly.

"Lookin' for a back way onto the Valentine farm, Shelly. Now you know. I was out at that farm last week and found me some clues. Somethin' peculiar goin' on out there. Has to do with that carved stick we found at Hazer's Field. I'm not gonna put up with that family anymore. As Orville told you, we had a run-in with some fellers out near Bunny Bayou blockin' the road, and we couldn't get through. I'm the law in this town. I can do what I see is necessary for the good citizens of Anker. Besides that, Shelly, that land is mighty valuable."

Shelly cast a knowing glance at the sheriff.

Percy stepped out of his truck. "You bring some of that jim-cracky rum with you, Orville?"

"Gonna be no drinkin' here tonight, hear?" snapped Neil. "Whiskey don't do nothin' but frazzle your eyeballs and make your mind ragged." He stood motionless, squinting through the mist of thick fog that was rolling through the swamp. "Follow me!" he commanded.

The men loaded their rifles and began to hike along the road, which wound up a steep incline. Frogs croaked, and crickets hummed, their night music reverberating through the marsh. The four moved cautiously along the narrow, rutted road. They came to a sudden halt as they rounded a bend.

"Dear God," intoned Shelly. Twelve knights in armor sat tall on their horses at the top of the crest, their great banner flag fluttering as if in a wind. Huge and silent, they faced the four terrified men. A full moon lit the area around them, casting flickering lights on their armor.

"They the same fellas we saw on the road," whispered Orville, his teeth chattering as he gripped his rifle. "What they doin' up here in the marsh?"

"I'm not stayin' around to find out!" shrieked Percy. He turned and ran back down the road, disappearing from view.

Shelly and Neil stood speechless, staring, shading their eyes against the blinding light from the armor.

Orville lifted his rifle to his shoulder, taking aim. "By God, I've got a mind to send these cock-a-boos to kingdom come!"

"Hold it!" Neil stepped forward, squaring his shoulders. "I got a thing or two to say to 'em, just to clear the record." He shouted at the horsemen, his voice hoarse: "Now you up there! I know you the same fellers I ran into the other day out on Bunny Bayou Road. Goin' to a costume party, weren't ya? Just head on out of the marsh now, and there'll be nothin' more said."

Neil straightened his hat and waited. The knights remained silent, watching them.

"We're wastin' our time, Neil," said Percy, reappearing from behind a tree. "I say we blast 'em. That's what we came here for."

Neil stood unmoving, chewing on a plug of tobacco. "All right, this is the last time I'm gonna warn you fellas! Come down off those horses!"

A wind cut through the humid night air, snapping the silken banner and the draped tunics. Neil turned to the men and nodded. A blast from their rifles shook the forest. The twelve knights and their horses suddenly shattered like glass, evaporating into the shadows. The men stood frozen as the wind reached an eerie pitch, whipping the trees around them and rumbling through the marsh.

"This the final act of your outlandish tale, Neil!" shouted Shelly, breaking into a run. "I'm headin' outta here!" The rest of them followed, Percy whimpering in fear, and reached the cars just in time to hear Soddy's voice in near hysteria on the radio.

Neil stumbled into the car and slumped behind the steering wheel, his hat askew. He shivered in a cold sweat. "Yeah, Soddy?" he asked, sounding tired and defeated.

"We got broken glass all over the county! Over." Soddy's voice squealed, repeating the message again and again.

Shelly squeezed close to the radio, suddenly alert. "Slow down, boy. Shelly Bowles here. Tell me what the chatter's all about … over." He straightened up, waiting for a response as he stared bug-eyed up the hill at the spot where the armored knights had sat not more than ten minutes ago. "We can't give in to panic," he said to Neil. "Got to keep our thinkin' level and not believe deranged stories. There's some sort of tomfoolery goin' on in this town right under our noses!"

The radio blared again. "Shelly, y'all need to tell Neil. We got broken windows, and I mean everywhere—stores, houses, the courthouse. Glass blew up like a hurricane not more'n ten minutes ago. I'm gettin' flooded with calls from here to Hattiesburg. Fella even called from over on the Tombigbee River and said his dry goods store got windows a-shatterin'. There's dogs barkin' and glass everywhere ... over." The radio went silent.

"What's he blabberin' about now, Shelly?" asked Neil wearily, mopping the sweat from his forehead and setting his hat straight.

"Plenty," snapped Shelly. "Maybe you oughta listen to Soddy, Neil, instead of pretendin' he's wastin' your precious time. He's plumb petrified. Glass tornado all over these parts of Mississippi—happened about ten minutes ago. About the same time the horse folks went to pieces," he added, glancing at Neil knowingly.

Both men turned suddenly, aware that the light on top of the car had begun to whirl and flash, swinging red into the darkened trees. Abruptly it exploded at the sound of thunderous horses galloping through the marsh. Then all was quiet, with only the sounds of dripping trees and croaking frogs.

At the top of the crest, the horses began to appear, slowly coming into full view from out of the moonlit forest. A small figure appeared among them, holding golden reins and adorned in lavender armor with a small helmet. Tobias lifted his gloved hand and raised his faceguard. He held a battle sword in his other armored glove, and he pointed it toward the three astonished men.

"Look up there, Neil!" Orville spoke urgently in Neil's ear from the backseat. "The purple boy is leadin' 'em!"

From the line of tall knights and the small figure of Tobias, a brilliant glow began to appear, shooting off a blaze of shimmering balls. The fireballs sped through the air, exploding next to the men in a shower of flames and sparks all around the road. The trees flickered in the tall shadows as the ground shuddered, spewing clods of dirt and rock.

"Move it, move it!" shouted Shelly from the passenger seat.

The men drove wildly into the night, frantic to get away from the exploding balls that fizzed and sizzled around them.

Shelly gripped the dashboard, watching in disbelief as one of them smashed into the windshield, lodging itself in the glass. "What is this thing?" he yelled, his voice faint in the chaos around him.

Neil didn't answer as he tore down the road. He turned to see Percy roaring past at full throttle. They all disappeared into the night, the clamor growing dimmer and finally fading to darkness.

CHAPTER 23

Blueberries,
Oh Blueberries

NEIL EMERGED FROM HIS car and stared wordlessly at Percy, who was sitting on his porch in the hot sun, chewing a wad of tobacco. His uniform had lost its crisp, well-pressed look. It looked rumpled now, his shirt stained, his hat dusty.

"Howdy, Neil," Percy drawled absently without looking up.

Neil sauntered toward him, hiking one foot up on the step and leaning down. "I see you got your window boarded up."

"Had to, Neil," he said, struggling to his feet. "Every window in this old house blew out—downright broke off and rode in the Mississippi wind. Look over there at Leota Claypole's house, and the school over yonder. It's just like Soddy said."

Neil sighed, glowering at Percy. "Same thing all over town, Percy. Not one house spared." He ground his heel into the shards of glass scattered at his feet. "I'm just steamin'—*steamin'*!" He stopped, strangling on his own words, his bloodshot eyes staring hard at Percy. "See, that Valentine boy, that peculiar purple child—I'm thinkin' he's behind all this. And Jewell, who says she's his mama—they're hatchin' a scheme, plottin' to take over. She's sendin' the boy out at night now with the horse fellas, threatenin' all us law-abidin' white folks to drive us out of the state of Mississippi!"

Neil paused and wiped his sweaty forehead. "That property of hers gonna be ours real soon now, Percy. You know, as sheriff I plan to make that claim. Town of Anker soon be ownin' that oil out there, and we'll be splittin' the proceeds around real friendly-like … if you catch my meanin'. But I gotta stomp down hard on these odd things that been happenin'. Who in tarnation was ridin' those giant horses up there at Danker's Marsh, Percy? Same fellers that was out on the road? Got any answers, huh?"

Percy shook his head and stared down at his shoes. "Dunno, Neil. Why ya askin' me?"

"Nobody has any answers!" he roared. "Seems to be *my* responsibility to find out!"

Percy shrugged. "You're the sheriff," he said languidly.

Neil ignored his comment. "Not only do I have those horse fellas to worry about, but ever since that creature—my eyes are still itchin' an' burnin'. I can't stand it … can't sleep for thinkin' about it."

"What creature, Neil? Never heard ya say anything about a creature."

Neil didn't answer. He jerked off his dark glasses and wiped at his eyes with a large handkerchief.

Percy glanced up at him. "Sorry to hear that, Neil," he mumbled. "Mighty peculiar." He shifted his wad of tobacco.

"Am I hearin' disbelief in your tone?" asked Neil.

"No, 'course not. But seems to me you're not mindin' yer sheriff duties. Too busy moanin' about a creature. That midnight ride up there at Danker's Marsh—how come you ain't called the army or the governor fer damned sakes? Or leastways talked to the judge?

Pinky Forrest, he'd tell ya there's laws to stop those fellas wearin' outfits." His moon-shaped face glistened with sweat, and he sat back, continuing to chew.

Neil sighed, carefully replacing his dark glasses. "Well, Percy, I called the National Guard. Called 'em and told 'em what we saw up at the Danker's Marsh. Army sergeant, he just laughed. Said to call him back if they started comin' around Marabelle's Hair Parlor and botherin' the ladies." He hunched over, inspecting his boots. "Then he hung up." Both men were silent, staring morosely out into the road.

"I know one thing, though!" exploded Neil suddenly. "That sergeant ... he can laugh all he wants. The purple boy was there. We all saw him—pointin' a saber at us, dressed up in a costume like the others—at midnight in the marsh. Those same fellas stopped me an' Orville out on the road." His eyes narrowed at the thought.

Percy fingered his pencil mustache. "Are you thinkin' the purple boy had somethin' to do with Ledyard disappearing? Heard he went coon huntin' the other day and never came back."

"Dunno. We all know that old bird had a twisted foot an' all, but he was tough. Didn't let nobody get the best of him—except settin' down in splinters when that chair busted!" In spite of themselves, Neil and Percy burst into loud guffaws, still delighting in others' misfortunes.

Neil stopped laughing and crammed his hat down hard on his head. "I know one thing, though. I'm comin' to the end of my rope!"

"I heard," said Percy sarcastically, picking at his tobacco-stained teeth with a toothpick.

"It's all on account of him ... you know who I mean." Neil bristled angrily again and headed back to his car.

Percy watched him go. "So there really be oil out there?" he called out. "Yonder, on that Valentine property?"

"Better than Texas-born," answered Neil, climbing into his car.

"I say we pick up the Snaught brothers, find Orville, and come in that property from all sides," said Percy.

Neil rolled down his car window and leaned out. "Yeah? What you got in mind exactly, Percy?"

"The way I sees it, Neil, them horse fellers can't be on every road at once. If they sees Orville comin' in from Danker's Marsh, and the Snaught boys comin' in on the front road … why, who's gonna know you and I are sneakin' in from the bayou?"

"Makes sense, Percy, but those Snaught boys are worrisome. Somethin' about them pasty boys I can't stand. Smell bad too. Did I tell ya I came across those two more than once talkin' some strange words, blabberin' just plain nonsense. And they sit in that shack with a roof made outa flattened tin cans, tinkerin' with radios—odd noises, static cracklin'. Every time I stop by, they're in there, just the two of 'em, starin' at me like I had some nail in my toe. Eyes flicker real funny too."

Percy heaved a sigh. "Well, got to keep it in mind that they just up from Louisiana, that's all. Country boys lookin' for a place to settle for a while. Maybe they just wantin' to mind their own business and have you mind yours." He chuckled.

"Get in," Neil said. "Might be you're onto somethin'." He swung the car around, and they disappeared down the road.

Neil leaned over the counter, watching Mr. Ricketts arrange ropes of black licorice in tall, heavy jugs. Herbert straightened his apron and ran his hand over his shiny bald head.

"Howdy, Sheriff. What brings ya?" He glanced at Percy, who stood at the squeaking screen door.

"Have you seen the Snaught brothers lately, Herbert?" Neil asked, removing his hat.

"Well, you know … funny you should ask. The two of 'em was in here this mornin', talkin' in a hush the way they do, when in walked Birdie Foy."

"Not askin' you about Birdie Foy," said Neil.

Herbert walked along the counter, quietly counting the jugs of licorice. "Bought themselves some hickory nuts and left. Said they were for a friend who was goin' away."

Neil's expression grew dark. "Now what would those two want to be doin' that for?

"Neighborly, I guess," said Herbert shortly, straightening the candy jars and rearranging the licorice.

"Uh-huh. Where you think they was off to, Herbert? Just curious, you understand."

Herbert paused and peered up at Neil. "Don't blame ya, sheriff," he said. "They was all goin' the same direction. Glad to see 'em go. Those boys gives me the dithers." He reached up, grabbed a big jug of jawbreakers, and set them alongside the licorice. "By the way, mighty good news about Pearl Wiggins, isn't it?" He beamed at Neil. "Strollin' around like she never knew a day wearin' those big old braces. Made her mean-tempered and downright ugly. She was in here the other day, and I tell ya, Sheriff, it's surely a miracle. She wouldn't say much about it, though—just pleasant and passin' the time with me." Herbert swiped a cloth over the countertop and headed to the back of the store. "But like I said, Sheriff, those brothers won't be missed around here. They smells rotten to me. Good day to you, now."

Neil turned and shouldered past Percy and out onto the boardwalk. "Could do without all that whoopin' and shoutin' about Pearl Wiggins," he huffed. "I tend to suspect that old woman been foolin' us all these years, and just decided to set this town a-gabblin'!"

The two men rode in silence down the main street of Anker, passing the courthouse and Ankers Saloon, past Marabelle's Beauty Parlor and the dingy hardware store. Neil slowed the car to a stop and looked over at Percy.

"Well, it seems Orville ain't in plain view, and neither are those creepy brothers. I'm fed up, Percy, just fed up. You and me are gonna pay a little uninvited visit to the Valentine place. We'll park over by Aberdeen Gulch by that grove of gum trees, cross over old Smokey's sweet pea field, slosh our way up Pencil Creek, and walk right up to the back of the Valentine property. We'll come in real quiet-like."

"Trouble is, them big horses and those fellas is likely to get wind of us trampin' around on that farm," said Percy.

"Stop bein' a weasel crawlin' on a sticky branch, for God's sakes," Neil replied unpleasantly. "Sloggin' up a creek bed is not in those fellas' noggins. They're horsemen, Percy ... need ridin' room."

"Yeah, mebbe they all over at Pearl Wiggins with the purple boy, washin' their capes!" Percy snickered.

Neil glared at him. Doing a quick U-turn, tires squealing, they headed toward Aberdeen Gulch.

It was late afternoon as Neil sloshed along Pencil Creek. He stopped and swatted at a raging bee that swept around his head, ducking and cursing under his breath. Percy sauntered behind him, humming to himself and twirling a twig between his lips. The afternoon sun beat down on them as they made their way up the creek, their boots making sucking sounds in the mud. They both stopped and stared at a small dam of rocks piled high across an upper pool. A high tinkling sound surrounded them as they climbed up into a clearing in the woods. Percy pointed at a huge, gnarled tree nearby, its brilliant-green leaves moving gently in the breeze, ringing like tiny chimes.

"Now, if that ain't the strangest lookin' tree I ever seen," said Percy. "Leaves be lookin' like they glass or somethin'. Hear that sound? They ain't real, though—is they, Neil?" Percy shook his head. "Whoever heard of a glass tree?"

"We'll see, mister." Neil stared up at the glittering branches. "Wait here," he announced importantly. He moved cautiously toward the tree trunk, crouched over, his eyes narrowed. Percy crept up behind him and reached up toward a cluster of glistening fruit that hung from the tree.

"Don't touch anything, boy!" growled Neil. "You seen how that lance we dug out of the ground on Hazer's Field whipped and jiggled around. This is mighty unusual. Gonna have to call my staff and report this." He looked up into the branches, rocking back on his heels. "Kinda pretty, though. Makes you want to ..." He stretched out his hand and gingerly poked at the tree trunk. Instantly an off-key chord vibrated through the underbrush, and he jumped back, clutching his finger. "Hotter'n yer mama's cookstove," he yelled back at Percy.

Percy didn't answer. He stared up into the vast tangle of glistening twigs and branches. "Must be a special fruit tree," he exclaimed, his face beaming. "Looks mighty tasty." He snagged off a cluster of berries.

"C'mon! We gotta move on!" Neil bellowed, fighting his way through the thorny bushes as he climbed down the slippery bank toward the creek.

Tossing the blueberries into his palm and popping a few in his mouth, Percy rushed to catch up with Neil. He smiled in delight as the berries slid down his throat. "Damn! Got my own candy store right out here in the woods," he murmured to himself, slipping a few more into his mouth.

A few moments later he jerked upright and let out a loud burp. A bubble began to form at his lips. It grew huge, stretching larger than his head. Suddenly it popped off his lip and floated languidly into the air. He watched in alarm as the bubble floated in front of him, forming strange eyes and a wide, smiling mouth that seemed to roll back and forth. The face laughed merrily and then exploded into a burst of showering sparkles.

He heard Neil shouting. "Somebody laughin' at us, Percy. Get away from that tree!"

Percy slid down the bank, losing his footing. He landed at Neil's feet and let out another loud burp.

Neil shook his head in disgust, and the two moved on, slogging across mud and jagged rocks until they passed into the pasture behind Jewell's house.

"Hunker down now," said Neil. "Can't tell if these folks are around here." He crept slowly around the corner of the house, staring at the deserted porch and the worn screen door. "Mebbe they just gone to town," he whispered to himself, "so we'll just have ourselves a little look for that property deed." He chuckled maliciously and disappeared into the house.

Outside, Percy began to stumble, his round, sweaty face was growing puffy and taking on a blue tinge. For what seemed an eternity, he stood alone and helpless, trying to call out to Neil. A bubble snapped away from his lips, this time forming the face of a grinning clown, which cackled at him and exploded in a sunburst of tiny sparkles.

Jewell's screen door burst open, and Neil jumped down from the porch as he stuffed a long envelope into his pocket. "Got it! Can't hide nothin' from Anker's sheriff," he said, chortling. "That oil money gonna be rollin' in!" He stopped dead in his tracks as his eyes fell on Percy.

"What you got there anyway, boy?" Cautiously Neil approached him, staring at another bubble that was emerging from Percy's mouth. "Did Herbert give you some special kinda bubble gum?" But now Percy was puffing up, staring at him wordlessly. His fingers formed into huge sausages, and his overalls began to tear apart, revealing blue and bulging bare skin. His normally moon-shaped face expanded, the cheeks growing like a huge blowfish, with tiny eyes and a knob of a nose caught in the middle. He peered at Neil, his eyes pleading.

"You ate some of them berries, didn't you—from that damned tree," said Neil accusingly. "Now look at ya! Can't say I didn't warn ya."

Percy nodded, barely able to move his head.

"Damn it, boy, that tree ain't normal. You ever seen trees lookin' like glass and makin' tinklin' noises, huh?" Neil stepped close to Percy's huge body, which continued to grow out of his shirt, his overalls, and his shoes. He was rapidly becoming a large blue blob that resembled a blueberry.

Neil stepped back from him and reclined on Jewell's steps. "There's nothin' I can do now, Percy. Should've heeded what I had to say and listened to your sheriff." A hint of amusement sounded in his tone.

Percy whimpered, his words lost in the mountainous folds of his face. Suddenly all his hair stood on end, each strand straight up. He fell over, rolling onto his side, his feet turning to blue blobs that kicked frantically.

"Looks like I'm gonna have to roll you back to Anker, mister," observed Neil, bowing his head in his arms, his shoulders shaking. "Wouldn't want to run you over any sharp roots!" He howled in glee at his own joke. "'Course, mebbe you might git to be air-bound and could float all the way past Punchy Green's place. Then he'll be callin' Soddy, sayin' he spotted some kid's balloon that has arms and legs!"

Percy's tiny eyes, now barely visible in his puffed-up face, flickered angrily.

"Punchy probably fill you full of buckshot, boy!" he continued, squinting at Percy, who now resembled a huge, knobby blueberry. Suddenly Neil jumped up, alarmed and feeling sorry for what he'd said, for Percy had begun to rise in the air like a child's balloon, just as he'd suggested. He floated above the ground, his hands and feet waving frantically, his body now a gigantic, bumpy globe.

Neil ran out into the barnyard, helpless to reach him. "Can't reach you, Percy! Stop holdin' yer breath. Mebbe that's why you bobbin' around up there. Might help you deflate!"

"That ain't funny, Neil," squeaked Percy from on high, his voice full of helium. He floated higher and higher.

Now Neil's shouts and taunts did not reach him, for the breeze lifted him up, tossing him this way and that as he rose to a distant speck in the sky. Soon he disappeared into the clouds.

Neil stared up at the sky, his mouth hanging open. Percy was gone ... gone up in the atmosphere somewhere. Plumb floated away like a big old blueberry. He wanted to laugh and cry at the same time. Ol' Percy, he thought somewhat sadly. He'd known him since he an' Ginger Lee first came to Anker. Got kinda fond of that moon-faced fella, even though his thinkin' wasn't too smart. Now look what he'd done to himself. Ate berries from that odd tree, and now ... Neil shuddered, still staring into the sky. He'd just plain departed, passed up yonder!

Shaking his head, Neil wandered off toward the pasture, hardly aware of where he was going. His thoughts were spinning, visions dipping in and out of his mind: the strange glass tree with leaves that tinkled and berries that puffed you up and floated you away; folks on horses wearin' shiny armor; horns blowin' over the treetops; and of course that creature, the big varmint with rolling eyes. He gasped just thinking about him. The other stories—he couldn't remember them all. But every one of 'em linked up with that purple boy.

And now Percy was gone. And his own wife was gettin' all lovey-dovey with the boy and his mama—and blazin' at her own husband. He rubbed his red, smarting eyes, clutched Jewell's property deed, and stumbled across the creek. Why me? He felt overcome with resentment and something like fear. Here he was, a shining example of a good town sheriff, makin' sure his townsfolk were happy, always polite, always fair and considerate. And now his career meant nothing. He had to get his hands on that oil. That'd change everything. All these strange incidents were overwhelming him. His anger bubbled to the surface as he climbed into his car. "Gonna get 'im!" he raged, beating on the steering wheel. "Gonna get that Tobias!" He gunned the motor and roared toward town, his shouts echoing across the golden cornfields.

The radio began to sputter with static. Neil grabbed the speaker as Soddy's voice once again assailed his ears. "Yeah, whatcha want now?" he shouted. "I'm tired of you, Soddy ... always whinin' at me. Get off your radio! Over."

"But I got Punchy Green here, Neil. He's wantin' to talk to ya, and some sergeant just called from that army base over near Natchez. You better listen up ... over."

"Yeah? Over." Neil's voice sounded wary.

"Says the Valentine boy, the purple one, well, he's got somethin' to do with that Huxley. You know, Punchy found it in the woods months back. Gonna put him on ... over."

Neil straightened up, his eyes taking on a hard glitter. Punchy's hard-edged twang assailed his ears, but he listened intently.

"Ah ... yeah, Neil ... uh, you paid me no mind months back when I told ya about that old tank I found in the woods. You're my sheriff, but you downright ignored me. If you were doin' your job, you'd have found that somethin' real strange was goin' on out there ... over."

Neil swallowed hard and cleared his throat. "I'm real sorry about that, Punchy. Why, me and Percy was just talkin' about you today. But bein' sheriff, well, runs me ragged. Haven't had time to think about some army tank up in the woods ... over."

"It ain't no tank, Sheriff. You can count on that!" Punchy shouted. "Hell, I knows a tank when I sees one. You're talkin' to a vet, you know, and I happen to know my war machines ... over."

Neil sighed heavily. "Well," he asked cautiously, "if it's not a tank, Punchy, then what is it? Over."

"Hold onto your britches, Sheriff, while I tell ya! Seems the purple boy and some of them folks he keeps company with—your wife, Pearl Wiggins, Tom Clausen and his little gal, and another little Negra boy—they been visitin' this Huxley right along out in the woods. Right under your nose. Can't believe Tom Clausen is doin' somethin' like this. Why, he's a good ol' boy. But I seen him—and your wife too—goin' on two days now: same place, same time. It's like they is preparin' for some kind o' fracas—mebbe a Holy Roller meetin', Sheriff. I seen 'em from the bushes, just standin' still, all together. Like they havin' prayers or somethin'. Oughta have a talk with that wife of yours, Sheriff. Mighty strange, if y'all ask me. This high staff feller from the army base says he's got a platoon standin' by. Over."

Neil leaned forward, gripping the steering wheel again. His knuckles turned white, and his tone was frantic.

"Where, Punchy? Where they holdin' these secret meetings?" Neil shrieked into the radio. "This some kinda cult? Chantin' an dancin' goin' on? *Where are they, Punchy?* Over."

A long pause followed with static. "South end of Hickory Road Bridge, Sheriff. A clearin' in the woods. Can't miss it. Over."

CHAPTER 24

The Lullaby

ROM DEEP IN THE forest you could hear it: a low, throbbing sound, soft as velvet. Climbing up from the gully, the tallest branches of the pines were radiant, the light scattered through the treetops. It stood in the clearing on the sun-dappled forest floor, huge and wing-shaped. The immense transparent doors revolved continuously with rainbow colors, but they remained closed, their lavender panels set in great friezes that were finely crafted in overlapping swirls and flute-shaped rosettes. Enormous golden lights from the ship beamed up into the forest.

They were all there, all those who had been to the clearing before: Ginger Lee and Pearl, Tom and Elma Mae—with little Chalmers holding her hand—and Birdie Foy and Jumper. Uncle Pete sat calmly in their midst. Jewell stood tall and stately, with a small, worn suitcase at her feet and Grampa Perry at her side. They had all known this day would come. They had secretly visited the clearing other times, gazing in awe at the huge spaceship—and then wordlessly slipping away. Now the day was here, and Tobias was leaving them.

Hovering just above the ship was Queen Trumpeter, her luminous wings like intricate spider webs in the glow of the lights. She carefully observed Tobias as he stood beside the vast doors in his freshly laundered overalls, the Five Stones of Royal Passage lying on his outstretched palms. Elo stood behind him, wearing his favorite lavender vest with yellow polka-dots, his spectacles newly polished and placed with extra care upon his tiny nose. He wore his lavender teaching gloves to match his vest for this important day, and he stood tall and solemn, concentrating on Tobias.

Tobias stared down at the Five Stones, his lips moving silently. Suddenly one lavender stone rose from his palm to whistle and fly around his head. It stopped directly above him, enlarging to the size of a bowling ball and shivering in midair. Then another one—a brilliant-lime-colored stone—traced a zigzag path before coming to a sudden stop. It began to buzz softly. A third stone, of golden hues, seemed to sigh as it left Tobias's hand. It floated lazily, turning over and over, and came to a standstill beside the "bowling ball." Tobias looked up at Elo, saying nothing, but his eyes were questioning, hoping for approval. "It is the way, Royal One," said Elo, inclining his head. "You have found the Passage."

The fourth stone swept around everyone in the group, grazing Chalmers's ear as it passed him. He gasped and reached out his hand, but the stone bounced and shivered, stopping next to the others. The last stone—magnificent and dazzling, with shooting lights and arrows darting off its surface—shot through the trees and disappeared for a moment. Then it was back to touch each of the others briefly before hovering above them all.

There was no movement in the clearing, and no sound except the pulsating of the great ship.

Then came Tobias's voice, clear and ringing. "This is the Royal Passage, Elo. The Stones are in position."

Elo bowed low, his tone reverent. "You have fulfilled your task, sire. The next step of your journey is at hand." He moved along the forest floor, his wings whisking leaves and twigs aside, and then turned to face the ship. The doors began to slide upward as a volley of musical notes exploded from the ship. Colorful musical bars, dazzling to the eye, floated lazily through the open doors. The sound of a gong rang out through the forest—a sound so vivid that the ground shuddered; pine cones fell from the surrounding trees; and half notes, whole notes, three-quarter notes, and eighth notes descended around them all, creating a child's lullaby. Queen Trumpeter swept high above everyone, her form moving to the rhythm of the music.

Elma Mae stood quietly, one hand over her mouth, and clutched Tom's hand. "Wow!" she whispered. She looked up and met her daddy's eyes. Tom nodded, smiling down at her.

Neil skidded to a stop in the middle of Hickory Road Bridge and slid cautiously out of his car, placing his hat on his head. Leaning out over the railing, he peered upstream and cupped his ear. "Hmm ... strange kinda music," he said aloud. "Nothin' like they play around these parts." He started down the river bank in the direction of the music, slipping on moss-covered rocks and swiping at bees. He might just walk in on these folks, he thought, and observe their secret hocus-pocus get-together. Sweeping past tall river reeds, he sloshed through ankle-deep water and started to climb out of the deep gully.

All at once his attention was caught by an enormous, bright-pink bullfrog, its skin pebbled with green warts. It sat clinging to the muddy bank, its bulbous eyes seeming to look right at him. Neil stepped over to it and leaned closer. The bullfrog had a curiously twisted stance, with one foot appearing oddly withered, causing it to tilt precariously in the gooey mud.

"Where'd ya come from, anyways," crooned Neil softly. "Ain't never seen a pink frog."

"Croak, croak." The sac beneath the frog's chin inflated to a huge sac, the eye protruding. "I'm Ledyard ... help me," came its garbled voice.

Neil squatted down, unable to believe what he had just heard. "You sayin' you're Ledyard?" He picked up a small stick and poked at the bullfrog, causing it to leap and land lopsided on a mossy rock. Nearby, a tiny pair of suspenders dangled on a thorny bush. Neil snagged them with his stick, waved them in the air, and started to chuckle. "Danged if you ain't," he said, shaking his head. "Talk in town is that ya drowned. But now, by gawd, you're just a frog!" He threw his head back and bellowed with laughter. He planted his big boots into the riverbank and swung up to the top. "You made a believer out 'a me, Ledyard. Enjoy the swamp!" he shouted over his shoulder as he disappeared into the forest.

The music still filled his ears. He was closer to it now, his curiosity aroused to a high pitch. Suddenly he found himself back at the same ivy-covered limestone wall where he had first seen that creature, that horrid, huge insect that had later showed up in the backseat of his car, making him count his fingers.

Maybe that big ol' bug got a bunch of pals together and they're playin' bug tunes. He chuckled to himself, but he glanced around nervously, wiping the sweat from his forehead. Directly above him were swirls of color; lavender, brilliant green, azure blue, crimson, and yellow streaked through the tree limbs. The forest air was filled with the sound of a beautiful child's lullaby.

I know it's that same— But he never finished the thought, for as he parted the branches ahead of him, he found himself staring directly at a group of townsfolk, all of whom he knew, one of them being his wife! They all seemed to be concentrating on something, their faces intent, with tears on some cheeks.

Neil crouched low behind a tree, staring in disbelief. Before him lay the great silver spaceship, quietly pulsating, and at the entrance stood the purple boy. The winged creature hovered tall beside him, a smile on his wizened face, the wiry fingers folded over a checkered vest—the same fingers that had tormented him from the backseat. His head pounded, and he struggled for breath.

But at the same time, he sensed an uncanny opportunity, and his hand closed slowly over the butt of his revolver. *I'll bring 'em all in at once,* he thought. *Herd 'em into town. I'll make 'em sorry—this Tobias and that big bug.* He began to meticulously pick tiny burrs and bits of forest debris from his shirt, conscious of his appearance as always. He carefully removed his hat and watched silently, planning his next move.

The musical lullaby stopped abruptly. Elo looked up at Queen Trumpeter as she whirred above them, motionless, her wings purring softly. Hunched low, Neil stepped cautiously out from the shadow of the bushes.

A new voice began—a loud, deep note in the bass clef, grating and off-key. From out of the ship floated two fat, red quarter notes bearing musical horns. They passed overhead, the sound of them like a loud foghorn. Elma Mae and Chalmers stumbled backward, knocked off balance by the sound of the great bass note. Ginger Lee glanced over at Pearl, who raised her eyebrows and looked over at Tom.

"That cuz of our Tobias, gal," Grampa Perry said to Jewell in a low voice. "He got lotta power now."

Tobias came among them, walked between Jewell and Grampa Perry, and looked up at them both. His expression was no longer childlike. Now it contained knowledge and confidence.

"The man who embraces evil, Mama—the Enriching knows of him," he said in a clear, even voice.

Neil ducked, looking up curiously as the cluster of big red bass notes floated overhead, blowing deep, discordant sounds in a minor key from strange silver horns that protruded from them. The sound of the odd notes whipped Neil's hair until it stood on end. Soon he could no longer stand against the might of the horns' deep bass chords, and he fell into a maze of hedges and tree stumps. The horns ceased. He struggled to his feet and reached for his hat, trying to attain a dignified posture, but he looked defeated and rumpled. Finally he began to bulldoze his way through the heap of twisted tree branches and brambly bushes.

No one moved as he stepped into the clearing. A crooked smirk curved his lips. His scratched face was smeared with dirt. Carefully he ran his fingers through his hair, his shoulders shaking as he began to laugh hysterically. They all watched him, their expressions curiously bland, for he held no importance in the remarkable events they were witnessing.

Elo placed one gloved finger to his chin, one antenna raised higher than the other, and one eye sweeping Neil from head to toe.

Soon the sheriff of Anker County was convulsed with laughter, his hands on his hips, his head thrown back. "This is it. This is what y'all been doin' out here, with this big ol' bug—and 'course it *would* be the purple boy!" He hooted with laughter. "Y'all havin' a sing-along this mornin'? Or gettin' ready for a hoedown? What's that hummin' contraption over there all about, anyway?" Neil began to pace back and forth, his thumbs tucked into his belt.

Tobias stepped forward. His voice was calm and self-assured. "I know you are the man who had my daddy killed, and my brother Josh."

Neil's eyes flickered and narrowed as Tobias came nearer. He laughed loudly again, tossing his head.

"You an that ol' pokey-eyed lizard, that's who!" Elma Mae shouted as she broke away from Tom's side and hurled herself at Neil to kick him in the shins.

"Gal got some wild spirit, Tom," Neil groaned, grabbing his leg. "I don't know nothin', boy, about your Daddy, and even if I did, I wouldn't be havin' a discussion about official police concerns—with a seven-year-old!"

"He's eight!" shouted Chalmers.

Ginger Lee moved quietly away from Pearl and stood next to Jewell, taking her hand. "You're lying, Neil," she called out to him. "You are responsible. Did you think I didn't know?"

Neil's eyes searched the group at the sound of her voice.

"And soon Tobias will be king of the Cripons!" announced Elma Mae proudly.

"Oh, is that right?" Neil said. "Cripons, huh? Just who are the Cripons? Part of your weekend sing-alongs?"

"I am," stated Elo, his tinny voice vibrating through the trees.

Neil jumped back, crouching low, his hand on his revolver. "Did that bug just say somethin'? Why're ya all dressed up like that? You just a bug." He stiffened in horror as Elo moved in front of him, treading slowly back and forth. At each turn he held up one gloved finger and shook his little walnut head, his eyelids half-closed. "Who are you, anyway?" asked Neil, mesmerized. "Did ya come from another—"

Queen Zinfoneth swept like a breath of wind between the two of them, leaving a trail of color and sparkles.

"Never mind where I am from!" Elo rasped. He planted himself directly in front of Neil, his wings pulsating. "You have sought to steal that which is not yours. By your wicked means, you have hurt many who stand here today. The measure of your actions is now at hand. A shrouded curtain shall overtake you. Tobias, soon you will be an ambassador. It is your responsibility to speak forth now."

"Am-bass-ador?" Neil repeated, his breath hissing. His face contorted into an ugly sneer.

"Not all things are under your power, Mr. Neil," said Tobias, turning from him. "From within I call, and from without. Bring forth the whispering of wings."

The great crystal doors on the ship began to rotate, sending out streams of blinding color directed at Neil. He lurched sideways, covering his eyes with his forearm. Blindly he yanked out his revolver. Suddenly hordes of butterflies emerged from the ship as the great clanging of the deep, red bass notes resumed. Elo and Tobias stood back. The massive throng of butterflies whirled around Neil, forming layer upon layer over his entire body. Ginger Lee cupped her hands over her face and turned away as Jewell's arm slipped around her.

Neil struggled silently under the weight of hundreds of butterflies as they covered him from head to toe. A strange cry erupted from beneath the winged creatures, and then the figure of Neil was still. After a few moments, they all dropped away and fluttered off into the sky.

A dead tree stood rooted to the ground. Its shape was that of Neil Swanny. His hat rolled off an upper branch and came to rest on a craggy twig.

The soft purring of the great ship changed now. It began to vibrate, and the wings began to shift imperceptibly, a tiny movement of lifting off. Jewell stood quietly, her eyes searching the clearing for Tobias. Elo stood tall beside him, one gloved hand resting on Tobias's head. He nodded in her direction.

"Yes, Jewell, he is here. It is almost time."

She moved quickly to his side, carrying the small brown suitcase. "Tobias," she said, stooping down to him, "Mama has packed two pairs of overalls for ya. They is fresh washed and neatly mended. I got some shirts for ya and … and yer toothbrush and …" Her face crumpled, and she brushed her hand along his cheek. "Oh … I gonna miss you so much." She looked down and swallowed hard.

"Here some pictures, son," Grampa Perry said, appearing suddenly at her side. "They brand new now. They was all dusty 'n' faded, but now they ain't. I suspects your friend there." The old man chuckled and glanced up at Elo. "You an' yer Mama in this one." He pointed a shaky finger at one photo. "And here be one of me. 'Course I a young twig then, but still …"

Tobias stood looking at both of them, a smile of love on his face. All at once a wet tongue licked his cheek, and he turned face to face with Cottonseed, who wiggled and whined with affection. Beside him stood Orville, his hair carefully combed, his face smooth-shaven. He cleared his throat loudly and began to stammer. "I ... I had ta come, and ... and ya probably wonderin' ... I need ta say I'm ... I'm sorry that I been a man of mean heart. Ya see, it suddenly come to me that you is a boy spreadin' love. My Cottonseed, he's healed up good as new. Got a spring in his step now. Tom, he bringed him back to me. Told me that hound just licked yer hand, and soon as he did, why, he was back bein' like a pup again. And them boys on the playground, why, I knows that be true now, that ya healed Darci. See, I was just all caught up in ... my eyes, they was blinded." Orville swallowed hard, looking awkwardly around at Elo and the spaceship, glancing with bewilderment at the small group who stood nearby. "Why, there be Miz Wiggins and ... and Ginger Lee, and that gal of Tom's," he whispered hoarsely.

Tobias laid his hand on Cottonseed's head. "I'm glad you came."

Orville bent down and whispered in his ear. "I brought somethin' for you. I'm bettin' it means a lot to you." He pressed a small piece of wood into Tobias's hand, the gift from Myron. "I was out a-fishin' the other day at Pencil Creek and found this stuck in the mud. I know it yours, cuz I knows how to spell your name."

Tobias closed his hand over the treasure. "Thank you, Mr. Orville," he whispered, looking up at him.

Tom stepped up beside them both. He pressed the little boy into his arms, his head bent low. "We'll be missin' you—me 'n' Elma Mae. You won't forget us, will you? Even when you're all grown up?"

Tobias looked up to see tears standing in Tom's eyes. "No, Mr. Tom, I won't ever forget! See, Elma Mae, she's my best friend—always will be—and 'tween the two of us, well ... we'll always be thinking of each other."

Tom kissed the top of his head and turned toward his daughter. Orville sniffled and dabbed at his eyes.

By twos and threes they came from the forest, riding tall and majestically, the sound of the horses drowning out the murmuring of human voices. Bowing to Tobias as they swept past him, the Cupbearers entered through the vast entrance of the spaceship.

Queen Zinfoneth appeared as the clattering of hooves diminished and the clearing became silent again. She shimmered in front of the giant doors, beckoning to Jewell and holding in her hand a single, slender trumpet. "This is for you, Jewell," she said in her composed lyrical voice. "With just three notes, you can call Tobias, and he will come to you. But use it with discretion and be wise. Count it as precious." She laid the lovely silver horn in Jewell's outstretched hands and brushed her cheek lightly with a wingtip. Jewell ran her hand slowly over the horn. Then she leaned down and kissed her son. Tobias wrapped his arms around her, and they stood quietly for a long moment.

The sound of the ship again shifted. Jewell slowly let go of Tobias and turned away as Grampa Perry took her hand. He lifted his arm in farewell.

Ginger Lee and Pearl stood together, overcome with emotion. "Thank you, dear Tobias," Pearl whispered to herself.

Elma Mae held tight to Tom's hand, tears on her freckled cheeks. "I loves ya, Tobias. I always will. Promise!"

"Always knowed, yep! From the beginnin'," chirped Birdie.

"Will ya ever come back and play?" called out Chalmers, scurrying to the front of the group. "If ya can, we'll prob'ly be in the glass tree, me 'n' Elma Mae."

Tobias lifted his hand as Elo draped a rich-purple mantle over his shoulders. He held the small brown suitcase close as he walked through the great doors. Turning back for a moment, he called out, loud and clear. "I *will* come back, Chalmers—for your seventh birthday."

They all watched in awe as the spaceship lifted slowly from the clearing, the wings moving gracefully, treetops bending from its force. The great horde of butterflies—the Enriching—followed its path. The earth trembled as it soared into the sky, trailing rainbow colors and musical notes. Then it was gone.

The End

ABOUT THE BOOK

THE SMALL TOWN OF Anker, Mississippi, is the setting of this enchanting novel, *The Enriching*. It is the early 1930s, a time when the Deep South is rigid and unchanging, laws are unbroken, white citizens hold sway in the land, and the Negro is ironbound in his inferior place.

Occasionally a white man breaks through those boundaries and reveals himself to be a kind and generous spirit. Such a man is Tom Clausen, whom we meet early in the story, a widower who is raising Elma Mae, his fun-loving, gregarious daughter with flying red pigtails and freckles. Her best friend is Tobias Valentine, an eight-year-old boy with rich purple skin the color of an eggplant, and unusual amber eyes that seem to hold a thoughtfulness, as if from another world. The story is rich in imagination and the wonders of childhood. We meet Elo, an enormous butterfly who has the capability to appear, large or small, beside Tobias at any time, to protect and teach him the power of Love. The Cupbearers, and the butterfly queen, Zinfoneth, are part of this magical tale, along with Jewell, his mother, and Perry, his blind grandfather.

Tobias's presence raises hostility, suspicion, and mean-spirited words ... until his love and special powers change the people and the town of Anker forever.

9 781480 834880